FAMILIAR
TERROR

Other Books by Evelyn Minshull

And Then the Rain Came
The Cornhusk Doll
Eve: A Novel
Familiar Darkness

FAMILIAR TERROR

—A Novel—

Evelyn Minshull

Published by Baker Books
a division of Baker Book House Company
P.O. Box 6287, Grand Rapids, MI 49516-6287

Printed in the United States of America

Library of Congress Cataloging-in-Publication Data

Minshull, Evelyn White.
Familiar terror : a novel / Evelyn Minshull.
p. cm.
ISBN 0-8010-5698-5 (pbk.)
I. Title.
PS3563.I476F36 1997
813'.54—dc20 96-18945

For my husband, Fred—
constant encourager and best friend

1

We found the body wrapped in a stained blue tarp behind the food tent. It had begun to rain—just a gentle shower, pattering on shade trees, green benches, and craft booths and tables clustered in the better-traveled areas of the park. But even such slight precipitation threatened the delicate quilling and scherenschnitte protected only by mats and plastic wrap and by the large green-and-white-striped beach umbrella one crafter held while another gathered both displays toward the center of their red-draped table. Raindrops, bouncing harmlessly from wooden and ceramic pieces, rolled and puddled on plastic throws drawn hastily to protect woven and knitted items. On invitation, the spinners and weavers, in pseudo-colonial garb, tugged their wheels, looms, and baskets of clumped wool beneath a leather-crafter's canopy.

Dee, my potter friend from Center City, held her dripping hands wide to protect her white canvas shoes from spatters of wet clay. Peering at the sky, she said, "We've lived through worse."

There were signs of clearing—a thinning to aluminum-hued clouds, though still no suggestion of blue. The rain was of no personal concern to either of us. Water was essential to her demonstration, and I'd draped my paintings at the first symptom of a moist breeze. But I knew that she, like me, suffered an unreasonable guilt. After all, we'd organized the show. Chosen this particular Saturday. "Next year," she said, "even if the show loses money, we rent large tents."

But in the meantime . . .

And then I spotted the tarp. "I wonder whose it is?"

In moments, fat raindrops splatted on pavement and splintered on clumps of grass. As we ducked beneath the flap of the food tent, scents of kielbasa and sauerkraut swirled around us. Meat sputtered on the grill. Amy Turkle, my poet friend, perhaps my best geographically close friend since Arden and I had accepted the three-church McClintock charge less than two years before, looked up from swiping barbecue sauce on thick, browning chicken breasts and drumsticks. Sweat trickled from beneath her polka-dot headband. "Get you something, Paula?"

"We were wondering about the tarp."

She frowned. "It wasn't there last night."

"It's not yours, then?"

"Nobody's I know of."

Of course it had to belong to someone. Probably the firemen, whose tent it was. With Firemen's Old Home Week only a week away, they'd offered to set up their tent and grills for our use. Nothing had been said about tarps. But dismayed squeals coming from unprotected booths seemed more pressing than protocol.

"Let's do it." Dee wiped her hands on the wet grass. "You take that end."

"I could help." But a minor blaze erupting in the largest grill aborted Amy's offer.

I'd known the tarp would be wet-slippery and awkward, but I hadn't expected it to be so heavy.

Puffing after only a few steps, we laid it down. One edge unfurled and a hand fell free. It was a slim hand, blue-veined, surely a woman's, patterned with liver spots and wearing a large ring that even in that dim light flashed gold and sapphire.

“Good lord,” Dee whispered, and it sounded like a prayer. “What do we do?”

Vomiting seemed like the best idea. Nausea rising in my throat reacted with the kielbasa smell. “Police?” I suggested.

“Do they have any in this burg?”

“Town constable,” I managed, not able to avert my eyes from that stiffened hand. “But he might not know what to do, either.” In quiet McClintock, a constabulary seemed almost an affectation.

“Find him,” she suggested, “before we attract a mob.”

I glanced around. Everyone was so busy adjusting displays to avoid rain that no one seemed to have noticed us yet.

Arden. If only Arden had come with me, instead of staying home to work on his sermon while Pam, our three-year-old, napped. Arden held an “okay here’s what we do next” attitude toward crises. Even during my deepest depression three years earlier—when panic paralyzed every joint and dread deadened every thought—he had remained forward-looking. Full of faith. But—even more pragmatic—mobilized. Just as certainly, he’d know what to do about this tarp, heavy with portent. All I knew was to mourn that hand, which might have been chiseled from marble, but was all too obviously flesh and blood. It belonged to someone. And the remainder of that someone, swathed in blue vinyl, might well be a woman I knew.

I prayed not.

“Snap out of it, Paula.” Dee was wearing her worried face. “The constable. Where would he be?”

Drawing a long, quivering breath, I went to the only place possible that day—to the far end of the park, where Joe Derrick and his wife arranged her ceramic pieces on long, steplike shelves.

"A *body?*" he boomed, then whispered, as though that might retract the earlier explosion, "A body, Mrs. Templeton? You're certain?"

I nodded.

"A . . . *dead* body?"

"It would seem so," I said dryly.

"I mean, as opposed to someone taking a nap."

"Wrapped in a tarp?"

He sighed ponderously. "I've never . . . except for road accidents. And a fire once. And that poor girl—a friend of yours, I believe?—who fell into the gorge."

I closed my eyes against ancient pain. "Lelia," I supplied.

He swallowed noisily, and observing his bulbous eyes and working mouth, I knew I wouldn't have his job for anything in the county.

"Is there anyone you want me to call?" I offered.

"Sam Westerman?"

The funeral director. I nodded.

"He could alert the county coroner." He looked up, almost questioningly, and I said, "I'll suggest that."

"But first . . ." He heaved himself from behind the display table. "Since you found the body, you'd better be there when . . ." He glanced almost longingly at his wife, at the unwrapped ceramics. "Guess you'll have to set up yourself, honey," he apologized.

She made no response.

Amy Turkle had left her station to join Dee, and billows of smoke rose from the grill, where chicken, untended, charred.

Food no longer seemed important.

Both women turned as we sloshed through the sodden grass.

"Constable Joe Derrick," I said. "My friend Dee."

Abruptly, he knelt by the tarp.

"Do we have to . . . here?" Amy's thin face was pale and twisted.

"The scene of the crime."

"Unless she was brought here. Doesn't that seem likely?"

Though he looked toward me, his glance seemed blank. "Call Sam," he said dully. "Tell him to bring a gurney. But you two'll still have to go with me, wherever we open her up."

Hurrying to the brick- and vinyl-sided mortuary, I found myself swallowing, then spitting out, vomit.

The woman was no one I'd ever seen. She looked fragile, like someone's great-grandmother or an elderly spinster accustomed to serving tea in fine rose-sprigged china inherited decades earlier.

Who could want to murder someone so frail and refined? And so brutally, at that? Her finely boned nose had been broken, one thin arm jerked from the socket. And, worst of all, she had only one small, high-arched foot.

Constable Joe had turned away; Sam Westerman, chin cupped in his hand, studied the woman's face. As though he knew her? Or thought he might?

Dee asked huskily, "Maybe an amputation? For diabetes, maybe?"

But the severed foot, still wearing its bloodied gray leather pump, hid in the folds of the tarp.

2

The craft show proceeded because it must. Surely artisans take a vow, I thought glumly. Neither rain nor snow nor sleet . . . nor murder.

But though people moved from booth to booth, from setup to setup, though purchases were made and carried carefully away, it wasn't what such days were designed to be. How could it be, with the memory of that ominous tarp and its quiet, frail burden? In shows I'd attended in the past, there'd been cracklings of excitement, explosions of discovery. Now only the whir of Dee's pottery wheel and the click-clack-click from the spinners' and weavers' display competed with hushed voices and footsteps muted by damp grass. The sun had emerged, but listlessly, and despite dripping foliage, even nature seemed to lack the will to restore joy. To resurrect hope. To encourage enthusiasm for objects crafted by hand.

The dead woman's hand—whatever it had turned itself to create or preserve—had been forever stilled.

Such thoughts were morbid. Worse than that, useless. I shifted a matted watercolor of dogtooth violets just fractions of an inch on its easel. And while it seemed fruitless to mourn so deeply for someone I'd never met—never, as far as I was aware, even heard mentioned—it seemed unavoidable as well. "No man is an island," John Donne had written, "any man's death diminishes me." We'd accepted such loss in magnified terms as TV broadcasts perpetuated images of carnage in Bosnia. In Israel. In London. Each newspaper photo of an overturned vehicle and sheet-draped body jolted us with a more personal horror also grown weary through repetition. Each posted notice of a missing child heightened a dread both achingly fresh and alarmingly ingrained. And Oklahoma City . . .

"Paula?"

My soul reached toward the warmth of Arden's voice. Its safe familiarity.

"Honey?"

Of course he'd know. Sam Westerman would have called the parsonage automatically.

Turning, I felt the patting of Pam's small hands near my knee. I reached down, allowing the softness of her curls to embrace my fingertips.

"I'm okay," I said, both grateful and annoyed that Arden still worried about the state of my emotions. I'd thought we'd established that I was firmly past my breakdown. As long as he sometimes questioned my stability, I was certain, I could never fully erase doubt from my own mind.

And yet there was such comfort in his constancy, in the unswerving faith he exhibited in God. In humanity. In me.

"Arden." It was Dee, hands slimy with clay. "Terrible thing." Her voice wavered into questioning. "You'd heard?"

"He's been to the funeral home," I said.

Despite the clay on her hands, she hugged herself. "Do . . . do they know yet who she is?"

Arden pushed back a wet lock of his cinnamon-colored hair. "Amy recognized her," he said, almost on a sigh.

"Amy?" I jerked toward the food tent. Head down, shoulders bent, she turned slabs of meat. Smoke rose in puffs and swirls. "She didn't say . . ."

"She didn't know, until just a bit ago. She got to thinking about the ring . . . and asked if she could see the body."

"And it was . . ." prompted Dee.

"I've forgotten her name. Antonia . . . something. She was organist at the Congregational Church in Simmons."

"About fifteen miles from here," I informed Dee.

Arden nodded. "I heard her play once, at one of the ministers' meetings. She made it look so effortless . . ." His voice drained off, and I pictured those porcelain fingers alive on the keys of a church organ, that spectacular ring catching and reflecting light.

And the severed foot.

I shuddered.

Perhaps as important as the skilled hands of an organist were feet which placed themselves accurately and firmly. What had the murderer meant to communicate with such cruel dismemberment? Could this symbolize a hobbling of the church? Hatred of music as a whole? Or had he or she simply sought to elicit shock?

If so, the effort had succeeded.

"How could anyone hate another person so much?" Dee was asking.

And I realized that I hadn't considered this a crime against an individual, but rather an expression of some broader rage.

In which case, this might be only the first murder.

"Cold, Mommy?" Pam was asking, looking up at me.

I forced myself to relax. Willed my trembling to ease. "It's the dampness," I said, and smiled stiffly.

"You're . . . sure you're going to be okay?" Arden, of course, his voice weighted with the familiar concern which both comforted and confined me.

"I'm fine," I said, too brusquely.

He paused, and I refused to look at him.

"Then I guess I'll go polish my sermon."

Pam wavered between following and staying, then spread her arms wide to the strengthening sunshine and suggested, "Cotton candy?"

And how could any world including both sunlight and cotton candy be fully frightening? Smiling, sublimating a small guilt at my coldness toward Arden, and allowing only a glance toward the setup where Dee worked her wheel for a small, silent group, I caught Pam's tiny hand and hurried her toward both.

Amy, face streaked with grease and tearstains, looked up later as Pam and I approached the cooktent. Amy's estranged husband, Turk, leaning against the center pole, scowled and moved away.

"We could come back later."

"Same old thing," Amy said, her voice a monotone. "All those years . . . and now he thinks it should be so easy. I should trust him when he says he loves me. That he'll let me write . . . even *breathe* without asking permission."

Shortly after we'd moved to McClintock, Amy and I shared her poetry and my art, and a friendship had begun and blossomed almost at once. She'd shown me the farewell poem she'd written—even before she'd given it to Turk, suspending their marriage. He'd aimed his rage at me, in blame, and still seemed to hold that view. But remembering Turk's restraint of recent months, his standing at a distance, watching with pain-filled eyes, I said gently, "There are times when he really seems to be trying."

"I know." She wiped her forehead with her apron. "But you know what they say about the leopard. I mean, try as he might . . . Turk is Turk."

"Take a break, Ame," Dora Kuhn urged. "You're lookin' like overdone chicken yourself." Dora worked as a checkout girl in the local grocery. Blonde, down-to-earth, steady, she'd been an anchor during our first rocky year in McClintock.

Gratefully, Amy moved from the grills and motioned me to follow. Pam offered me her hand, sticky with blue cotton candy. Or what had once been that cloudlike substance and now seemed more the texture of new pine sap.

We'd reached a break in the tent where a breeze flowed. The fragrance of something blooming nearly canceled the smells of kielbasa, sauerkraut, and barbecue sauce. "There are whole days," Amy said, "when I wonder what God expects of me."

"No more than you can bear," I said, and thought, How sanctimonious. "Or so they tell us."

Often, following my breakdown, during those bleak, despondent days hospital personnel had misnamed "recovery," I'd heard the maxim and received it in the same spirit Amy's grimace suggested.

"The trouble is, I still love the jerk. We did have good times, too. Especially at first." She smiled. "He brought me blue chicory once, for no reason at all."

I'd never seen the blue chicory side of Turk's character. But with his dark good looks—more Irish than Polish—I could envision some distant forebear in a wide-sleeved white shirt and dark cummerbund, black close-fitting boots and gray breeches, overlooking some glen or glade or gentle sea, a wild rose in his hand, a sword at his side, and a love poem on his lips.

But I knew that—except for the sword—Turk would disown such a person.

"He felt so threatened when I wrote. And more than that, when I talked about it with friends. With you. What is it with men, anyway?" she finished angrily. "Why do they think they can't be manly and watch a sunset . . . or speak gentle words . . . or . . ." She smiled softly. "Why can't they be more blue chicory and less bluster and booze?"

I thought of Arden and knew—again—how fortunate I was. Arden, with his warm eyes. His gentle voice and hands. His nurturing—

Pam tugged stickily at my wrist. Turk was striding toward us, his shoulders hunched slightly forward, his eyes smoldering. "I'll call you later," he said, aiming the words at Amy, "when you ain't so . . . busy." His eyes flicked to me.

"We should go."

"Yeah, you should," he muttered. "Or should never've come in the first place."

And I was certain he meant not just to the park that day, but to McClintock. Ever.

Amy placed a greasy hand on my arm. "Call or not, as you please, Turk," she said, "it'll make no difference. The way you are now—angry because you can't control—proves you haven't changed."

"You ain't given me a reason to change."

"No, Turk," and she transferred her hand to his arm. "You've got it backwards. You change first, *then* we'll talk."

He jerked away. "There are other women not so picky."

"There always were."

He stiffened, hands balling into fists. "Not till you shoved me away. Never! Never another woman, till then!"

"Turk," she began wearily, reaching out again.

But he caught her hand, bending her wrist backward, bending *her* backward toward one of the tables, clothed in red-and-white checkered oilcloth.

Pam whimpered. Looking down, I saw her wide eyes, her quivering lip.

"You're . . . frightening . . . Pammie," Amy said with difficulty.

"It's you I mean to scare."

I yearned to slap his smug face.

But that quickly he released her, and she stumbled, falling sharply against a corner of the table. "And that will convince me . . . to take you back?" she asked quietly.

He swore under his breath, scanned her hotly, shoulder-line to toe, and stalked away. She watched him go, then sank onto the nearest bench.

Moving behind her, I prodded her tense neck muscles with probing fingertips. Sighing, she leaned into them. "That . . . and Mrs. Porter," she said, glancing up, "all in a day."

And new tears trickled. I bent to touch my cheek to hers, then returned to Dee, shook off the dropcloth, and exposed my paintings to the sun.

"Antonia Porter's life," began the memoriam in the *Danvers Bugle*—a local weekly paper delivered each Tuesday, and intermittently between—"was a celebration in song."

> Like many of you when you were young, I practiced scales in her airy studio. Sheer beige curtains billowed near potted ferns on shining brass pedestals. Two gray and white cats—perhaps the parents or grandparents of her current companions—unwincingly groomed themselves in an atmosphere of mutilated Mozart. Even those of us who endured piano lessons as a necessary penance of youth, however, respected Mrs. Porter, who so obviously loved and respected music. Who among us can listen to classical music, even today, without closing our eyes and reliving the tap-tap-tap with which she rectified our rhythms?
>
> Though we decry the casual violence so prevalent in our culture, though we cannot deny that our lives are made poorer by her passing, we must resist grieving this dedicated teacher in dark chords, like Bach at his most mournful, or in anger, like Handel at his most bombastic. Instead, we shape our epitaphs from melodic strains of Liszt and Brahms. To consider Mrs. Porter in any terms but her music is to trivialize her life. Her life *was* music, a music which will continue to throb and flow in fugues and chorales, in oratorios, in hymns of energy and vibrance as long as memory itself survives.

"Beautiful."

Mary Lynn herself had dropped by the parsonage to

show me the article, so fresh that the paper still smelled of printer's ink.

"How pleased her family must be."

"No family," Mary Lynn sighed. "She was childless, widowed long ago. Her music was all she had. That and her cats. And her students. An endless parade of students, present and past."

"I wish I might have known her." But that was only half the truth. I coveted for Pam, when she was old enough, that kind of teacher.

"You'd have loved her. Her house, too. Victorian, with even more gingerbread than your parsonage, and a new coat of white paint every other time you turned around. She did the porches herself, the floors always a battleship gray enamel that stayed on her fingernails for days." Mary Lynn sighed. "It's beyond me how anyone could have killed her. Her, of all people. So gentle—" Her voice broke, and she turned away.

I handed her a tissue.

"Thanks."

"Robbery?" I suggested.

"Nothing missing, that they could tell." She paused. "No sign of a break-in, either, and the cats were fine, just hungry."

"Then . . ."

She shrugged. Blew her nose. Dabbed at her eyes.

"Another tissue?"

She shook her head. "I need to remember her joy," she said with a lopsided smile. "And the joy she created for others. For . . . for me." Her face darkened. "I wish I had him alone—whoever did it—for just five minutes."

I wondered if they'd determined that the murderer was a man. Or if it was merely a common conjecture that such acts require a man's strength . . . and a brutality most women don't like to believe that women possess.

"Though I suppose . . ." she began, then shook herself and asked, "Have I told you this is my last week at the paper?"

It was difficult to imagine the *Danvers Bugle* without Mary Lynn's byline. We'd met when Arden was first assigned to the three-church McClintock charge, pastoring tiny East Danvers and Peachstone churches and the McClintock congregation, with twice as many members but still small by conference standards. She'd appeared then to do a story on us, but discovered something infinitely more intriguing in the mural Dean Kettering, a then-troubled boy, had created on the annex wall.

Since then, we'd been friends. Not close ones. Not as close as I'd have liked—nor, as she often indicated, she'd have enjoyed if only our paths crossed more frequently.

And now in less than a month she was leaving, though for happy reasons—to accompany her soon-to-be husband in his air force transfer from Texas to an even more distant Germany. "Still, I'll miss it. Everything. Everyone." She looked about, as though memorizing the town—not just the seen, but the unseen, the guessed, the remembered. "Still, the pony express runs this far. Maybe we could write, once in a while. I've asked them to have the *Bugle* sent."

"It won't be the same without you."

"Maybe even better."

"Never!" I protested. "This story is *marvelous!* No one could do as well!"

Grinning, she said, "You hadn't noticed, had you?"

"Noticed?"

"It's not my story."

"Not yours?" I half-exclaimed, half-questioned. I hadn't even glanced at the byline. "Matt Culhaney. Matt Culhaney . . ."

"You might have heard of him. Minnie Kelp's his great-aunt."

Minnie—who hadn't quite forgiven Arden and me for being Arden and me—would never have mentioned him. Not to us.

"Someone else, maybe."

"Matt was almost a folk hero here—basketball and track star, merit scholarship runner-up, won states in debate—before he went to journalism school and his folks moved away. Now he thinks he'd like to 'come home.' He won't last long, though. Too good. Today the *Danvers Bugle*, tomorrow the *New York Times* or the *Washington Post*—or beyond."

"Sounds like a worthy successor to the Whitman tradition," I said, and she hooted.

"Just wait. This guy's a literary meteor. Ten years from now, we'll all be saying, 'I knew him when.'"

That evening, Mary Lynn brought Matt by to meet us. "He knows nearly everyone else already," she said.

He was a strapping young man, easily six foot four, but built like a beanpole—or, more accurately, a stringbean, since he was curved in that manner, perhaps from perennially accommodating his height to low doorways.

"Great to meet you!" He shook hands so energetically that even Arden had to brace himself.

But he hunkered down to take Pammie's hand, ever so gently.

She seemed enamored, even offering him her favorite teddy to hold on his lap while we continued our conversation over coffee and spice cake.

"Your story on Mrs. Porter was exceptional," Arden said.

"Poetic," I added.

Matt nodded. "I've been hearing compliments all day." There seemed neither modesty nor arrogance in his tone. Just matter-of-factness.

Mary Lynn said, "Get used to it! This is only the beginning!"

The last crumb was scarcely eaten when Matt stood, stretched to unbelievable heights, and said, "We have to drive to Simmons. Constable Derrick wants to question some of the carnival hucksters. They've been there all week. You knew, I suppose."

"You mean they were there—"

"Before the craft show," Mary Lynn said quickly.

"And before the murder."

"Does he . . . Mr. Derrick . . . suspect that someone in the carnival killed her, and brought her all the way over here?" It didn't make sense. Did it?

"Nobody knows what to think, just yet," Mary Lynn said, her eyes troubled.

"Though if you're looking for a criminal type," Matt drawled with what was surely youthful insensitivity rather than journalistic callousness, "where better to find it? And," he finished darkly, "they come here next."

3

In the park, grass trampled by craft show participants and customers was straightening in time for the onslaught of Firemen's Old Home Week, to open with traditional vespers Sunday night. The year before, the ministerium had imported a men's gospel octet from a small town north of Pittsburgh. The year before that—our first summer in McClintock—the headliners had been "homegrown," a community choir gleaned from all denominations within a ten-mile radius.

As planning began for this year's Old Home Week, the town council, apparently perceiving an upward movement, had contacted Samantha Crane's agent. Reeling in shock when she'd accepted, they'd scurried for funds to cover her substantial fee, suggested local backup and sound technicians, and asked that Arden and I provide room and board.

No problem. I'd been impressed by her tapes and looked forward to meeting someone our staid bishop had found "electrifying, with a cosmic ministry." Someone less ecclesiastical might have cited her pose on the cover of *Today's Christian Music*—model-lovely and just a few points short of provocative.

The Women's Society met Friday noon in the annex. Long before I arrived with my potato casserole—still steaming fragrances of green pepper and cream of chicken soup—I could hear the buzzing, punctuated by periodic bursts of sharp opinion.

I sighed.

The murder, of course. And until something definitive had been discovered, I truly wished the topic would subside. What could be gained by repeating the head-shakings, the clucking disbelief, by rehashing the lurid details, by determining, still once again, that Joe Derrick's investigation was going nowhere, that no one could or should relax in supposed safety until the murderer had been apprehended?

Still, I'd cautioned the baby-sitter to keep the doors locked while I was gone; to reject pleas for a walk past the park where the carnival was assembling by telling Pam she'd be seeing everything a few evenings later, when the lights were finally on and the merry-go-round running. Connie, bubble gum snapping and gaze attached to TV images, had nodded. I hesitated only slightly. She'd never let us down before. Perhaps teenage attention was capable of a three-way split.

". . . nearly blasphemous," Minnie Kelp was saying as I moved through the church kitchen toward the meeting. "That saintly woman scarcely cold in her grave, and such pagan rites within spit-throw of where her body lay. And," and her voice lowered a half-notch, "not to mention our own esteemed minister to deliver the invocation!"

Sighing, I maintained my pace.

And there would be no frontal assault, for dear old Mrs. Bancroft, my dependable ally, had straightened her slender arthritic shoulders and raised her snow-capped head in challenge. "And what would you have instead, Minnie Kelp? Devil-worshipers intonin' gibberish?"

Minnie shrugged but turned away. "More suitable than the church condoning sin."

"Like the little kiddies' rides, I s'pose. Or the saltwater taffy. Is that it, Minnie? The ferris wheel. Oh, I know! The pet parade! All them shameless animals marchin' naked."

Minnie charged again, but halfheartedly. "You know very well what I mean."

"S'pose you tell me."

"The games of chance!" Minnie, stout hands fisted at her sides, fairly shrieked the indictment.

"Oh, that." Mrs. Bancroft's voice softened. "And I do believe the Historical Society's rafflin' off a quilt . . . ain't we?"

Actually, the afternoon did bring some scant new light on the murder investigation—that, too, announced by Minnie, whose grandnephew had apparently supplied facts and rumors too fresh to have appeared in Tuesday's *Bugle.* Or even in the daily *Center City Times,* to which most people in town subscribed for national news, sports, and weather. It would take more than a murder investigation to attract the *Times'* attention to us. Even Center City's own murders—averaging one a night—drew only ho-hum coverage.

Though the site of Mrs. Porter's murder remained a mystery, her body had definitely been transported, probably in some small truck or van.

"Dear Matt will certainly be writing about it," Minnie said, fairly glowing. "Did you ever in your life read articles so . . . so . . ." Apparently, words failed her, but pride brightened her eyes as she dispensed information. Cecily Jones, a deputy, had obtained one imperfect impression of tire tread, possibly identifiable by brand name and uneven wear. And there'd been something pressed into the grass beneath the body—a scrap of poster advertising the carnival.

"Not too amazin'," Mrs. Bancroft drawled, "seein's how they've been blowin' all over town for weeks."

A triumphant glow lit Minnie's smile. "Not for the carnival coming *here,*" she contradicted firmly. "For the one at *Simmons.*"

There was a silence broken by indrawn breaths. Almost audibly, all heads turned to Minnie.

She visibly savored the attention. Basked in it. "And what does that suggest?"

"That Antonia Porter lived near Simmons. Which we already knowed."

For once, no notice spun to Mrs. Bancroft. Minnie, firmly in charge, leaned forward, eyes glittering, lips pursed. Like a cat, I thought, and indeed she nearly purred her conjecture. "And who better to have their posters than carnival people themselves?"

Clearly, only Mrs. Bancroft and I found such a statement too sweeping. A murmur of assent caressed the room. And I knew, long before sewing-box lids were closed, and casseroles claimed and covered with foil, the carnival had been indicted, tried, and convicted of Mrs. Porter's murder.

How cozy, I thought, for the real murderer, and resisted the possibility that Minnie might indeed be right, that it did seem a stretch of coincidence that violent death and the carnival should arrive together.

Small guilts intruded. Just because the concept had originated with Minnie, should I dismiss it summarily?

After I'd paid Connie—rapt in the credit lines of a soap—I zapped the TV to discourage lingering and sat down with a special edition *Bugle*. Both Mary Lynn and Matt were represented with articles so beautifully written that I wondered if management realized what a treasure it was losing in one, and what a bonanza it'd found in the other.

For this issue, both had interviewed carnival people, while the murder was given only slight coverage, and that on page four. Mary Lynn's feature introduced Sylva Raines, the teenage daughter of big-cat trainers, who saved her summer earnings toward college. Planning a career in art, she spent her off-time sketching the animals. Some of her drawings, Mary Lynn noted, would be on sale during Old Home Week. The photo showed the young artist bent in concentration over a half-finished sketch of lion cubs.

Making a mental note to encourage the girl, I turned to Matt's byline—front page, center, with a color photograph of a woman bent over some sewing.

"Although the carnival retinue seems composed wholly of individualists," the article began, "for this reporter Monique Toulouse dominates."

> Well past middle age, her rust-hued hair streaked with tarnished silver, her face set in apparently placid lines of acceptance, resignation, and a benign passivity, she hums tunelessly at her work—the mending of costumes for those who perform on the rings, the high wire, the trapezes to which she can no longer aspire. It isn't until she stands and endeavors to straighten that the reason becomes obvious. In response to my questions, she turns luminous eyes in my direction, though not fully focusing, and confides in a voice both gravelly and ingratiating that when she was younger—perhaps in her twenties—she was a star of the circus high wire. One day her partner lost his footing, jolted against her and sent them both spinning, netless, to the sawdust. He was killed. Later, she wished that she had been.
>
> "Only see," she invites, tugging back a dry swatch of hair to disclose a concave temple, an angling scar. "My thoughts have been muddled since. And the scars I can't show, the ones inside," she touches her forehead, her chest, "those yet wrench so that when others perform I scarce

glance above ground level, lest panic and pain roar back." She turns from me then, and noting the grotesque promontory of her upper back, the unevenness of her shoulders, the hitch in her gait, I try to imagine that graceless body shaping movements of beauty and fluidity through the expectant air of a striped tent.

Impossible.

"They think me a joke, these new ones," she says, peering past that deformity—her eyes suddenly narrowed to glittering, her mouth twisted, her voice like splintering ice. "Them that remembered, while they remembered, they showed me respect. But these new ones—not just the young—treat me useless as cobwebs. Those long hours, just me and my needle alone in shadows, when the music grates like sandpaper on my spirit, and the laughter like acid, eating, I remember. And I plan. For they won't always laugh, that I promise. One day . . . one day . . . the music will die. And them that laugh now, they'll envy poor old crippled, useless Monique . . . one day . . . soon."

I spoke with Monique for perhaps thirty minutes, but she'll remain forever a unique puzzle in my mind—a paradox of limbs limp and halting, yet retained in her misshapen upper arms a strength still capable of lifting her weight without effort, a contradiction of calm passivity and openness and that shuttered coldness, those muttered plans for vengeance.

I marvel at her courage while I shudder at her potential for hatred.

Finishing the article, I found myself frowning. Certainly Matt had a way with language. Certainly he'd painted an unforgettable portrait with depth and texture. What troubled me was that he described a real flesh-and-blood woman, not a character in a short story, a character without the power—beyond that orchestrated by the writer—to feel and wince and cry. I imagined Monique's reaction, should she see this issue of the *Bugle*. And she certainly would see it, if, as she felt, there were those in her troupe who scorned her.

Rereading both articles, Matt's and Mary Lynn's, I weighed their approaches. While both styles were polished, Mary Lynn drew a more positive, more encouraging line. A warm "we're in this together and aren't we lucky" air. Matt seemed more self-consciously literary. Out to impress. Perhaps he felt he needed to be, in a small town not always alert to the genius it had spawned, and for readers more excited about Matt's past slam dunks than any present potential. Yet his more sensitive piece on Mrs. Porter had earned him accolades, and a privileged position for this article. I could nearly hear Minnie Kelp crowing, "And did you see where my Matt's article was placed? Just wait and watch! That boy will go far!"

And I was certain that he *would.* But surely farther, I thought, if his work bore the imprint of compassion.

He'll learn, I comforted myself; then, at the sound of Arden's steps on the back porch, folded the paper and went to begin dinner.

"Well," Arden said over dessert—rice pudding sprinkled with nutmeg, "I just spent my afternoon with the volunteer fire department, helping to clean out the fire hall and hearing the solution to the murder."

"Really?" I asked, though his tone indicated otherwise.

"Without a doubt it was some 'carnival creep.' Unless it was someone from around here. A stranger, unless it was someone who knew her, in which case it was almost certainly accidental. That is unless it was—"

"Premeditated," I supplied, laughing.

"How does it sound so far?"

I shrugged. "Who could argue?"

"And the motives range from attempted robbery to vengeance—someone with perfect pitch who wanted kids to stop coming for lessons."

"We shouldn't joke—"

"He wasn't."

I felt my eyebrows elevate. "Really . . ."

"Everyone agrees, though," he said, more seriously, "that it's inconceivable anyone should want to murder such a fine lady. And that the mutilation means one thing. Insanity."

I toyed with my spoon and nutmeg merged with milk. Perhaps those who'd never been emotionally ill could afford to be judgmental. I couldn't. I'd been submerged in blackness for too long to have anything but compassion for those who felt themselves smothered by it, entangled in it, filled with it, warped by it. I'd known intimately some of the demons who could infiltrate and whisper and engender doubt. How often I'd demanded of God, Why me? and then, less selfishly, Why anyone? In vain, I'd waited for answers, but all I'd ever discerned was that—once cured—anyone who'd ever explored that hell would have a deeper understanding and sharper sympathy for those currently afflicted. A foolish reason, I'd chided God—in reality no reason at all, for if no one's emotions were twisted, it followed that no one could require that particular forbearance.

Arden put his hand on mine. Through unexpected tears I noticed his sprinkling of freckles. "Sorry," he said.

I tried to smile. "It sneaks up."

"Well, we'll just shoo it away again," he said. "And besides, yours was never even a first cousin to real insanity."

"Close enough," I said, and we'd begun to clear the table when the telephone rang.

"Samantha Crane," Arden said when he returned. "Her flight's been changed, so she'll rent a car at the airport and be here by midafternoon Sunday for a short rehearsal with the local guys running the soundboard."

"She'll still stay with us Sunday night, though?"

"She says not. Something's come up with next month's tour, but since I assured her your nut brownies are world famous, she'll stop by for those and some vanilla ice cream before she hits the road again."

I laughed. "She won't be the first beautiful woman you've bribed with my brownies. Guess that makes me a codependent. Or facilitator. Or something."

"Accessory before, after, and during the fact," he said, his breath warm on my neck, his hands firm at my waist. "And the only beautiful woman I'll ever care to bribe."

4

With the concession lights dimmed, spotlights immersing the temporary plank stage, Samantha Crane made more of an excavation than an impression.

"Vespers?" I heard Minnie Kelp mutter. "More girlie show, I'd say, flopping around that brassy hair and swinging her hips." Even Madge Pears—her characteristic excitability dulled since the tragic death of her granddaughter Lelia—exclaimed, "But vespers is supposed to be . . . soft and sweet! Ain't they?"

I thought of vespers I had known—muted and candlelit. Worship slowed to a softened beat and cushioned in muffled organ strains.

Samantha, vivid in a jogging suit of glittering silver slashed by fluorescent fuschia and turquoise, gestured, stomped, swooped across the small stage and into the audience, her long hair swirling, her microphone cord snaking in her wake. Her voice throbbed, soared to unbelievable heights, then plunged to baritone range—equally at home, it seemed, at all levels—while her amplified background recording thumped, rattled, exulted in emotional runs and rivulets. The lyrics—many of them her own—wheedled, accused, comforted, confessed, triumphed by turns. I'd read that hers was a performance either widely acclaimed or deplored, and I observed ample evidence of both reactions. There were more toe-tappings and swayings than frowns, though, and when she invited the audience to clap in rhythm, a groundswell developed. A few young people closed into a circle and danced.

Even Joe Derrick, lounging against the half-open door of his official vehicle—the radio bubbling and crackling during moments of relative quiet—moved in a bulky, off-rhythm response.

I expected Minnie to have an apoplexy, but she seemed beyond that. Mouth gaping, eyes frantic, she stared about—searching, I assumed, for her grandnephew, who was busy at the moment shooting photos from improbable angles.

Poor Minnie, I thought, and yearned to go to her, either to ease her culture shock or to lead her to a safe distance from its source, but she hadn't come to a sufferance, yet, even of my Sunday handshake. Or Arden's.

Just then, her eyes met mine, and her face twisted. "You . . ." it seemed she was saying, and I knew the word accusatory.

I was being blamed for Samantha.

I couldn't help but smile, which surely angered Minnie further. She pinioned me with narrowed eyes for a beat or two, then turned a rigid shoulder. But it was ludicrous to blame—or credit—Arden and me for Samantha's appearance. It had been arranged by the town council and the *Bugle,* who'd asked us only if we could put her up for a night or two. It seemed strange that such uncompromising bitterness could coexist with her unqualified pride in her grandnephew.

Oh, well. Minnie's well-being seemed to depend on a steady infusion of hatred.

Without warning, my mind swung to Monique Toulouse, to Matt's story about her. Easing to the edge of the crowd, I looked about. Many of the carnival people were there. Some lounged almost listlessly with an air of indifference; others turned away, conversing in swirls of cigarette smoke; only a few actively responded. A young girl—surely the budding artist—leaned forward, hands clasped. And a muscular young man with tangled tan hair and the face of a Hummel shepherd boy beat an intricate rhythm with his fingertips on the lopsided lid of a trash can. But Monique?

I caught sight of her at last, huddled in shadow. She moved in quiet agitation, but I couldn't see her expression. How must she be affected by this lithe performance? The vibrance which spun itself without inhibition, which entangled and enthralled, as once she had done. How must it pain her to see such power, and she herself long powerless?

The mood of the performance had altered.

Samantha stood quietly, then, and her audience silenced. Stilled. Constable Joe's radio intruded with high-pitched information about a loose cow, and he silenced it with an awkward twist.

Hands clasped loosely about the mike, eyes raised, expression intense, Samantha sang the opening phrases of "How Great Thou Art," and long before she'd finished the hymn, tears were running down her cheeks . . . and mine. I heard soft snifflings about me, the shufflings of people reaching for tissues. For one another, a hand to hold.

And when Samantha gave her testimony, I saw Turk. If Minnie had been angry, he was livid. Rage seemed to emanate from him. Though he stood on the verge of the crowd, I wondered that Samantha herself wasn't seared by it.

The brownies would never stretch far enough.

"I've cut them as small as I can," Amy confided, lifting a bite-sized chunk from the pan as proof.

"We have lots of ice cream, though," I said.

"But your brownies are the big draw."

No. Samantha was the big draw, the reason our living room bulged.

"Everyone's so quiet," Amy whispered.

They were still absorbing.

Dora Kuhn, her blonde hair disheveled, joined us, her tall frame nearly filling the doorway. "Need help?"

"A miracle," I laughed, "of the loaves and fishes variety."

"Who'd ever have expected . . ." she began, opening a cupboard door. "Any microwavable goodies in here?"

"Cupcakes and muffins?"

"Good enough." Pulling down three boxes, she glanced at me, apparently for approval.

"Go to it. And bless you."

Ripping open a box, she said, "Some folks think this is the way Jesus did it, too."

"In the microwave?" giggled Amy, then said, "You mean by people sharing."

"Not me, though." Dora helped herself to a bowl, measuring cups, and a stirring spoon. "I have no trouble with the original version."

"The whale, too. And the ark." Amy placed a miniscule brownie on a plate and scooped ice cream over it. "Pitiful," she sighed.

"Give Samantha mine and Arden's," I suggested. "Under the ice cream, no one can tell how many anyone has, and Arden's reputation depends on her being able to taste them!"

"Then she can have mine, too," Amy said, "and Dora's."

"Thanks, Ame," Dora drawled. "It's nice to have friends."

During refreshments, while Matt interviewed Samantha, those gathered in our living room interjected their own questions, comments, and expressions of gratitude. During the interruptions, Matt listened actively. Scribbled busily.

One awed teenager said, "It took such guts to tell us all you did! I think *I'm* bad—often—and that God must be throwing darts at my picture. But you were into drugs and even kinda prostitution—and look how you serve Him now! When I get home, I'm gonna . . ." the young voice trailed off.

"Why wait until then? I'll pray with you now."

"Would you? I mean, you wouldn't mind?"

"And neither would He." Two bright heads bowed together, long hair mingling; four hands—two of them nail-bitten—clasped, and a voice rich with sincerity and belief interceded.

Moving quietly into position, Matt snapped a photo. And another.

Why did that trouble me at some deep stratum? Because such a moment should be private? Because journalists intrude on every human emotion without hint of apology? Because if Jesus were crucified today, TV cameras would record every nuance of His agony, to be dissected later and discussed dispassionately by psychiatrists, sociologists, biologists, historians—and to extend the celebration of His enemies? Not enough that it be suffered and observed once, it must be preserved and thrust forever before the eyes of the grieving, curious, sneering, and exultant alike.

The moment passed, the prayer ended, conversation resumed—but a dull unease smoldered within me.

The plates had long ago been cleared of refreshments. A few older people, hiding their yawns, said quiet goodbyes. Still, sharing continued.

"Such love here," murmured Amy. And tears threatened.

I hugged her.

Finally, Samantha stood.

"Are you sure you can't stay overnight?" asked Arden.

"If you knew what I have to do tomorrow . . . and how early!"

"Me, too," Mary Lynn said. "Greg's flying in from Texas." She colored. "We're ordering flowers, the cake . . ."

Matt was standing, too. Somehow, when he was vertical, the room grew squatter. "I need to polish this story so I can file it in the morning."

"Make it another great one," someone said, and he only nodded.

Then gradually the room emptied until only Amy, Arden, Samantha, and I remained. From the kitchen, sounds of dishes and water proved that Dora was still cleaning up.

"Thanks," Samantha said huskily. "You folks are great." She hugged me, then Amy, and extended her hand to Arden.

"You're allowed," I said, and she hugged him, too.

"You've given this town a precious gift," said Arden. "A new perspective."

"One some weren't quite ready for," she said, laughing, "but I'm used to that. Except . . ." Her eyes sobered. "There was one dark-haired man—I've never seen such hatred on a face before. It fairly blazed."

"Turk," Amy moaned. "I know it was Turk. I hoped you wouldn't see."

Samantha shuddered. "It was 'feel' more than seeing. There was a tangible pull, a force—almost malevolent—" She broke off. "I'm sorry. Is he related?"

Amy paused. "Only by marriage." She looked stricken.

For a moment, Samantha studied her. Then, patting Amy's hand, she promised, "I'll pray for him. And," she added, "for you."

With her presence removed, the house seemed drained. Together, we watched her down the steps to the rental car and into it. Saw her buckle her seat belt, adjust the mirrors, and lock the doors.

"Good girl," Arden said, "especially on the interstate."

But she never made it that far. Her car, abandoned with two flat tires, was found by joggers early the next morning at the edge of a cornfield just a few miles from town. Constable Joe found her crumpled body—throat cut and wrapped tightly with her long hair—a few rows into the field, where it had been dragged, her heels dredging bloody twin lines in the earth.

"No footprints good enough to cast, though," said Mary Lynn. She and Matt had come to tell us before we'd learn from someone less sympathetic. Their eyes held a haunted look.

Arden had taken Pam for a post-breakfast walk. I wished they'd hurry. I needed to feel Arden's strength, his quiet sanity, surrounding me.

"Let me get you a stiff cup of coffee," I offered around tears. "I know I need one."

At first, they refused, then sank onto kitchen stools. Matt propped his elbows on the table and dropped his head into one hand.

"Why?" I asked.

"And how?" added Mary Lynn.

"She'd locked her doors," I remembered.

"Really! Then even more . . . how?"

"Going for help?" suggested Matt.

"Maybe . . . yeah, I suppose that's it."

"Unusual, though." Matt frowned. "How do *two* tires blow?"

"Maybe spikes in the road? Or glass? Or . . . something."

"He'd have to know she was coming," I said.

"Or that *someone* was coming. Maybe any victim would answer . . ." Mary Lynn didn't finish, just swallowed noisily.

But why Samantha? I wondered. Why someone whose effervescence had caused us to love her out of all proportion to the time we'd known her?

Where was Arden?

The kettle whistled, tentatively.

"Just a few minutes," I said, and reached for mugs.

"Make mine tea, instead?" asked Matt.

"Decaf?"

"No way!"

I agree, I thought, as I spooned a double measure of instant coffee into my cup and handed can and spoon to Mary Lynn. Caffeine and prayer might be all that would get us through the day. Not in that order, I amended, and apologized silently to God.

Throughout the day, I found myself remembering Chaucer's tale in which the little Christian boy, ambushed and murdered in the ghetto, was unable to stop his sweet, worshipful singing because of a grain placed in his throat . . . had it been by the Virgin Mary? The details were jumbled. Maybe he had to sing until a grain *was* placed there. Perhaps he wasn't dead yet, couldn't die until . . .

No matter. From the time I'd first read it as a senior at the university, the story had disturbed me, and during my breakdown it had often recurred, summoning its sadness, its futility, to flap through my darkness. No matter that Chaucer's purpose had been a prejudicial one; the main focus for me had been oppression, that depressing imbalance between any innocence and any evil. The small boy's throat had been slit as well, before he'd been thrown into a sewer.

And Samantha had been discarded in a muddy cornfield, her body surrounded by ears of formed grain, her blood blotted and song muffled with her own hair.

I wondered if the murderer had ever read Chaucer.

And if so, what classic had caused him to sever Antonia Porter's foot?

I wasn't alone in seeing parallels between the two murders. An editorial in a Monday special edition of the *Bugle*

listed them—both victims women; both well respected, widely loved, hugely talented; both involved with church music.

Mary Lynn, in her final article for the paper, grieved that what was to have been a gentle, loving farewell to a gentle, loving community should instead seek for reason in such senseless crimes.

Most of the issue, though, was Matt's. The front page featured his photo-essay—a collection of color shots of Samantha in performance at the park and in prayer in our living room surrounding a photo, mercifully black and white, of her body in the cornfield.

I cringed. Though Joe Derrick had tried to shield the worst of it with his bulk, the contrast remained vivid: glittery costume under spotlights, animated movement, vibrant life, juxtaposed with the stark result of violent death.

Woodenly, I turned to Matt's article on page two. Of course it was beautifully crafted. And though the phrases had obviously been chosen to elicit horror, I caught none of Matt there—his deeper sensibilities. Perhaps journalists must steel themselves against that—or at least resist expressing it—but I would have welcomed some signal of youth's vulnerability, a willingness to weep in public print.

While there wasn't much new information, Matt's article mentioned something I hadn't heard as yet—the absurdity of the tires, not blown at all, but slashed with the bloody knife already used in the killing.

What did that do, I wondered, to the theory that Samantha had been going for help when the killer found her? And while neither the editorial nor any of the articles indicated that a serial killer might be involved, the implication seemed inescapable.

5

I was amazed that evening—and a bit appalled—by the apparent curative powers of whirling lights, swirling calliope music, the blaring, glaring, barking, coaxing, pressuring of the carnival atmosphere.

With the children, it was understandable that such enchantments might banish thoughts of recent death. Surely most parents had withheld details, perhaps even those least damaging. By common consent, Arden and I had folded the *Bugle* photo side in and placed it on a high shelf.

Breathlessly Pam tugged me from one wonder to another; then, when I tired, enlisted Arden. The other children were similarly enthralled, similarly wide-eyed and insistent. But even among the adults, I could find few symptoms of sadness or fear, though special care was taken that no one stray from a group. That no one walk home unattended. To watch and hear the laughter, the banter, at food tent and baseball throw, at games of chance, to listen to delighted screams from the ferris wheel and wide-swinging rings, to note the rapt silence exploding into cheers and applause when leopards and lions snarled to obedience, a stranger would never have guessed the twin acts of violence which had dominated all conversation.

Until the lights. The music. The coaxing.

Hadn't I seen that same resilience, that reluctance to dwell on tragedy, in funeral homes? Had, in fact, been repelled by it at my own father's funeral, as normal conversation and light laughter swirled—

"Mrs. Templeton."

I turned. "Dean!" I was tempted to say that he'd grown inches since spring, which he had, but remembered in time that as a teen I'd hated such chronicling by aunts and neighbors. "Having a nice summer?" It was good, I found, to be tugged to normality—and I tagged myself with hypocrisy.

Dean was tanned and relaxed. "Sure am. Are you?"

I smiled. Summer for a minister's wife, with Bible school, church picnics, and church cleaning, was as busy as any other season, but I'd enjoyed working in the flower beds, as opposed to dusting shelves. And I'd loved taking long, bootless, gloveless, coatless walks in the woods beyond the senior citizen housing development. With a twinge, I knew that such solitary excursions were out of the question now. I felt a sharp sense of loss. Surely, surely only temporarily. I said, "I've missed my favorite muralist, though."

He shifted. "I know I shoulda been coming to Sunday school—"

I touched his arm. "I'm not keeping attendance, Dean. It's your company I've missed. Drop by sometime, and we'll have cold milk and warm—"

"Chocolate chip cookies?" he interrupted, looking at ease again.

"Chocolate chip cookies," I assured him, and added, "with vanilla ice cream."

He took a moment to absorb that. Then, "Whattaya think of the animal drawings?"

"I was just going there." I glanced to be sure that Pam and Arden were still together. She was astride a lethargic spotted pony plodding about a well-worn ring while Arden cheered as enthusiastically as though she'd tamed a rodeo bronco. She'd be deliriously weary by bedtime, I thought, and followed Dean. "Have *you* seen the drawings yet?" I asked.

"They're great! But I didn't have a chance to talk to her." He paused. "She's real pretty," he mumbled.

I smiled inwardly, thinking that Sylva Raines was also probably three or four years Dean's senior. Not that it mattered. Sometimes a first love was safer when its object stood well out of reach.

But as we neared the booth where Sylva's work was displayed on small, individual easels, I saw that she was both younger than I'd expected and as pretty as he'd observed. Not with a model-like assurance, nor a china doll delicacy, but with that wholesome, clean-skinned, hazel-eyed, not-quite-perfect prettiness that spoke of good food, a loving family, and a self-esteem just emerging from shyness. Contact with the carnival had not taught her callousness. Vulnerability proved itself in the way she made eye contact slowly, then held it unswervingly. In the clasping and unclasping of her slender hands, the tentative way she pushed back her long honey-colored hair, and the slight quaver in her voice—until she spoke of her drawings. Or until someone else did.

"Amazing," a dignified older lady was saying as we approached.

"So lifelike," I added, and Sylva lifted shy eyes to catch and return my glance.

Dean said, "I read where Michelangelo took the skin off dead people and dissected them—to learn about the muscles and bones and stuff."

I started.

Sylva's expression stiffened.

"Sure looks like you might've."

She propped her hands on her hips, and her eyes narrowed under straight dark brows. "I couldn't do that to our animals!"

Dean, Dean, I thought. And felt embarrassment for him.

He colored. "I meant . . . it was a compliment, honest. I can see the muscles under the fur, gatherin' t'leap. I mean, your drawings come alive on the page."

She seemed slow to forgive.

"They're great," he finished weakly and glanced appealingly in my direction.

"Handling the animals must help," I offered.

She turned a warm smile on me, and a dimple formed in one cheek. Poor Dean, I thought. "I do when they're babies," she said. "And when they get older if Papa and Mama hold them. But books have taught me a lot. Let me show you!" She turned in a swirl of long denim skirt to enter the canvas-draped booth.

"I sure messed that up," Dean mumbled.

He certainly had, I thought, but patted his shoulder encouragingly.

She was back, thrusting some well-worn texts toward me. Several were familiar from my university art classes—page after page of drawings illustrating bone structure, then bones plus muscles and tendons, finally with flesh and hide or fur added. "Look at these, Dean," I said, and explained, "Dean's a very talented artist, too."

Her expression didn't soften. "I watch how they move," she said. "At first, I sketched from life mostly when they were resting—so I had time, you know. But now I can pretty much catch them in motion."

"Like that one," Dean tried again, almost but not quite touching a drawing of a tiger leaping toward a flaming hoop. She'd used black marker, and her lines were sure and spare.

Removing it from the shelf, she handed it to me. "It's one of my favorites," she said, with a grudging glance toward Dean. "Rexxon. That's what I call him. He's regal, and he's high octane."

Dean laughed nervously. Miserably.

She turned back to me. "Dad gets prints made of my best ones. You can have that, if you want it."

"It's wonderful. And I'd meant to buy some. Dean, is this the one you like best?"

He was sunk within himself. I knew how he felt. I'd been there myself, at his age and even beyond, wanting so desperately for my older brother and his friends to approve of me, to admire me—at least to *endure* me—and as a result moving with consummate awkwardness and making only the most graceless, bumbling observations. Even now, I could blush with remembered shame—as Dean was coloring. Even after all these years, I could wonder what they'd thought of me—then remind myself with even more debilitating certainty that they hadn't considered me at all.

Be nice to him, I thought toward her. Can't you see how he wants to impress you?

Surprisingly, she *was* looking at him more tolerantly. "Go ahead, take it," she urged. "And don't feel bad. I do dumb stuff myself, all the time."

His expression spoke abject adoration. "Thanks," he mumbled. "I'm sorry. About . . . what I said."

Obviously, he was afraid to remind her too clearly of what that had been.

She shrugged. Pushed back her lustrous hair. "Are you any good at animals?"

His shrug was an echo of hers. "Not near as good as you."

"You want to sketch tomorrow afternoon?"

"With you?"

A smile tugged at her lips. The dimple flashed again. "If you want to."

"Yeah! Sure! Thanks!" He could have looked no more deeply honored, no more elated, if he'd been invited on a field trip to heaven.

"Three or so? When they're a little sluggish?"

"Thanks!"

"And bring your own drawing stuff," she called after us. "Moving around, we don't have room for much of mine."

As we walked toward the pony ring and Pam and Arden, I didn't interrupt his euphoria.

At last, sighing deeply, he said, "I'll have to keep my mouth shut, though. What if I say something stupid again?"

I couldn't help it. I hugged him around the shoulders.

He didn't resist but asked in a muffled voice, "What's that for?"

And I answered with something stupid myself. "Because you're growing up, I guess. Do you know you've shot up at least three inches since spring?"

Closing the parsonage windows against the muted medley of distant carnival sounds, Arden and I settled for a few hours of together time. His busy schedule and my own involvements allowed too few periods when we could simply sit, perhaps hold hands, and share quiet thoughts, silence, or contented laughter.

Precious time.

"I forget," he whispered against my ear, "just how special it is to be with you."

Tears stung my eyes.

In those long months when I'd struggled to escape the cloying strands of blackness, when dark whispers had insinuated that any escape was preferable to no escape—

"What did you think of her?" he was asking.

Her? Samantha? No, he wouldn't be speaking of Samantha in such equable tones.

"Sylva," he said. Perhaps repeated.

"She's wonderful!" I added, "Dean's smitten."

"It's time."

"I suppose." I wondered, but didn't ask, when Arden had first thought himself in love.

"My first grade teacher," he offered, "had long straight hair that looked like a black vinyl curtain and lips the color of eggplant. One of the guys said she'd had them tattooed, but I knew they were natural." He pulled me closer. "It broke my heart when she showed us her engagement ring."

Except for monthly newsletters and periodic reports, we hadn't been in contact with Dr. Connelly, district superintendent overseeing Arden's pastorate, for quite a while.

Dr. Connelly's voice had always been more dependable than a meteorologist's report. When things were humming along—causing *him* no concern—his voice vibrated with well being. But the tone I heard over the phone Tuesday late morning could denote only one thing. A complaint of some kind. And not just a generic complaint. Something major.

"Just when things seemed to be going so well," his barometric tones continued, and I mentally amended that to read: just when Arden had kept his problem charge quiet for nearly another year.

"I don't suppose you could tell me."

In a longsuffering mode, "You know the protocol, Paula."

Which didn't mean I had to agree with it. "Arden's helping at the food tent. It's Old Home Week here."

"Yes, yes. So I understand."

"He won't be back until late this evening."

"He couldn't get away long enough for a phone call?"

It would be a temptation, I knew—simply to learn what we faced this time—but Arden wouldn't duck a commitment.

"No."

He sighed heavily. "Commendable, I suppose. Still."

I lost patience with him. "This isn't the first time we've been penalized for his dedication."

"This complaint has more to do with . . . judgment."

"And there's nothing wrong there, either."

There was a beat of silence. Then, "There's no call to be defensive, Paula."

"Really? How can I be otherwise when I don't know who's on the *offense?*" Of course I could make some educated guesses. "Does this have anything to do with Samantha Crane?"

It was essential that I fill his silence with words. "She was wonderful," I chattered, "but then, if you've ever heard her—"

He cleared his throat. "*Of* her, of course, especially since . . . since her death. But . . ."

His silence told me all I needed to know.

"Surely Minnie isn't accusing Arden of her *murder.*" I was deliberately talking nonsense, yet when he didn't answer, the flesh on the back of my neck began to crawl. Dear God, I thought, dear, dear God—surely even Minnie Kelp couldn't suggest something so preposterous. So unjust.

I spoke very carefully. "I'd never have dreamed of asking Samantha here, to such a small town. Nor would Arden."

Silence.

I continued, "The town council suggested her, and the local newspaper made the contact. They shared the expenses."

"But—"

"They asked if we could house her. That was all. And then she couldn't stay."

"Too bad."

Yes, I thought. If she'd waited until morning, she might still be alive. Still performing those glorious runs and trills. Still striding through an audience, a visual portrayal of energy and joy. Still bending her head with a troubled teenager in prayer.

"Paula? Are you still there?"

"Oh. Sorry. I was . . . remembering."

"This has to be difficult." Was it significant that his tone seemed more personal? Had he discounted the complaint? Or simply shelved it for later? "You will have Arden call at his first opportunity."

And I knew that nothing had been fully dismissed.

After an early lunch, when I'd settled Pam in with Connie, cold milk, warm cookies, and the expectation of a nap, I reported for my shift at the Historical Society booth. Minnie Kelp was just leaving. It was obvious by her swift coloration that she'd rather have missed me.

"Good afternoon, Minnie," I said.

Grunting, she turned away, but a grinning Mrs. Bancroft stood in her path.

"How are ticket sales going?" I asked.

Minnie sighed, shifted, and muttered, "Well enough."

No eye contact.

Significant.

"Dr. Connelly called."

She started, and her color deepened.

I said, "Perhaps he'd seen Matt's photos—do you think? He's a talented photographer, perhaps as gifted as in his writing."

Brazenly she straightened. Faced me squarely. "You know very well who called him! Don't be more mealy-mouthed than usual! And it grieves me that Matt seems so taken with you . . . and with such as that Crane woman. I know we shouldn't speak ill of the dead, and

I'm sorry as I can be that she had to face her Maker like a slut—"

"A sl—"

"Yes, prissy Mrs. Templeton! A slut! Perhaps you're too close to being one to recognize one—"

"Minnie Kelp!" snapped Mrs. Bancroft, pulling Minnie about despite the difference in their sizes. "Now, you apologize! That was uncalled for, and you know it."

"I'll apologize for nothing!"

"Oh, yes, you will, too!" Mrs. Bancroft was leaning forward, her hands propped on her slender hips, her neck elongated. She fairly vibrated with wrath.

"And who'll make me?"

I felt a smile tugging. They were so like children squabbling on a playground.

"*I'll* make you!"

"*You!* Hmmmph!"

"And don't think I can't. There are skeletons in your closet I know about and few others do—"

"Why, Sara Bancroft! That's blackmail!"

"And better'n character assassination any day."

Slowly, Minnie turned, her eyes not meeting mine. "I don't think of you as a . . . slut, exactly. But that Crane woman was, dead or not. No nice girl swings her hips that way. You know what all those men were thinking—"

"Mrs. Kelp," I began softly. "Minnie, did you listen to the lyrics?"

She didn't answer.

"They were worshipful. About sacrifice and redemption and love."

Her lips firmed. "I know the kind of 'love' that one wanted!"

"Minnie Kelp, you have a dirty mind!"

Minnie's lip quivered. "Do not."

"Do too."

"Not."

"Too."

The playground again. Who knew how long it might continue? "Please, Mrs. Bancroft. Minnie just has . . . a deep moral concern."

Minnie glared at me. "I don't need defending in my own town! And particularly not from you, who wouldn't know 'a deep moral concern' if one jumped up and banged your nose! The first thing you did when you came here was allow that young delinquent to desecrate the annex wall! And just the other week—you and your artist friends! Hmmmph! I only pray you don't corrupt my sweet Matt! And that husband of yours. *Poetry* at Sunday service? What place does *poetry* have in a church?"

I couldn't resist. "The psalms—"

"Psalms are different! They're . . . uplifting, not this modern—" She broke off. "How dare you grin at your elders and betters!"

I'd been thinking of the Song of Solomon.

But there was neither need nor opportunity to mention it. Mrs. Bancroft did. "I often think," that sweet lady said, fingertip to her lips, "if those who talk about bannin' books ever once read the Bible—I mean, really *read* it!" She clucked. "Why there's everything there! Violence to curl your hair. And sex . . . and more sex. Solomon wrote some X-rated things, for sure."

"Solomon," Minnie said sanctimoniously, "was the wisest man in history."

"Except he was addicted to women." Mrs. Bancroft struck an exaggerated pose. "'The joints of thy thighs are like jewels. Thy navel is like a round goblet, which wanteth not liquor—'"

"Sara Bancroft!" Minnie gasped.

"'. . . thy belly is like a heap of wheat set about with lilies. Thy two breasts are like two young roes—'"

"Sara!" Minnie's voice was choked. Both hands pressed against her own ample bosom, she struggled for breath.

"'. . . that are twins,'" Mrs. Bancroft finished. "Oh, Minnie, don't be silly!"

"Are you all right?" I placed an arm about Minnie's shoulders, and she leaned into it.

Which showed, I thought, just how serious the situation could be.

"Minnie, it's an analogy," I explained gently, "comparing human love to Christ's love for the church."

That seemed only to make things worse.

Of course, I berated myself. Her image of Christ was formed by the paint-by-the-numbers replica of *The Last Supper* hanging in the annex. Prayerful, passive, and two-dimensional, He was safe there—and she safe from any possibility that He might tolerate sensual terms.

She was breathing in heavy gasps.

Mrs. Bancroft, face pinched, looked suddenly penitent. "I only wanted . . ."

Whatever it was she had wanted to accomplish, she'd succeeded—and beyond.

"Here, Minnie, dear, do sit here," she urged. "I'll get you some nice cold water."

"The least . . ." gasped Minnie, ". . . can do."

Always gracious, I thought, carefully withdrawing my arm and moving to sell tickets to a young couple who gushed over the quilt and patted their money before releasing it.

Mrs. Bancroft was at my elbow. "I truly am so sorry," she murmured. "I knew she was prudish, but . . . good thing I didn't get to the part about climbin' the palm tree and takin' hold of the fruit."

"A very good thing," I agreed, hiding a smile and wondering what—or who—had ever encouraged sweet little

Mrs. Bancroft to commit portions of the Song of Solomon to memory.

"And from the King James Version, at that," I finished, retelling the scene to Arden and Amy that late afternoon.

I'd invited Amy to join us for dinner, and she'd agreed, once I'd promised not to go to a lot of trouble. As it happened, Arden had bought barbecued chicken dinners at the food tent and carried them home in plastic containers more commendable for their size than their stability.

"I've never had the nerve to preach on the Song of Solomon," Arden admitted. "It's really very beautiful, but open to misinterpretation."

Amy giggled. "Was Mrs. Bancroft misinterpreting it?"

"Interpreting it very narrowly," I suggested. "But making a valid point."

"Clarify," invited Arden.

"Well, Minnie'd been upset about Samantha's performance. All she remembered was swinging hips, and that set her off on modern art and poetry."

Amy winced.

At dinner, Arden had asked if she'd read some of her work at all three churches the coming Sunday. "I'm preaching on loss," he'd explained, "and some of your recent work—"

"Certainly fits," she'd agreed. "Sure, if you think no one would be offended—"

"If no one's offended by my sermons," Arden said, "I figure I've served up pudding."

She leaned forward. "You don't mean . . . you deliberately *try* to upset people?"

"I mean," he repeated, "deliberately to speak the truth. And the truth usually makes someone flinch." He grinned.

"Christ often poked holes in people's smugness. Why should I be less controversial? Or," he added, "safer?"

"And yet," she offered thoughtfully, "then you get calls from Dr. what's-his-name."

"Exactly," he agreed, leaning back. "Maybe he needs to get jolted, too, occasionally."

That evening, after another short visit to the carnival, we sat comfortably—Dr. Connelly's calls behind us, his concerns soothed. I nursed a cup of spiced tea, knew that Pam slept safely in her bed, and listened to Amy reading her work in shy, intense rhythms. More than half a week of celebration and excitement stretched before us. It seemed endless. Harmless. Though the thought of Samantha Crane, sitting here just days before, brought jolts of pain, danger seemed far away.

6

Where warmth empowered,
now earth lies cold . . .

impossible for me to recognize if
there beneath that shallow shell,
within that frigid womb,
lies only barrenness—
a vacant gloom—
or
fallow seeds
which,
when I least anticipate,
may quietly germinate,
may reach with threadlike roots
toward sustenance . . .
may pierce the crust
to thrust their supple, slender green
toward atmospheric chill,
toward light
I view as midnight, still. . . .

while I—
enmeshed by fears,
and groping through a vacuum
splintered by tears—
may stumble there,
may grasp direction,
may realize epiphany—

a resurrection
of all that joy and pain
I'd mourned as lost—
that pain and joy which shape the cost
of loving . . .
of being loved.

Matt shifted on a kitchen stool. He'd read this poem and two others sensitively, stumbling over a few words. Not as though they were awkward or illegible. More as though they'd awakened some unexpected chord. As though he were inexplicably moved.

It was a side of Matt I hadn't seen before. His references to the carnival workers, his feature on Monique, had hinted of brittleness. Of a casual, almost callous, indifference. Even his stories on Samantha Crane, though of high literary quality, had read more like press releases than observations by someone who'd experienced her effervescence firsthand, however briefly. Minnie should have found comfort in the objectivity which I found more than faintly distressing.

For some reason he might never disclose, Amy's poetry had touched him as Samantha's music had not. Sipping my first coffee of the morning, I wondered why. How.

He rested his fingertips on the pages. "She wrote these? Mrs. Turkle?"

"Amy," I said. "Yes."

"Why?"

"Why?" The unexpectedness of his question had jarred me.

Mary Lynn, who'd been sitting quietly, sipping at her coffee, asked, "Why do any of us write anything?"

He didn't look up. "Some of us," he said, "write for money."

Mary Lynn reached to place her hand on his, and his fingers convulsed, curled in the way that grubs, when discovered, seek to make themselves smaller.

What an analogy, I thought, repulsed by it. Matt's hands were large and strong and capable and tan. Where had the grub image come from? Still, there had been that kind of passive resistance.

Mary Lynn was saying, "Advertising agencies write to make money. Pornographers write to make money. You couldn't possibly—ever—write as you do just for money." She patted, withdrew her hand, and his gradually resumed its natural dimensions.

A shiver spun up my spine.

Amy's poem had revealed a vulnerable dimension Matt had successfully hidden before—perhaps even from himself.

Poetry seemed to have that power.

Frightening.

And wonderful.

Still studying the pages, Matt reached for his coffee mug. "You should do a feature on her. On . . . those."

"You forget," Mary Lynn laughed, "I'm an *ex*-star reporter!"

It was as though she had freed him to be himself. "Right!" he said lightly. "The *Danvers Bugle* is now my oyster! Mine alone!"

"And welcome to it." She spoke more gently, though. Almost sadly. "She'll be as good to you as she has been to me. Maybe better." She blinked rapidly. "Good grief, I'm not going to cry, am I?"

"Probably," Matt teased. "You're coveting my future Pulitzer."

"Surely not merely a Pulitzer!" she scoffed fondly. "Minnie will fight for a Nobel in literature, at least."

Sighing deeply, he nodded, his expression guarded.

To me, Mary Lynn confided, "The *Times* asked to reprint Matt's photo-essay, had you heard?"

"Congratulations!" I said.

He murmured a response.

Silence hummed. The cooling stove ticked. The house settled. It seemed a companionable silence—why did I yearn to break it?

And then Pam broke it for us. Overhead, I heard her feet thump to the floor, then scamper in the direction of the bathroom.

Mary Lynn giggled. "Lucky you."

I nodded. I well knew how fortunate I was to have Arden and Pam. "In a year or so . . ." I began, allowing Mary Lynn to finish the thought for herself.

"Greg wants five, at least."

"Five—what?" teased Matt.

"Five children, you oaf!" She punched his arm, and her coffee sloshed. "Oops. Sorry, Paula." She mopped with her napkin.

"Forget it." I went for a dishcloth.

And, thankfully, we were fully back to normal.

"What happened here?" I asked, when Pam had finished juice and cereal and was humming over toast and grape jelly.

Mary Lynn had stayed. I'd offered to help with wedding favors. She looked up from shaping a peach satin rose. "With Matt?"

I nodded. "And what you said about Minnie."

"Oh, that." She smiled. "Matt lived with Minnie for a while. His parents traveled a lot."

"She . . . resented him?"

"Far from it! She doted on him! Spoiled him rotten, as a matter of fact. When his parents returned from one trip, and he kept casting up 'Aunt Minnie this, Aunt Minnie that,' they swore they'd put him—and her—up for adoption."

"Poor Matt."

"Poor *Minnie!* They set her off-limits for a while. But you know how hard it would be to bar Minnie from anything she wanted to be a part of!"

I smiled grimly.

"At piano recitals, his parents might not attend, but Minnie would—listening with her eyes closed and her face glowing. When he had a game, she was there—berating the refs. Even telling the coach he was wasting Matt's potential."

"But he made all-stars . . . someone said."

"And Minnie was sure it should have been states."

"Of course he *did* in debate."

"And she'd planned on his winning nationals."

"Poor Matt."

Admiring the completed rose, she handed it to me for leaves. "There are worse things than having someone who's totally, firmly, enduringly on your side."

She was right. Arden had been all of that for me. I couldn't have survived my breakdown without him.

"And you've seen how tenacious Minnie can be. Speaking of which?"

"A lull in the storm—for now, at least. But it took Dr. Connelly to convince her that we hadn't bodily dragged Samantha here to corrupt the minds of our youth."

"Poor Minnie."

In a way, Mary Lynn was right. It was sad that Minnie—that anyone—couldn't have seen past the modern trappings—the exercise suit, the microphone, the background music—to realize that Samantha worshiped the same God, exulted in the identical glory that Minnie could accept only through phrases and tunes of an earlier century.

"'Be not the first by whom the new are tried, nor yet the last to lay the old aside.'"

"Alexander Pope," Mary Lynn said, beginning a third rose, this one burgundy. "You don't suppose he'd met Minnie!"

Due to the placement of the gazebo and fountain, and because vintage oaks and maples so liberally populated the park, high-wire acts were to be held in a barricaded street. There, too, both height and breadth were limited. Still, long before dusk descended, the children were preparing to be amazed.

"High!" Pam's tiny finger wobbled as she pointed to the wire.

And it *was* frightening!

There wasn't height enough to allow for a net, and surely in the event of an accident the mattresslike pads roustabouts had spread beneath would prove insufficient protection. With my own intense fear of heights, I wasn't sure I could bear even to watch.

And then I turned and saw Monique.

Her hands stilled on her ever-present sewing, an unreadable expression twisting her features, she rocked slightly in a lawnchair and stared at the empty wire.

What memories spun behind those shadowed eyes? I wondered. What music did she strain to hear, what gasps and roars of the crowd? What remembered breezes stirred her, what exultation of supple limbs and trained grace—

Suddenly I was aware of her eyes turned to study me.

I felt warmth climbing to my face. "I'm . . . sorry." I spread my hands awkwardly. There could be no acceptable defense for staring. She must think me fascinated by her deformity. My face burned.

As she struggled from her chair to hobble toward me, I resisted the impulse to step back. To hide Pam behind me.

Instead, I extended my hand. "I'm Paula Templeton," I said, startled by the power of her frail-looking fingers.

"The Reverend's wife and little girl." Her voice was deep and grainy, as Matt had described it.

I wondered that she would have known us. Or Arden.

Pam clutched my knee.

"She's a pretty one."

"Thank you."

"And you. You're pretty, too." I felt her glance scrape my face, scan my hair. "I was pretty once," she added.

Surprisingly, vestiges of that beauty survived.

"You have lovely eyes," I said. They were gray and clear, despite hours over her mending.

Matt's article had described them as luminous.

"They see more than they ought," she said tiredly. "No one's eyes should be forced to read pity or scorn . . . and I've yet to decide which is worse. But you . . ." her eyebrows arched. "You looked at me different. Not disgusted or haughty. More as though you saw beyond what I am—"

"To what you were!" I finished. "You're very perceptive!"

"And you," she said slowly. Contemplatively. "I never felt those thoughts on me before—not so gentle—not since just after the accident, and my own mother hovered above me, her tears falling hot on my face and hands. All those long, long years ago." She pulled her attention fully back to the moment. To me. And she frowned, surely in questioning.

"I read Matt Culhaney's article," I explained.

She spat to the grass. Huddling closer, Pam made a sound more of delight, I thought, than alarm.

"He's . . . young," I said feebly.

She grimaced. "He used me. Used my deformity and pain and turned my own words against me." She glanced over her shoulder. Roustabouts adjusted lights; barkers tested mikes; performers tugged at costumes. Checked makeup in lighted mirrors. Her voice deepened to a husky whisper. "Before, they ignored me, walked by as though I was shadow. Now, there's a difference. They notice me now, and it's an uneasy noticing. There's fear in it. And youth or not, he caused that."

The dark mood passed as quickly as it had come. Stooping, she coaxed Pam, "Come to me, pretty little girl, and let me touch your straight limbs and soft curls."

Surprisingly, Pam released my leg and obeyed.

I wanted to snatch her back. If Matt had been right about the streak of violence . . .

"So sweet," she was cooing. "So lovely. And your name is . . ."

"Pam," I supplied, around the clog in my throat.

"Pammie. Sweet Pammie."

Inwardly, I shrank still farther. Not so surprising, reason told me. Pam. Pammie. What other softening would occur to a stranger?

Pam reached to touch the brittle hair. Pushed it back, revealing the concave forehead. With small fingers, she gently stroked the scar. "Hurt?" she asked sadly.

"Yes. It hurt. So very, very badly." Her voice broke.

"Poor lady." Pam caught the wizened face between her chubby hands, stood on tiptoes, and kissed the scar.

"There," she said, pulling back, but only slightly. "All better, now!"

Monique's beautiful eyes glazed with tears. Her voice was strangled. "Oh, God. Oh, merciful God, *yes!* If healing could ever come, it would be . . ."

And it seemed she could go no farther. "Forgive me," she sobbed, and rushed awkwardly away, her deformity underscored by her haste.

"Lady cry," Pam said, her own eyes filling. Sighing, she clamped herself to my leg again, releasing me only when Arden joined us, his late supper shift in the food tent ended.

While Arden and Pam watched the high-wire performance, I stood well back, where—in breathless moments—I could turn my attention elsewhere.

And there was much to observe.

Matt was everywhere, it seemed—stooping, angling, questioning, scribbling.

The rides and games continued unabated—a rhythm of sound, color, and movement which seemed the blood and breath of the carnival.

Most of the people were known to me—not only the residents of McClintock and surrounding areas, but carnies grown surprisingly familiar during the several evenings. There were, though, some strangers—and one of those intruded himself into my thoughts for no other reason than that he wore a charcoal-gray felt hat pulled low on his forehead. It was too warm for a felt hat. Other men wore the baseball caps that seemed almost a uniform, though in every color and with every conceivable legend.

This man was set apart, as well, by attitude. There seemed no joy in his brow-shaded eyes, in his long face, set in deep, wrinkled patterns. No carnival spirit. Morose, he slumped on one of the small benches in the gazebo and fingered, rather than ate, his wilting french fries. If he was interested in anything, it was in the activity near the street.

Dean and the young artist approached together, languidly, sharing a cone of multicolored cotton candy.

"Mrs. Templeton!" Dean called, and tugged her after him. "Baked anything lately?"

"I could manage tomorrow," I said, "if I had a good reason."

He grinned. "I could bring Syl with me."

"Sylva, really," she corrected, offering her hand, then drawing it back. "I'm sticky. We met, remember? But it's Sylva. Don't ask me why."

"It suits you. It's lovely." Uniquely old-fashioned, I thought . . . and comforting.

She flushed. "It's a lot of trouble, though. I'm always having to spell it—"

An explosion of drumrolls clattered from the street.

"We're missing the high wire!" Dean grabbed her hand, and she didn't resist.

"See you tomorrow!" she called over her shoulder. "Deannie says your chocolate chip cookies are stupendous!"

Ah, I thought, smiling. Deannie and Syl. Shared cotton candy. It looked promising.

But how would Dean handle the end of the week . . . the closing of the carnival?

Standing by the bole of an oak, its crisp foliage drifting between me and the action of the high wire, I could experience the excitement, once removed. The crowd was energized. Responsive. Both the performance and the reactions seemed choreographed, rather than reflected, by drumrolls and trumpet blasts. Earlier, I'd seen the trumpeter—an elderly man in a wrinkled red jacket missing several brass buttons—sneaking surreptitious sips from a bottle-shaped brown bag. But there was nothing fuzzy about his fanfares.

The drummer was young, his tan-gold hair shining in a halolike frizz about his head while one clump hung long and straight down his broad back. He wore tight, ripped jeans, a buckskin vest, and no shirt. His upper arm muscles gleamed with sweat as he plied his drumsticks and stroked the cymbals with metal brushes.

I'd seen him before, I realized, accompanying Samantha Crane's last performance with imaginary drumbeats on the lid of a metal trashcan. Then, I'd been struck more by the cherubic appearance of his face than by his muscular arms. Observing him from behind, I tried to imagine his expression as he played, as his body wove its own rhythms, then relaxed in wary waiting until another climactic moment must be underscored.

Certainly he'd been caught up in Samantha's music. Perhaps any music transported him.

As I watched, Matt crouched and waited, camera poised, shooting only when the drumsticks blurred again.

Dean and Sylva sat on a grassy spot nearby. Once, in a lull, she looked up to say something. I saw the drummer's shoulders shaking, heard his robust laughter. Dean drooped.

Poor Dean.

And then the drums rattled again. Sylva touched Dean's arm, and he straightened, tugging her close.

No problem. Dean would be fine.

I came upon the drummer later, just as I was recovering from the shock of seeing Turk and Amy together, their hands entwined. Drumsticks protruding from his vest pocket, he leaned on a counter displaying stuffed animal prizes and talked with the young man tending the stand.

"How'd the show go?" I heard the other man asking.

The drummer shrugged. "A coupla slips. No falls. Good thing, too. We'd've had another Monique, for sure. Whoever thought those mats'd cushion a fall—nuts."

"So what's new, Clint-o? Tell me, what's new? Who cares about safety here—'cept maybe Monique, and she's batty." He swirled his fingers around his temple.

"Still, not a bad old girl," Clint insisted. "In fact—"

By then, I was past, though keeping at a distance behind Amy and Turk. Thinking how awkward it could be, having Turk see me, I veered aside—barely avoiding a collision with the felt-hat man—and into the crowd near the kiddie rides. Arden would be ready for some relief.

But Pam wasn't with Arden.

Heart thumping, I rushed toward him.

He smiled, nodding. And there was Pam, bent close to Monique, who plied her needle to the ripped shoulder of a lime-green sequined concoction.

"Strange attraction," he said.

And I thought, Beauty and the beast, but kept it to myself.

Matt aimed his camera skyward, through drifting foliage, and pressed the shutter. It should be a good shot, dark clouds lit faintly by carnival lights.

"I saw Turk and Amy," Arden said. "Looking cozy."

"How would you feel," I asked, wondering what I'd answer if the question were put to me, "if they'd get back together?"

"If he truly valued her . . ." His voice drained off, and I wondered if he thought, as I did, that there was more chance of Guernseys giving banana splits instead of milk.

The next hour was busy with merry-go-round adventures and strawberry shortcake, trainrides and popcorn.

Twice I saw the drummer Clint in conversations. And, in the same vicinity, the felt-hat man in morbid concentration.

In the distance, lightning flickered, just as Pam held her tummy and said, "I tired."

Another flash, followed by another and another. Even over the carnival sounds, I heard the rumble of thunder. I held my hands to her, and she lifted her arms.

"Time to go home," I called to Arden.

He nodded. "The storm sounds close."

In fact, the first drops pattered as we passed the ferris wheel, where the quality of squealing altered swiftly. Funny, I thought. They're not afraid of heights that would drive me frantic, but a few raindrops . . .

A deep voice called Clint's name—first tentatively, then with authority. I saw him freeze in place, turn slowly to face . . . why was I not surprised? Felt Hat.

"Can we make it?" Arden asked.

Already, the tempo of the carnival had changed. Rides screeched to a shuddering halt. Loud voices called and concession frameworks banged in shutdown. Hunched figures, some with newspapers or carnival posters protecting their heads, scurried for their cars or for cover—anywhere.

Still, I heard voices raised in anger.

Turk's and Amy's.

". . . no use! . . . never change . . ." The wind caught segments of their speech and hurled them toward us.

". . . wish . . . *dead!*" That had been Turk.

I slowed, glancing toward Arden, but either he hadn't heard or read no genuine threat there.

". . . never!" Amy's voice shrieked.

I glanced back. Turk was reaching for her, she retreating. He followed until he'd backed her against a corn-dog trailer. And still he pushed. Metal clanged and buckled beneath her slight weight.

"Arden!" Cuddling Pam close, I tugged on his arm, and he turned. Rain coursed from tendrils of his cinnamon-colored hair.

And lightning flashed. Again. Again. Strobelike.

"Wait here!"

But I followed, as swiftly as wet grass and Pam's weight allowed. There were three people, then, and one—blonde and burly—struggled with Turk.

The drummer?

I thought so. And certainly Turk was no match for him. After only moments, he pulled away, backed off, shouted and gestured, then strode toward us. Clint—I was nearly certain it was Clint—enclosed a sagging Amy in his arms and moved toward shelter, where I was sure—or almost sure—Felt Hat waited. I shuddered. Impressed by Clint's sensitivity to music, his fondness for Monique, I thought that Amy might be safe with him. But would Clint be safe from Felt Hat? And Amy . . .

And then I felt Turk's presence, barring Arden's path.

Shadows and slashing rain hid his face, but there was no questioning his mood. He lunged, shoving angrily at Arden's shoulder and knocking him off balance against an electric pole, where Arden stood stunned, for a moment, as Turk turned to me. I thought he would push me, too. But Pam whimpered in my arms, and he only shouted, "You done this—you and him! Since you come here—"

And he raged into rain, now driving in cold sheets.

"Arden," I gasped. "Amy . . ."

"Where?" His voice was weak. Uncertain.

Poor Arden.

But Amy . . .

With Pam huddled against me, I sloshed toward the spot where I'd last seen her. Last seen *them.* All but a few dim lights had been extinguished. Rain clattered on tarps, pinged on metal, splatted in puddles already brimming.

"There," Arden said at my shoulder, and peering into shadow layered in shades of deep and deepest, I caught the pale flicker of Amy's blouse.

"Amy!" I called, and wind whipped the syllables into shreds.

But she turned. Waved. Called something in a tone that seemed reassuring.

When she and one figure—only the one—moved away easily, bent together against wind-driven rain, and Arden said, "They're okay, honey, let's get Pam home and into a hot bath," I agreed with only minimal reluctance.

7

Suddenly, the week seemed endless. It was only Thursday morning, and the carnival would close down Saturday midnight. With all the emotions already erupting, would we make it?

And Amy.

I'd tried to call—twice. No answer. Could I have misinterpreted what had seemed assurance? Clint was, after all, a carny. Felt Hat still an unknown quantity.

Taking one pan of cookies from the oven and inserting another, I longed for the relative rightness of precarnival life—not just because of the murders; after all, the first had predated the carnival's arrival—but for the known quality of tensions. Of familiar interpersonal stresses.

I was reaching for the phone again when I heard the tap on the kitchen door. I breathed relief. Too early for Dean and Sylva. Amy? Surely it was Amy. But it was Mary Lynn who called from the kitchen door, "I know you're in there. I smell embryonic calories."

"Come in!" I said, striving for lightness. "I have half the table cleared for rose makings." I'd call once she got settled.

She opened the door, set in a sagging tote bag and her purse, and said, "The rest's in the car."

"Need help?" I slipped the cookies on racks for cooling. Their surfaces rippled; melted chocolate chips dulled.

"Just get those cookies made. My system cries for caffeine!"

"There's always coffee." But she was gone.

When she returned, I asked, "Where's your partner in journalism?"

"He's doing some interviews at the park. The drummer, I think, for one."

I paused, spatula suspended. Clint. And Amy? Surely they weren't still together—of course not! Spent with emotion, she'd simply slept in. Not heard the phone.

"What's wrong?" Mary Lynn sounded suddenly very tired.

I shook my head. "Nothing . . . really." I forced a smile. "Really. Nothing."

Frowning, she turned away, and I said, "I hope Matt doesn't run into Monique Toulouse."

"Oh?" Slowly, she arranged materials on the table.

"She seems . . . upset by his article."

Mary Lynn didn't answer.

"I tried to appease her."

"Maybe you shouldn't have."

My spatula clattered to the stove top.

"It's just," she explained haltingly, as though shaping her thoughts as they occurred, "that maybe he needs to *know* when he's stubbed his toe—or somebody else's. I mean, we can't protect him forever."

"I wish we could," I said, surprising myself. Wanting to protect all of them. Clint, Amy . . . not Turk . . . and Matt, of course.

Mary Lynn teased gently, "You and Great-Aunt Minnie."

"Ouch." I regreased the cookie sheet, still warm, and plopped spoonfuls of dough in equidistant globs.

"What's the occasion?"

"You're here," I teased. "And Dean's coming . . . and bringing his new friend."

"Ahhhhh."

"Have you seen her drawings?"

She paused. "When I did the interview . . ."

"I'm sorry." I felt a swift warmth that had nothing to do with the oven. "I'm losing it."

"No problem. So much has happened since then. Besides, mine wasn't the memorable article."

"It was gentle."

"That's part of it. But look, if you're going to take forever with those, I'll have to postpone the wedding!"

I handed her three of the cooling cookies. They were still limp. By the time she'd finished murmuring satisfaction, I'd made another call—still unanswered.

The last cookies were in the oven, Pam in her high chair, and Mary Lynn and I well into production when a knock rattled the door.

"Dean?" I wondered, and glanced toward the clock.

"It's me." Amy's voice. Her sad voice.

"Come in." Tears of relief clogged my throat. I was aware of Mary Lynn's puzzled glance from Amy to me. To Amy. Still, I said, "I was worried."

Amy looked haggard. Her eyes had a haunted look, and a dark bruise marred her cheek. "You saw, last night." It was half-question, half-statement. "Turk, I mean."

A fly buzzed. Drawn by the baking, no doubt.

"We were just about to come to your aid when . . . someone else did."

"Clint."

To Mary Lynn, I said, "The drummer."

"Ahhh." She laid another completed rose on the pile. Peach, burgundy, and pale green satin glowed dully in the scant light.

"Nice," Amy said. "Could I help?"

"Uh . . . sure." Mary Lynn scraped her chair to one side to make room.

"Later," I said, restraining her. Needing to know.

"When you shouted," she began, "when I told you I was okay?"

I nodded.

"He took me to Monique's tent—"

"Monique's!" Mary Lynn and I said together.

Amy said gently, "She was really sweet."

"Sweet!" Only Mary Lynn echoed her this time. I was remembering Monique with Pam.

"She made tea—sassafras, I think—and patted and fussed." When she smiled, the bruise was less obvious. "Between the two of them, I felt more cherished than—" Her voice broke. "Than I have since I was a little girl, being rocked and crooned to." She laughed nervously. "I could work while I talk. Please."

"Do leaves," I said. "I'm behind anyway, and Dean will be here any time."

"Maybe I shouldn't stay."

"Sit," I ordered.

As I opened the oven door, unwelcome heat stroked me. Chocolate scent flavored the air.

"Ummmmmm," murmured Pam from her high chair.

Startled, I realized that she'd been uncharacteristically quiet. That I'd forgotten her presence. The tension was changing all of us.

"Ummm, indeed, Pammie dear," Mary Lynn was saying. "I hope your mommie made enough."

"Four pans," I reminded her.

"Three for Pammie and me . . . and one for everyone else?"

Pam giggled and rubbed her tummy. "One for *me!*"

"Vandal," I said, "teaching my daughter greed. If you bulge out of your wedding dress, it'll serve you right."

Amy sat quietly, rubbing a length of ribbon between thumb and forefinger. "I thought I could do this."

Mary Lynn placed a hand on her arm. "Take your time," she said, and then, "Would you rather talk to Paula alone?"

Amy shook her head. "You're . . . fine."

I handed her a tissue.

She sniffed and blew. "Yesterday was just so perfect. We spent the whole day together. Turk's idea. A long hike. Then we bought stuff at McDonald's and took it to the woods for a picnic. I was a little worried about the woods—remembering—but Turk insisted I was being silly; he'd almost enjoy a one-on-one with the murderer." She shrugged. "He . . . said he'd protect me, and I knew he would . . ."

I wondered if she might be thinking, as I was, that he was capable of protecting her against anything but his own jealous rage.

Softly, she continued, "The food was cold by then, but it didn't matter. We walked to that . . . special place I told you about once, Paula. And later, to the gorge and the swinging bridge."

Shuddering, I wondered if that site would ever lose its horror for me. If I'd ever forget how my friend Lelia had plunged to her death there.

"Sorry," Amy said.

"It's . . . mostly because of the height," I lied. "Go on."

"When we got back home, it seemed Turk couldn't bear to leave. He did, once, but came back with a bouquet."

"Blue chicory?" I guessed, knowing it was past its season.

"It was mostly dried-up blossoms. But that didn't matter either. And then he said let's go to the carnival. And that was fun, too, until—" Her voice broke again, and she groped for another tissue.

To fill in, I said, "We saw you together. You were holding hands."

She nodded, and tears flowed freely.

Mary Lynn threw me a chiding look that said, "That was stupid." And I couldn't have agreed more. I bit my lip.

Fortunately, Pam chose that moment to demand attention. Mary Lynn and I offered more than she required—and so gave Amy a chance to reclaim self-control.

There wasn't actually a great deal more to the story. They'd ridden the ferris wheel.

"Twice," she said. "He always puts his arm around me."

And they'd eaten hot sausage sandwiches and saltwater taffy.

"And talked," she said. "We talked a lot. And it really seemed that he could be . . . what I'd thought he was, when I first fell in love."

"And then," I prompted into a long, sniffling silence.

"And then I told him. About reading poetry next Sunday. And at first he said, kind of stiffly, 'That's nice.' And then he asked what it was about. I was feeling so *safe* with him then!" She broke off. "I know that was stupid. Some people never learn, I guess. But I had a copy with me—in case I wanted to revise anything—and I gave it to him to read." She paused. "Turk never liked poetry. I should have known he'd never catch the *hope* there. He thought it was just about us."

And of course I'd seen the remainder of the scene played out. Turk's anger. His attack. His repulsion by a younger and stronger Clint.

"Clint was so gentle," she said. "Said he knew what it was like to be hurt, but that he understood Turk, too—how he'd feel, losing . . ." she paused, and finished lamely, "someone as special as me."

"Ahhh," Mary Lynn said, in almost a sigh.

I hid a smile. Perhaps all soon-to-be brides were such incurable romantics.

"And Clint said that when he gets that angry, he takes it out on his drums."

I laughed. Although he *had* gone after Turk as though he'd brawled a time or two before, it was difficult to imagine that cherubic face twisted with rage.

Amy added, "And he *does* get that angry, he said, especially at his father—or when anyone else calls him an ex-con."

I dropped a half-leafed rose.

Mary Lynn's "Ah" seemed startled out of her, like a grunt.

"I was surprised, too," Amy said. "He looks so . . . *innocent.* He was a user, he said, long enough to get him kicked out of school. And home." She sighed. "And he peddled for a while. But he says he's clean now. And I believe him," she finished quickly.

I said, "Then so do I."

"Monique accepts him. *Loves* him, I think, sort of like a mother. She couldn't seem to touch him enough. His shoulder, his hair. His hand." She cleared her throat.

"Anyway, his father's here, all the way from the Coast. At the carnival, I mean. He'd thrown Clint out, when he first told him, and Clint said he could handle that. But Clint's stepmother died not long ago, and his dad never even let Clint know so he could attend the funeral." She formed a leaf, frowned at it, and tried again. "And now his dad wants to make up their differences."

Mary Lynn said dryly, "Sounds like a lot to make up in one week."

"The worst was his stepmother," Amy said. "Clint really loved her. She'd tried to keep in touch, but his father admits he tore up the letters."

"Sad," I said, and remembered the moroseness of the man I assumed to be Clint's father. "Does he wear a felt hat, pulled low on his forehead?"

Mary Lynn threw me a "what does that have to do with anything" look.

But Amy answered, "How did you know?"

I said, "He was the saddest human being I've ever seen in my life."

Amy sighed. "Even sadder than me?"

The last cookies were still warm when Dean and Sylva arrived. Mary Lynn began gathering her things, but I said, "Just shove them to one side," and we all crowded about the small table—Pam scrambling back into her high chair and securing the tray herself. While melting vanilla ice cream pooled and dribbled over the cookies, we chatted. Occasionally someone closed his or her eyes and mumbled appreciatively, but often the only sound was the scraping of spoons on bowls.

"Decadent," Mary Lynn pronounced, picking up her final crumb on her fingertip, "even to the last."

"Wonderful," purred Sylva, patting her stomach. "I'd like to curl up like a big old tiger and take a nap!"

"Nap," Pam repeated, and lifted her arms to be taken. Just in case her intentions might be misread, she yawned widely.

Sylva laughed. "She's neat."

"Would you like to take her up?" I asked. "Pammie, would you like for Sylva to take you?"

Pam nodded with false shyness, then as soon as she was down from her chair, raced off yelping, dragging Sylva behind her.

Soon, though, she was back. "Forgot," she said. "Matt tooked a picture."

Of course Matt had taken hundreds of photos!

"That's nice," I said. "Nite-nite."

Mary Lynn asked, "A picture of you, honey?"

Pam nodded. "Me and the lady."

My hands stiffened on the silverware I'd been carrying to the sink. "What lady?" I asked, determinedly calm.

"Nice lady," she said, and pushed back her hair to expose her forehead. "Hurt lady."

I left the silverware on the sink board and went to kiss her. "Have a nice sleep, Pammie." When she and Sylva were gone, I turned to say heavily, "Matt took a picture of Pam and Monique. Together."

"What do you suppose he's up to now?" Mary Lynn asked. She didn't seem worried.

But I remembered Monique's anger. "He used me," she'd said. "He used my deformity."

And I wondered what angle he might take with an article on Pam and Monique together. My own flippant thoughts returned to haunt me. Beauty and the beast.

By the time Arden, Pam, and I had arrived at the carnival that late afternoon, I wondered why I'd been so reluctant. All remnants of the previous night's storm had disappeared—puddles dried, small limbs gathered into garbage bags—and the mood was festive. I stopped to buy another of Sylva's drawings, this one for me, and bought three instead—one of a lioness and her cubs as a wedding present for Mary Lynn and Greg, and another of a self-important jaguar to send to Dee, partially as a peace offering for not having written or called since the craft show.

Though she tried to appear collected—as though triple-sales were an everyday event—Sylva's whoops as she relayed her news to her parents followed me as far as the pony ring.

Pam was riding her phlegmatic favorite once again. "Time for my shift at the food tent," I told Arden, and he nodded. He looked tired.

But perhaps he was "thinking through" his sermon.

My shift was uneventful—only moderately busy—but warm enough that I returned to the parsonage to change into something dry, unrumpled, and unstained.

The phone rang while I was in the shower. By the time I'd reached it, dripping and shivering, it had stopped. And no message had been left.

"Probably one of those siding or water-testing calls," I muttered, but kept my ear tuned while I dressed. Somehow, any unanswered call carried more portent than all but the most serious answered ones.

I was tying my tennis shoes when it rang again.

I caught it on the fourth ring.

"Hello?"

"Matt. I was just ready to hang up again."

"Oh. Then it was you—just a bit ago?"

"Ten minutes. Maybe fifteen."

I breathed deeply with relief.

"Just wondered when you thought I might be able to interview Amy Turkle."

"Well, you'd have to ask her, of course—if she even *wants* to be interviewed. But she *is* reading her poetry Sunday." Running a brush through my hair, I tested neatness by touch.

"I'll cover that for certain. That might be a good time. Just to flesh out the story. Thanks."

"Matt . . ."

I could sense his bringing the receiver back to his ear. "Something else?" he asked, then laughed. "Oh. Forgot . . . *I'd* called *you!*"

I laughed, too, but it sounded self-conscious, even to me. I tucked the brush in my purse. "Pammie said . . . you'd taken a photo of her and Monique."

"Haven't developed it yet, but it should be good. Why? Did you want a copy?"

"No . . . well, yes, probably. But I was wondering . . . what you planned to do with it."

"Any suggestions?"

"Park it in a file somewhere." I'd said it quickly, before I could change my mind.

The silence was so deep I could hear the humming of the connection. "Why so?"

I sighed. "I thought Monique might have said something to you today."

He snorted. "If looks could shout, I'd be deaf. What's her problem? I mean, beyond the obvious."

"She was . . . hurt by the story."

Silence again. Dear God, I thought, I do hate to wound him. Help me to say the right words.

"It was a *good* story," he said at last. "At least I thought so."

"Beautifully written . . ."

"But?"

"I guess we can't know . . . how another person feels about a sensitive thing like . . ."

"Like deformity?"

"Each of us has one—of one kind or another."

"Not me," he said lightly, then added, "Only kidding."

But he hadn't been, I was sure. He was so young.

"What's yours, Paula?" he asked, his voice still light. And, when I didn't respond at once, he added, "Your deformity?"

"I have a million," I answered, striving to match his casualness, "and I guess what I'm saying is—I wouldn't want to read about any of them in the *Danvers Bugle*. Or anywhere."

Silence. Then, a small "Ouch."

Miserably, I said, "I don't mean to . . . reprimand."

"Yet you do it so very well." His tone was quiet. Level. Careful.

I felt tears gather. "Oh, Matt! Don't make me feel smaller than I already do!"

No answer.

"We love you, don't you know that? If we didn't, I'd—"

"Not have said anything?"

"Probably not."

"Love has its price tag," he said, and his voice wobbled, too.

Blinking rapidly, I yearned to be done with the conversation, to go off somewhere to cry. "I wish . . . I wish I hadn't heard the phone."

He said tightly, "No problem. Everyone needs a kick in the teeth once in a while. Teaches us humility." He asked quietly, "So what are you saying? That I should apologize to Monique?"

I didn't think that an apology would make a difference.

"Because I won't, you know," he said with new strength. "One thing a journalist has to do is stick by his instincts. I mean, right or wrong, I wrote what my guts dictated."

I could have wished that he'd reached farther north, into his heart.

"And even if Mary Lynn asked me," he was saying, rapidly now, "I wouldn't back down. Or Aunt Minnie." He paused, breaking into strained laughter. "Aunt Minnie would be tougher. Not because I value her opinion more. Just because she gives no room for rebuttal."

"She means well. I . . . I did, too."

"I suppose I know that," he said. "Later, I'll probably appreciate it."

"As soon as you pick shoe leather from between your teeth?" I forced a smile, which of course he couldn't hear.

"More likely when I'm an old, old man, looking back on a successful career."

There seemed no point in further discussion.

"I've got to go." But we'd said it together. And we laughed unconvincingly in tandem as we hung up.

That evening, an aftertaste of sadness—of guilt?—tinged the carnival for me. It was all I could manage, during my stint at the quilt booth, to sustain a pretense of excitement about the truly lovely coverlets on display: Dresden plates, broken stars, maple leaves, and one nearly threadbare crazy quilt—under glass—which had once graced a trundle bed in the governor's mansion and which reflected—through its brocades and satins and moires—the merged opulence and thrift of a century ago.

Once the shift was over, I wanted nothing so much as to go home and to bed, to assume the fetal position and seek the release of uninhibited tears.

Foolish.

I'd said only what needed to be said, after all, to protect Monique, to . . . instruct? . . . Matt. How pretentious that sounded! What right had I to interpret brashness and strive to curb it? Who did I think I was? Aunt Minnie?

That hurt.

Home. Home sounded so inviting. Yet I'd promised to help again at the food tent . . . I consulted my watch . . . in another hour.

I sighed.

An hour. How to kill an hour in an environment which assaulted me with color, music, laughter, activity—each an impetus to gaiety my spirit rejected? Almost, I could sense an echo of those dark times of my depression, when I'd felt victimized by the happiness of others. Powerless to survive.

Again, I sought the stand of oaks from which I'd half-watched the high wire show a night earlier. No street performance was scheduled until later, and light and sound from the distant excitement reached me dimly.

I was alone. Blessedly alone. I basked in the solitude. A breeze stirred. The medleyed sounds and scents were muted, pastel, as blurred as the shadows altered by shifting foliage.

Wonderful.

I hadn't realized how tired I was. How drained. Not with a debilitating weariness, in this mode of relaxation—half-kneeling, half-sitting on cool moss—rather an impression of numbness, near-bonelessness, my thoughts a formless thrumming, not demanding shape or expression.

I felt myself smiling. This was as comforting as the fetal position in bed—or anywhere—and untainted by that consuming stigma which characterizes surrender.

At some point—I was unsure when—comfort diminished. Only slightly, at first, then with a stealing sense that aloneness had dissipated as well. My ears strained, catching only that same rattling-whishing of foliage, those identical diluted musics and laughters which had previously lulled me. No footstep . . . was there? Though could a footstep be identified, if cushioned on grass and earth?

Surely . . . only imagination!

Yet the crawling chill on my arms and neck couldn't be denied—the primal certainty that something . . . someone . . . was there, observing me with a degree of . . .

Of what? Malevolence? Come on, Paula! This is McClintock! Petty malice, perhaps, but malevolence?

And yet there'd been Samantha.

It was all I could do to suppress a shudder.

How foolish I'd been to isolate myself, even in daylight.

At least there had been daylight when I'd come there. When had dimness begun?

A stirring, not of the breeze.

A shifting—to ease muscles? To gather for an attack?

I'd been more than foolish. Reckless. Stupid. Irresponsible. Solitude was a conceit canceled by two murders.

I waited.

No further movement.

No symptom of intent—friendly or otherwise. If it were someone I knew, surely by now he—or she—would have spoken my name. Even a stranger should have made some generic comment.

I would get to my feet—slowly, as though unaware—and move casually—*impossible*—toward the fringe of oaks, toward the street, then by some well-traveled route to the food tent.

Stand, Paula.

My muscles had forgotten how!

Push up on your palms.

Moist earth, cool and solid.

Now, gather the knees. Up. Up. You can do it.

I can't.

You must.

I must. Where are you, watcher . . . waiter . . . murd—

I wouldn't permit completion of the word.

Now was the time for some friendly voice to speak my name, to say, "I thought you'd fallen asleep. You're due at the food tent soon."

Nothing.

Dusting off my seat, my knees, I felt fragments of leaf mold crumble. My slacks would be stained when . . .

When my body was found?

No.

When I worked at the food tent.

I breathed shudderingly.

And then he . . . she . . . moved a step closer and I wouldn't, couldn't turn.

Dear God.

Dear, dear God.

And as though He'd answered that precipitately, the lights on the street below blazed to brightness, laying pathways of illumination even among the outer oaks.

Still, where I hesitated . . . where he waited . . . dense shadow survived.

"Arden!" I called, unevenly, to the indistinguishable figures swarming within light that layered the pavement. "I'm up here!"

Someone turned from the street, though, peering toward me.

Toward us.

And I heard a sharp intake of breath, and swift movement away—thankfully, *away!*—a crashing of twigs or branches, and eventually nothing save the hushed conversation of breeze and foliage renewed, and—from the street—the dialogue of setting up.

Long before I'd forced myself to turn, I knew that I was alone, and could have convinced myself—nearly—that there'd been no one lurking there had not the brush of casual malevolence remained on my skin. In my mind.

Working the tables in the food tent, its glaring lights consoling, it was as though I operated on two planes—the public me, responding to lighthearted banter, the warmth of friends, and the Paula still restrained by tentacles of fear. Clawing. Chiding.

Gradually, that chill receded—to be dealt with later. Not, however, to be shared, even with Arden. Not yet.

". . . and curly fries?"

"Wh—"

It was Clint, leaning lazily, elbows on the counter, his eyes twinkling. "I *thought* you were half asleep!" His smile faded. "You okay?"

"I'm fine. Just . . . tired, I guess."

"Tired, maybe. But . . ." He didn't complete the thought. "Somebody gonna walk you home later?"

I'd been turning away, but I felt my stiffening. "Yes. Thanks. My husband."

His voice lightened then. "The Reverend . . . right?"

I set his drink before him, and he found it without breaking his glance. "Seems like a nice kinda guy."

"A *very* nice guy." And so, I thought, are you.

That impression was confirmed as most of the crowd scurried to the blaring loudspeaker and we continued to talk.

"Don't you have to play your drums?" I asked later, when someone had doused the barbecue, and the tent lights dimmed halfway. Nearly time to go home.

"Off tonight." He stretched his fingers. "I'm . . ." His glance lowered. "My dad's gonna meet me here. Is that . . . okay?"

"That's fine."

"Not really," he mumbled. One hand clutched his mug; the other flexed in spasms.

I resisted the urge to cover it with mine.

It seemed he knew. "Thanks," he said softly.

"And thanks for . . . worrying about me earlier."

"Don't mention." He drew a deep breath. "Scary stuff goin' on."

"Scary, indeed."

Finally, I allowed myself to shudder.

Friday passed—with Turk avoiding Amy, Matt avoiding Monique—and, it seemed, me—and Dean and Sylva, their arms tightly linked, walking, sitting, talking, eating, laughing, always together. Dean wore a look of mingled ecstasy and impending doom—not an easy mixture, I thought, either to attain or sustain—except, perhaps, for a preteen in the throes of first love. Sylva seemed sad, but not heartbroken. I wondered how often before she'd walked this route.

And then it was Saturday, and though Saturday evening's crowd was the largest since opening night, some of the edge had dulled from the corporate excitement.

I'm not the only one, I thought, who needs this to be over. To get back to whatever normality was—or could be, given two murders.

I could see it even in the postures and strained expressions of the carnies. Already, it seemed, they were winding down—preparing to gear up once more for the next stop.

I didn't even want to know where that might be.

Seeing Monique, I planned to say good-bye. Something stopped me. Perhaps it was the intensity of her expression—surely pure anger—as she listened to the high-wire music and swayed erratically, in shadows, to its rhythms.

Moving toward the gazebo, I came upon Clint and his father in a low-toned argument.

Amy, selling tickets at the Historical Society booth, could scarcely count the money for the tears in her eyes.

With swift resolve, I found Arden turning burgers at the food tent and told him that I was going to leave, that I'd take Pam home with me.

"Not alone," he insisted, concern darkening his eyes.

I promised that I'd wait for a group, for safety. I would have anyway.

Pam didn't resist, even though it was barely dusk, and I didn't mention the fireworks we'd miss. There'd be less emotional ones, I thought, Labor Day weekend.

So I was at home, in bed, and deeply asleep when Arden shook me awake to tell me that there'd been a third murder.

8

He'd been found, Arden told me—with obvious reluctance—hanging head down from a seat of the ferris wheel, his legs propped along the back and his ankles secured there by binder twine. With the fireworks over and the crowd thinned to nearly nothing, carnies had already begun breaking down a few of the game booths. The riding ponies had been herded into trucks, high wire apparatus disassembled.

"I'm not even sure," Arden said, "why they started the ferris wheel again. Maybe some late customers. But he'd been . . . arranged, more than anything . . . into a seat back in shadows. And I'm not sure who saw him first, but I heard a shout—distressed, sort of choked—and saw somebody pointing."

He paused, and I found I had suspended breathing.

"When I looked, he was coming over the top. They pulled the switch, stopping him there, and I just stared. Everyone did. In shock, probably—I know I was—trying to make sense of it. The seat swinging, back and forth. Back and forth. His tangled curls catching the light . . . the wind stirring them. He was wearing purple socks—"

His voice broke, and I reached to steady him. The sleeve of his sweater was damp, and I wondered—abstractedly—if it was only night dampness or if it had been raining again. If the murderer had waited, hunched against falling rain, first for the moment of murder; then for the fulfillment of disclosure.

"Some of the carnies thought it was just somebody showing off. One of them yelled—something I won't repeat—and touched the lever again, and the wheel turned. Almost like slow motion in a horror film. That was when I saw the blood, especially on his hands—they'd been battered, and the drumsticks strapped to them with round after round of elastic cord."

Poor Clint. I wondered if his father had been there, had seen, and how he'd find comfort—here in a strange, friendless town.

Of course, he could be a prime suspect. He and Clint had quarreled.

And my mind swung to Amy, to Clint's kindness the night of Turk's attack. And Turk—Turk would be questioned, and that could only add to Amy's sadness. Once before, I'd suspected Turk of senseless violence. He hadn't been guilty then—but certainly the potential lay within, smoldering. Often venting in hot spurts of verbal abuse. Occasionally—as Amy's bruises attested—in more than words.

If he had killed Clint, Amy would blame herself.

"Joe Derrick looked beaten," Arden said. "Three murders in just over two weeks." He shuddered, then gave me a quick hug. "We need to get some rest, honey."

Sleep seemed an impossibility. I felt a slight resentment as Arden huddled in bed, tossed a few times, then snored comfortably and steadily. Knowing that he'd have the three services in the morning, that somehow he'd have to deal with this latest intrusion of tragedy into the complacent mind-set of rural McClintock, Peachstone, and Danvers, I tried to lie quietly.

But there was nothing quiet about the emotions that roared through me or the scenes that spun behind my closed lids and when I surrendered and stared into darkness, reshaped themselves there, despite all efforts to dismiss them.

I imagined Clint, draped in the scarred seat of a ferris wheel, descending from shadowed dimness into muted light. His sightless eyes overlooked the park—first the upper foliage of oaks and maples, then tent canvas and striped vinyl awnings, empty rides—pathetically gaudy when stripped of eager crowds and bright music and enthusiastic, insistent hawking. Next, they blindly scanned the few remaining revelers. The fragments and litter of weeklong celebration. And, as the wheel shuddered to a stop, as his seat swung and creaked in place, there was the grass, bruised by hundreds of feet—including his own. The solidified mud, scuffed and polished.

Remnants of food smells hung in the air like tattered banners—hot sausage, buttered popcorn, french fries, and vinegar—mingling with the burned stench of spent fireworks. Hammer blows sent tent poles to the ground, hinges clanging, startling big cats already slumbering in cages loaded on a flatbed and secured by locked and tested chains. But Clint heard neither that metallic sound, nor the grumblings and sharp retorts born of weariness. Not a crying child or two, bedtime long past. Nor the reactions of onlookers suddenly alert to what was happening and had happened, what Clint's limp peacefulness signified. His fixed gaze. His lack of reaction.

Poor Clint. What had he done to attract such a hideous death?

He'd told Amy that he'd used and sold drugs. That he'd spent time in prison. Yet how many would have known? Or cared? His father, certainly—since he'd banished him from home for that reason. And surely those with whom he traveled. Carnies would shrug. Many would think his record mild.

But if one or more of his coworkers had despised him for any reason, why McClintock? Why not kill him en route, dumping his body in a field? Why take a chance at discovery? For despite the distractions, it had been risky, wherever the murder itself had been committed—and Clint would not have succumbed quietly—to strap the body into the ferris wheel for its grisly, undeniably dramatic disclosure.

Nor did my pondering stop with Clint. Three murders—all bloody. Unrelated? Possible, of course, but probable? I remembered how Samantha's death had brought Chaucer's tale to mind. What of Clint's mutilated hands? An effort, surely, to silence his music, rather than to imitate some long ago classic. Then Samantha's slashed neck had been designed to stifle her song in the most obvious manner. And Antonia Porter's—

What kind of monster could envision, much less orchestrate, such atrocities?

Could there possibly be three murderers, all equally depraved? Surely not. Inconceivable as the thought of a serial killer among us, mocking our grief, a corps of such ghouls was even less acceptable.

But who?

Despite Turk's obvious flaws, his incendiary temper, I couldn't think him capable of such passionless calculation.

Clint's father—an unknown quantity—hadn't been around, at least not obviously, for the first two murders.

Monique possessed sufficient strength—and anger—but toward a gentle piano teacher? Or for Samantha Crane—though the litheness of her performance, contrasted with Monique's disability, rose to call this conclusion into question. But according to Amy, Monique had loved Clint.

The digital alarm clock blipped minute after minute, one hour into another, as questions battered. Rolled. Formed and destroyed conclusions.

I wondered if the murderer, who had also murdered my peaceful sleep, lay wakeful too, reviewing his handiwork.

Or hers? And perhaps crafting the details of still another horror.

Just as sleep seemed within reach, another inescapable possibility intruded. If I had not called out to Arden from the oak-patterned dimness, would he—or she—now be reliving the details of *my* death, rather than Clint's?

Early Sunday morning, Amy called in tears to ask for a postponement of her participation in the service. "I know Arden wanted those particular poems because of his sermon on loss," she said, "and I hate to back out . . ."

"I understand."

There was a beat of silence.

"So will Arden," I added. "We're not feeling so solid ourselves this morning."

Her voice wobbled. "Clint was just so . . . sweet. And we didn't even know him. Not really."

I remembered his gentle concern for my safety, his defense of Amy, his energy at the drums, the various moods evoked as he stroked the cymbals with brushes, tapped their bright metal with drumsticks or lifted and clanged them at the climax of some daring act.

Again, the murderer had taken his toll in talent.

"Why musicians?" Amy asked.

I shivered. So often, we seemed on the same wavelength. Once, Dee and I had shared that quality of closeness. Now, stretched by miles, by inconsistent communication—

". . . do you think?"

"Sorry," I said. "I can't keep my thoughts together."

"I've been like that all morning. Even before Turk called."

Another chill. "To . . . apologize?" I asked, but not as though I believed it.

She laughed shortly. "To ask if I'd heard what had happened to my 'Superman.' I hadn't."

So of course he'd told her.

"Oh . . . Amy . . ."

"I know. I'm so afraid . . . so worried . . . and yet," and her voice strengthened, "I know Turk. He might *talk* about killing someone, but to actually do it . . ." Her voice trailed off. "Unless the victim was me," she finished, laughing nervously.

She didn't sound all that convinced, I thought.

"At least if he killed anyone, it would be without thinking. I mean, the hands—that had to be planned. It's sick. Like . . ."

"Like what happened to Mrs. Porter. And to Samantha."

"It *is* too much of a coincidence, isn't it?"

"It has to be." Unless, I added, only in my thoughts, someone had tried to make this murder appear to be one in a series.

"And Turk wouldn't've had anything against Mrs. Porter. He didn't even know her. And Samantha Crane—well, he'd have been more likely to make a move on her than kill her."

Unless, I thought, she'd repulsed him?

And of course she would have.

I didn't like the way my thoughts were moving. Hadn't I decided—only the night before—that he couldn't be a suspect?

Tears choked Amy's voice. "Nobody knows Turk better than I do. And I just *know* . . ."

I asked gently, "Why do you think he called you?"

"To shake me up. To make me do just what I did—back out of reading this morning. I shouldn't let him get away with it, should I? But every nerve in my body is quivering." Again, that nervous laugh. "Of course, they would be anyway—but this isn't just stage fright. It's grief—not an isolated grief, just for Clint, though I keep remembering how we talked that night. How gentle he was . . . and sad. And it's not just that I'm afraid for Turk—though I am. I can't help it. Much as I'm afraid *of* him, I'm more afraid *for* him. If he were choking me to death, my last thought would be, Please don't catch him. Don't hurt him. And what does that say about me?"

I thought, It says that you still love him.

God help her, I prayed.

"But it's more than any of that," she continued. "It's for what's happening here. In McClintock. That people can do such cruel, senseless things to one another."

Amy's sentiment was echoed in Matt's article for another *Bugle* extra, released Monday.

"Music has suffered another tragic loss," he wrote, "and consequently so has humanity."

> For if there is anything in society which nurtures the sacred and bans the bestial, it is that celestial coalition of instrument and voice—and, similarly, the poetry of language and those visual musics, art and dance.
>
> Surely the illogical crimes which have recently brutalized our small community loom larger because of their unwonted viciousness and their unlikely victims. Antonia Porter was a woman of sensitivity and gracious talent—not a talent which hugged itself to itself, but one which—openhanded—shared both the joys and the proficiencies of her craft. Surely only a base monster could have wanted to rob us of her gifts.
>
> And reconsider Samantha Crane—another giver of herself, another spontaneous sharer of musical joy. Any who saw her perform must wonder what twisted mind could have quieted that glorious voice, stilled that exuberance, blunted that impact on a world hungry for spirituality.
>
> And now a young man of lesser outreach and milder flamboyance—but a talent, nonetheless, though still in the processes of refinement—Clint Wyse has become a third victim.

I spoke with Clint several times during carnival week. More impressive even than his rhythms were his humility and his humanity—honed, perhaps, rather than diminished, by his brief submission to the drug culture, his subsequent imprisonment, and his staunch determination to reclaim his life. Unlike Samantha Crane and Antonia Porter, Clint was not actively involved in church. "Used to be," he told me, the last time we met—just hours before his death. "Did my time in Sunday school where some gray-faced biddy listed the 'Thou shalt nots' but showed negative smarts in what kids go through today. And I skipped and tripped and yipped through vacation Bible schools. A coupla times I looked for God. Thought maybe I'd found Him, and prayed that He'd find me—and not throw me away like my dad did. Times I felt as close to God as the air and grass. And there were other times . . ." A look of infinite sadness marred his expression. "And then, in prison, I didn't just *pray;* I *yelled* to God. I didn't *ask* why He'd let happen what guys told me they'd done—and never regretted. I *demanded.* And y'know what? No answer. Not a whisper. Not a whimper. Now I'm an atheist," he concluded. "Least I think so." Without a pause, he said, "Come here. I want t'show you something." From a battered briefcase in the rear of a nondescript van, he withdrew a sheaf of sheet music, scrawled closely with uneven notes. "You Are My Light" was one hand-printed title. Another, "Walk Close by My Side." And still another, "When I Feel Darkness Gather."

"Love songs?" I guessed.

He smiled. "Sort of. To God. From my pre-atheist period."

No musician myself, I asked, "Have I ever heard them?"

"And won't," he answered, returning them to the briefcase and closing it with what seemed like finality. "Why play a love song to God when you're ninety percent sure He can't hear?"

Later, when he was pulled from the seat of the ferris wheel, when he was lifted to a gurney and covered by a sheet, I wondered if I shouldn't have challenged his doubting. If I shouldn't have insisted that we search out a pianist to translate those scribbled notes into sound which might—just might—have reignited for Clint Wyse that belief that had once inspired him to create.

Those notes, though unheard, will reverberate in my conscience for a long, long time to come.

That afternoon, Clint's father brought the briefcase to the parsonage. Slouched, his felt hat crumpled in one hand, he stood waiting on the front porch while I called Arden.

"He won't come in," I said. "Poor man."

Arden tugged me with him to the porch. A slight breeze ruffled maple leaves and stirred Mr. Wyse's thin, silvery hair.

"I want you to do a funeral here," he said, his voice flat and worn, "before I take him home to rest beside his mother. His carnival friends deserve that. And your organist . . ." He opened the briefcase. Extracted the sheets. "What that reporter wrote about these never being heard. Well, I couldn't bear that. I didn't have much patience with his music—" his voice broke, "or with him. But he was a good boy." He lifted his head, and his gray gaze was level. Unblinking. "Whatever he did wrong he paid for."

I couldn't help thinking how sad it was—especially for him—that he hadn't reached that conclusion earlier.

"He used drugs," he said, the words directed to me.

I nodded.

"And *sold* them." He paused. "To *children!*"

He waited.

What was it he wanted from me, I wondered. "I can't condemn him," I said quietly.

He slumped, suddenly, and Arden reached to support him, but he shook himself clear. "I thought different of you," he said, and there seemed as much disappointment in his tone as surprise. "I'd have expected a minister and his wife to be more—" He broke off.

"Judgmental?" I asked softly.

His glance unswerving, his lower lip unsteady, he said only, "There was a lot of good in my boy. When you preach over him, Reverend, just say that. Only better."

"This is beautiful." Marian Sells, our church organist, touched a tissue to the corners of her eyes. "No one can tell me this boy doubted God."

I'd felt the same as I'd listened to her tentative renderings of one song after another. The musical phrasing was poignant, worshipful, often majestic.

Marian said, "I've been as accurate as I can—so many scratchovers." She raised the tissue again. "If I had more time . . ."

I reached to hug her shoulders stooped from decades of bowing above keyboards, inclining to consoles. "Clint would be pleased."

Again she ran her fingers over the keys. Repeated the theme of one of Clint's pieces. "What a waste. What a tragic, sinful waste." Her hand fell heavily, exciting a discord. "How can anyone do . . . what's being done here?" she demanded. "How can God allow . . ." She shook her head. "Sorry."

"It's understandable," I said.

"Where will it stop?"

Shivering, I wondered.

A few of the carnies, camping in their vehicles near the park, had delayed for the funeral. Seeming uneasy, they entered the church in a cluster, studiously wiped their shoes before shambling down the carpeted aisle to the flower-banked casket, then quietly filed past for the final viewing. As they turned away, one dabbed his eyes. Some wore expressions of anger.

Understandable.

Even we, who'd scarcely met Clint, had both wept and expressed rage.

Only Monique, who'd come alone, touched the corpse. She stood for a long while, rubbing her hand back and forth across Clint's forehead, down his cheek—then touching his battered hands, which Sam Westerman had camouflaged with a spray of lilies. At last—when Arden entered—she stooped awkwardly to kiss Clint's bright hair.

What had forged the special bond between them, I wondered, the closeness Amy had indicated—two wounded souls seeking mutual comfort? Or would Monique have grieved as deeply, as openly, for anyone cut off in youth with a finality she had once coveted for herself?

I half-rose to go to her, but by then she had limped to a front pew where she huddled alone.

Clint's father, entering late, took a seat farther back.

Only a few of the townspeople had come. Constable Joe stood off to one side, his relaxed posture deceptive, I thought. His eyes seemed alert. Active.

I gained new respect for him.

Just as Arden began to speak, Amy and Dora slid in beside me. I took Amy's hand, and she held mine tightly.

For the second time in three days, Arden spoke of loss—and I knew from notes he'd shown me that the following Sunday's sermon would continue the theme.

When the Scripture had been read, prayers said, and gentle thoughts spoken, the music came. It began in tendrils and trills, then progressed rapidly to a crescendo that was pure and pleading and palpably triumphant.

Oh, God, I thought—withdrawing my hand from Amy's to swipe at the tears. Why? Who? Three beautiful people are gone from our lives.

What I was thinking merged on blasphemy. Who was I to question?

Yet how could we not question?

Help us, I prayed, beneath the music. Help us—and I couldn't suggest *how* He help us overcome this evil, root it out, dispel it from our lives before it could steal even more.

Not since the abyss of depression had I felt so helpless.

So fearful.

9

Later that week, all evidence of the carnival erased, even the grass repairing itself, life also struggled to resume normality.

Yet could it ever, truly?

"It will," Arden assured me. "It must."

"Surely," I'd heard someone say, "now . . . with the carnies moved on . . ."

But I noted how neighbors reacted at footfalls behind them. How sharply they commanded the closeness of their children, even required a measured quietness in their play. There were a caution, a hesitancy, a somberness—indelible symptoms of fear.

And I felt them in myself.

"Some great environment for a wedding," Mary Lynn said glumly. She'd asked me to go with her to the sanctuary, to help plan where to place flower arrangements and candles—in the event of rain. "Maybe Marian should play a dirge, rather than 'Here Comes the Bride.'"

Sunlight, slanting through stained glass, cast spots of color to carpet, velour cushions, polished wood.

In light of recent events, such cheer seemed almost obscene.

Sighing, Mary Lynn sank into a pew. "Tell me the truth." She waited. "Should we postpone?"

"The *wedding?*" I gasped.

"It just seems—I don't know. So much death. Not that I think it will jinx us or anything. But do we have a right to ask people to force a wedding kind of joy—with all that's happened here?"

"Maybe," I answered slowly, "a wedding is what we all need."

She seemed to think that over. "Life in the midst of death."

"Rather, not allowing death to dominate. Whoever's doing this . . ." My thought drained away.

"Is nuts?" she finished.

"More than that. What does he want—really? I mean, the act of killing—" I shuddered. "Whatever excitement that provides is over so quickly. Even the grieving—the worst of it—and the funeral are over in days. But what if what he wants is to hold us in a kind of . . . perpetual mourning?"

"And fear," she added. "Dreading what might come next."

I nodded.

The light had moved slightly, mellowing new spots of oak and velour.

Mary Lynn moved her hand into a liquid wash of rose and gold.

"We make a conscious choice," she mused. "Darkness or light. Death or life."

"Freedom or fear. Dread or . . . faith."

"Faith is hard just now."

I covered her hand with mine.

She turned, the pew cushion rustling slightly with her movement. "What *does* come next, Paula?"

I shrugged.

"Does he kill again . . . and again . . . and again . . . until there's no one left? Of course, that wouldn't work. There'd be no audience to shudder and scuttle in fear." She asked intently, "What is it he really wants? Guess it's the reporter in me, but—there doesn't seem to be any reason, does there? I mean, if murders happen at all, there ought to be motive—greed or vengeance or a hunger for power . . ."

"He has the power now—whether that was the original motive or not."

"He . . . or she."

"Or she."

"It *could* be a woman. Women aren't the poor simpering weaklings men liked to suppose for so long. We never were, most of us."

"The power of the press. Tell them often enough, and they'll believe it."

"And that's another thing!" Her frown deepened. She looked distinctly unbridelike. Brides should be vivid, I thought. Glowing. Unlined—as she'd been before.

"Matt's articles," she said.

"Matt's . . . articles?"

She gestured broadly. "Professional jealousy, I suppose. But they're so *good* . . . they attract so much attention." She colored. "I'm not saying this well, but couldn't *they* be giving the killer just what he—or she—wants? Keeping the grief and fear fresh—oh, I'm not making any sense, and I know it!"

But she was! "Of course!" I agreed. "The media always glorify the sensational."

"Give the terrorist the audience he lusts for," she picked up the thought. "The hostage-taker an arena for his particular brand of diatribe. The small-town crazy an aura of mystery, millions asking, 'When will he strike next? What depravity can outdo broken hands and a slit throat and a severed foot?' And so—he *can't stop*. He has to get more and more bizarre—to keep his audience dangling. To feed the gut of the media." Her face was flaming then. "I know it sounds like jealousy—and it's not. At least I hope not. I hope it's just concern—not only for everybody else. For Matt, too. What happens to *him* when the killer's caught?

When he has to go back to covering town council meetings and high school track meets? Did you know a dozen big newspapers have run parts of his articles? Not just Pittsburgh and Philadelphia—but D.C., Houston, Denver. New York. Even, I think, London—all salivating for sensational stories to fill space. Nobody admires Matt's talents more than I do, except—"

"Except for Matt?" I teased.

She laughed, and her expression cleared. "I was going to say Great-Aunt Minnie!"

"Her, too."

She tipped her head to one side. "For a minister's wife, you're delightfully catty today."

"Sorry."

"No, you're not."

"No, I'm not," I agreed, and knew that I should be. "I love Matt, too," I said, then remembered his reaction when I'd mentioned Monique's pain at the article he'd written about her. "When he's gained more experience—in living, I mean, not in writing . . ."

"The story will still be most important," she said. "That's the way a good journalist *must* be—single-minded. A bit callous where sensitivity could get in the way." She sighed. "Matt has what it takes to shoot him to the top. I don't. So . . ." She stood and scanned the sanctuary. "Guess it's a good thing I'm escaping into marriage."

Sunday, at all three services, Arden invited everyone present "to the marriage of Mary Lynn Whitman and Greg Stremboski, to share in their joy." He was reading from their wedding invitation itself, and the phrases injected a needed spirit of well-being. Of peace. At McClintock, all about me I saw people relaxing. Smiling. Sneaking looks to note the couple's embarrassment. It was the first I'd seen Greg, and if aesthetics had been Mary Lynn's sole criterion, she couldn't have done better. Tall and military slim, he wore his uniform more easily than his status as bridegroom. The flush underlying his tan invaded the roots of his crisp black hair and tinted his close-set ears.

There were other visitors in church. When Arden and I arrived, Mr. Wyse already sat toward the back on the far side. I'd been surprised when Arden said that he wouldn't leave until Monday to return Clint's ashes for burial. This might well be the final time we would see him. He had rolled his felt hat and stuffed it into the pocket of his dark jacket. Neither hat nor pocket could ever again be the same. He wore no tie, but a dark flannel plaid shirt, open at the throat, its unpressed collar turned awkwardly over the lapels of his jacket, its unbuttoned sleeves jutting unevenly past his wrists. He crossed and uncrossed his legs and constantly ruffled the pages of a hymnal. During the prelude, Minnie Kelp, sitting two pews ahead, glanced back pointedly once or twice, then rose stiffly and moved toward the front of the sanctuary, where—pausing for only a moment—she slid in beside Matt, who looked up, smiled, shifted a bit to the right, and then studied his notepad again.

He had said that he'd cover the service—specifically Amy's reading.

Amy sat alone in the choir loft on the left, where Arden had suggested she wait. "When you're already nervous," he'd said, "climbing those few steps to the platform can really make the old heart race."

Amy's glance flicked often to one spot in the congregation. I followed it.

Turk.

Of course.

He wouldn't have missed such an easy opportunity to rattle her.

A surge of something close to hatred twisted my thoughts.

"Okay?" Dora Kuhn, next to me, asked.

"Turk's here," I whispered.

"Maybe he'll learn something." But she didn't sound hopeful. Or concerned.

When the choir entered, Arden following, another visitor slipped in. I started. Monique Toulouse!

"Didn't you know?" whispered Dora. "The carnies kicked her out. Or she decided to quit, whichever. She's living under a bridge outside town."

Under a bridge.

Arden had initiated the call to worship.

"Later," Dora promised, and joined in with uncharacteristic fervor—delighted, I knew, that she could look forward to filling me in.

And then, after the opening hymn, Arden read the invitation—and all discomfort seemed to melt in the joy of the upcoming wedding.

Too bad it couldn't last, I thought, not long after.

Following the offertory, when the strains of the organ trembled into silence, Arden announced, "That beautiful etude was composed by Clint Wyse."

At East Danvers and Peachstone, the announcement had elicited murmurs of wonder and vague sadness.

A slight stirring began somewhere, I thought, in the area where Minnie sat, but its ripples spread quickly and, at first, in relative quietness.

Perhaps the silence of shock.

"The prelude was his, too, and following the benediction Mrs. Sells will play a third composition."

"Why?" demanded a strident voice.

Arden, not visibly startled, turned toward Minnie.

She was standing, looking not so much toward Arden as into the congregation. "Why must we submit to . . . to something written by a young man so sinful any *real* Christian might blush to speak his name?"

Arden asked patiently, "Mrs. Kelp—did you hear this morning's Scripture?"

She bristled. "I read the Scripture every morning of my life, mister—and again each night before I go to bed."

"Then you know that we're warned not to judge—"

"*Nor* to embrace evil!" Her voice was throbbing. She leaned heavily on the back of the pew before her. "And you, a supposed minister of the gospel! Defending a convicted *drug dealer?* You should tremble in fear of damnation!" Her hand rested on Matt's shoulder, perhaps in benediction. "You read Matt's article, I assume."

For all Matt's height, he seemed to have shrunk from view.

Poor Matt.

"Then you read—in that young man's own words—that he'd rejected God! It's an abomination, is what it is—playing that . . . atheist's . . . songs here, in the hearing of decent God-fearing people!"

Arden asked gently, "Tell me truthfully, Minnie—what did you think of the music before you knew—"

"That's one of Satan's tricks, mister, one you ought recognize—beguiling us to accept what we know is wrong!"

"The *music* . . . is wrong? You find it flawed in rhythm? In phrasing? In what way, exactly, Mrs. Kelp?"

"I find your thinking flawed—and not for the first time! You try to change us. To twist us." She paused. Nodded grimly. Said with quiet malice, "Maybe the reason you hold such high regard for . . . that person . . . is you're just like him."

A sharp gasp—half of excitement, half of horror—left no doubt that she was understood.

Though Arden's voice showed no sign of anger, he gripped the pew. Leaned forward.

"Birds of a feather . . ." Minnie pursued smugly, and I knew that she'd caught his tension. "Two peas in a pod. And who would be the greater sinner, I ask you—that one who denies his God openly, or him who disbelieves in his heart while lip-serving from a pulpit? Need I clarify further, Reverend Hypocrite?"

Matt was physically tugging her into her seat, and she struggling in a way that would have been comical, if any conflict within a church body were less tragic. When she was quiet, Matt rose slightly. "Please accept our apologies, Reverend Templeton." His voice trembled.

Arden nodded and paused while quiet restored itself through diminishing murmurs. I imagined him using those moments to regain his own composure as well. Mine would have to wait for later. How dare she—how dare anyone!—accuse Arden of anything less than total honesty with God and with his parishioners? And how dare she judge gentle Clint, who—though he'd been guilty of sin—had risen above and beyond it?

Arden spoke clearly and compellingly of loss, of how the loss of health or property or reputation—here, he seemed to glance toward Minnie—or the death or separation of loved ones could threaten faith. It was at that point that he asked Amy to read.

And at that moment two people in different sections of the sanctuary stood swiftly. Minnie Kelp and Turk. An unlikely pair, they stalked up two separate aisles—Minnie with chin high, arms stiff at her sides, purse swinging, while Matt stared helplessly after her; Turk, firm-lipped and scowling as he stared over his shoulder at his pale wife—even then approaching the lectern.

Amy joined us for lunch. It was a quiet, thoughtful meal, nearly silent once Arden had commented still again on the poignancy of her poetry. "People were touched," he said.

She sighed—thinking, I was sure, of Turk.

We were still at the table when Matt arrived.

"I called Mary Lynn," he began, "but . . ."

"She and Greg were visiting his parents."

"I don't know how I'm going to function when she's gone." Settling on a stool, he looked like a praying mantis. But I couldn't even smile, the emotions of the morning lay so heavily on my spirit.

Pam yawned widely.

Good idea, I thought, wishing we could all just nap away the doldrums of the day.

When I came downstairs after putting Pam to bed, Matt was apologizing again.

". . . don't know what gets into Aunt Minnie sometimes," he said. "I like to think it's the strength of her convictions, but it's often more like just plain balkiness. Like a mule." He sighed and added, "She's not a bad person."

Arden said gently, "We know that."

"But if she knew I'd come here, she'd whip me." He grinned. "For my own good, of course."

I remembered what she'd suggested—that I'd corrupt him.

Arden smiled and changed the subject. "It was another fine article you did on Clint. His father appreciated it."

"He . . . told you so?"

Arden nodded.

"I was a little worried . . ." Matt shrugged. "That he might be offended." He threw me an unreadable look. "As you said Monique was."

Not "as Monique was," I noticed, but "as I'd said."

His shoulders sagged. "I didn't mean it that way."

"We're all a bit edgy." I patted his hand.

Amy laughed nervously.

Matt said firmly, "You read beautifully."

She murmured her thanks.

"You *did,*" he insisted. "You've got to believe that. A writer needs . . . confidence."

Was it my imagination that his glance rested on me—in reproof? I felt my color rise.

"Artists are the same way, aren't they, Paula?"

So I'd misinterpreted. Maybe. I cleared my throat. "There's a wire-thin balance, though. Too much confidence, and performance suffers." That warmth again—the barometer of my conscience. He could easily interpret what I'd just said as still another swat at him. "I remember hearing—" and my voice was too high, too loud. I deliberately leveled it. "Some famous opera singer insisted that if she wasn't nervous before she went on stage, she wouldn't do well. Over-confidence would dull the edge."

Matt relaxed. "Good point. When I sit down at the word processor, I always feel those butterflies swarming. If they ever come up missing, I'll know I'm in trouble." Lifting his cup, he sipped coffee that must be nearly congealing.

"Warm that for you?" I offered.

But he shook his head.

Arden excused himself. "Just watch, you creative types, that the butterflies don't become a swarm of bleeding ulcers."

I heard the front door swish behind him. "He's gone to tame his own butterflies."

"Him, too?" Amy sighed. "He always looks so—glued together."

"Preaching's creative," I reminded her, "and there's a lot of responsibility."

"Just so none of his ulcers are Aunt Minnie's fault."

I smiled. "She's contributed her share. But more of them come from a nagging wife."

Amy said fondly, "You wouldn't know how to nag." Then she grinned almost impishly. "I could give you lessons!"

Later, while Matt asked Amy to answer more questions for the interview, a groggy Pam and I walked toward the park. Strange, I thought, that the same shrubbery which might well shield a murderer past dark was so welcome now—the shadows cooling, rather than chilling.

Just ahead, a sound rustled, and I paused, startled. Pam stifled a yawn, then pointed as a squirrel, full tail horizontal with speed, swept across the street.

Safe enough. Surely, McClintock was safe in daylight. Even in the city—where streets were familiar—I'd walked without fear. Holding my purse close, of course, ears tuned to uneven patterns of sound, of movement.

And here, where danger was such an innovation—surely here it hadn't learned to invade the sunlight.

Still, I checked carefully at cross ways, listened with sharpened awareness to scrapings and scufflings, the murmurs of traffic and far-flung voices, and the ever-present watchfulness of dogs.

Pam stumbled a few times over broken sidewalk, then held up her arms, wordlessly, and I lifted her.

"You're getting so heavy!" I said, and settled her more manageably against me.

"Not heavy."

"That just means you're getting to be a big girl."

"Not a big girl," she insisted peevishly.

"My, you're in a good mood!"

"Not in a good mood," she murmured, and her thumb went into her mouth.

Oh, well, I thought, yearning for a park bench. Some days are like that.

When we finally reached the park, all the benches were taken. So others, too, refused to be denied sunshine, and by their unity intensified the guarantee of safety. On one bench, someone slouched alone, and I decided to risk asking for a share. My arms were throbbing.

He turned, then, and I knew there was no chance I'd be refused.

Dean.

I decided not to ask how he was doing. Instead, I ventured, "Nice day."

I almost expected him to argue, as Pam had.

"I guess so," he said.

I would not ask about Sylva. It was all too obvious that he suffered withdrawal pangs. "Have you done any drawing since—" Oops. I'd almost said it. "Since the craft show?" I finished lamely.

"Yeah, as a matter of fact." He fished in his pocket and unfolded a tight square of white unlined paper. "Whattaya think?"

It was of a chipmunk, and I could almost see its eyes sparkle and its tail flirt. "Oh, Dean! It's marvelous! This could be a whole new direction for you!"

"Yeah," he said, enthusiasm fading. "Before, I always thought I wasn't that good at animals."

Of course I knew who had changed him. Challenged him. Given him confidence—of more kinds than one.

"She said what I shoulda knowed already—just look at them as shapes, the different parts—like drawing a tree or anything." He sighed.

I reached out to touch his shoulder, and, surprisingly, he leaned against me. "You can keep in touch, Dean."

"She said we would."

"Don't you believe her?"

He shrugged. "Guess so." Again, he sighed. "She was writin' to a dozen other guys while she was here."

When we returned—Dean finally coaxing Pam to a better mood, the two of them walking just a bit ahead, hand in hand—Amy waited alone. She looked concerned.

"He'll do a great article," I assured her.

She nodded. "Even Mary Lynn doesn't write better."

"But you're worried . . ."

"Not about what he says! Just about how . . . Turk might react."

I turned on the front burner. "Tea?"

"Thanks. Then I'll have to get home—before dark."

Suddenly chilled, I sat down to wait. Dear God, I prayed inwardly, let everyone be safe tonight.

"Sooner or later," Amy said, "I've got to decide about Turk—do I want him in my life or not. This morning, I thought I knew."

I remembered the cold look he'd turned on her.

"Like he hated me," she said, and I had that eerie feeling, again, that our thoughts were in sync. "If he'd just make up *his* mind—then it'd be easy for me."

10

I needed Dee.

In the days before Arden—when I'd worked in a small framing shop and Dee had designed for a pottery outlet specializing in mixing bowls and heavy, utilitarian mugs—we met at least once weekly. Calls—frequent and often brief—bridged the gaps. Sometimes, after work, we met at McDonald's and called it dinner. Occasionally, Sunday afternoons, when the weather allowed, we took long strolls in the park, or hiked or biked the trails beyond town.

Or, on a rainy Saturday, we might have coffee in her basement workshop, where dried clay was the color, if not of choice, of necessity. Thick tabletops, supported by a forest of two-by-fours, were slathered with the dusty dried gray or grayed red. So were the shelves, lined with drying pieces, looking faintly leprous. With damp, rag-draped pots in progress, with forms, with half-filled bags and crumpled boxes. With jars and cracked vases holding grubby tools. Clay coated the floor—thicker blobs spattered everywhere—the deepest, freshest near the potter's wheel and Dee's working stool. Always her jeans, smock, and apron were clay-patterned. Invariably, clay streaked her face and hair and matted beneath her fingernails.

Only when the kiln was freshly emptied, before completed pieces had found their way to customers or several consignment shops—when bowls, pitchers, vases, plates, vivid and glowing with glaze, designed a vibrant, disorganized still life—was there anything to relieve the oppressive gray-whiteness of the place.

Yet we met only rarely in my more colorful but crowded apartment, where one small room doubled as studio and bedroom and offered what little storage area I boasted.

"I'd fire the maid, if I were you," she'd say, peering past the door of the miniscule kitchen into the general clutter.

"Can't. She's a . . . relative."

"Seriously," she'd ask, her forehead wrinkling, "how do you stand it?" She'd shudder. "Makes me claustrophobic."

"The light's good, though." I'd thought I was in heaven when the landlord, apologizing that it sometimes leaked in heavy rainfall, had pointed out the streaked, leaf-littered skylight.

"True." Dee would lean back grinning. "My basement feels like something from 'The Pit and the Pendulum.'"

"Sounds like it, too."

"My creaking wheel," she'd guess.

"And the anguished groans when a piece doesn't go right."

"No scurrying rats, though," she'd say, and add fervently, "thank heaven!"

We'd sit companionably, sipping coffee or hot chocolate. Nibbling week-old cookies from the convenience store one street over. Occasionally smiling or sighing in contentment.

"Nice," she might say.

Or, "I'd know you if I didn't know you."

"Hmmmm. Have you considered a career in politics?"

"I mean . . . you always wear oil paint. And now, since the framing shop, usually a Band-Aid or two."

"Have you looked in a mirror lately?"

She'd grin. "Why ruin my illusions?"

The illusions we'd shared then were comfortably illogical—she with a successful line of her own designing. An apprentice or two, clustering to learn from her while willingly performing the more menial tasks which frustrated her. A clientele with limitless resources and an unquenchable thirst for her fine pieces. And I, of course, would be an artist—exciting such references as "Rembrandt-like" or "reminiscent of Monet at his best."

"Rembrandt or Monet? Which?"

I'd shrug. "Maybe both."

"Hmmmm."

"Or maybe neither. I'm still exploring."

And my exploration in techniques was still occurring when I'd met Arden, when I'd fallen in love, when I'd dismissed my mother's firm assessment that I'd never make a satisfactory minister's wife—I was too self-centered and scatterbrained—and her staunch prediction that he'd turn from me in less than a year, and then where would I be?

I'd wondered sometimes since if Mother had ever fully forgiven Arden for ignoring her dark expectations.

My friendship with Dee had survived the change nicely, and while we'd lived in the city, Arden and I, serving the lovely old church there, our closeness had—if anything—intensified.

During my breakdown—which my mother had faced by refusing to acknowledge it—next to Arden and dear Dr. David, my gentle psychiatrist, my guiding angel, Dee had been my sturdiest mainstay. When my gratitude shaped itself in apologies, she'd argued that I was her best therapy as well. "Artists are all a little off-base," she'd said, "especially us geniuses." She'd laughed, and my hiccuppy giggle had nearly succeeded. "But seriously—would you accept a trade-off? Would you surrender the creative urge—merely to be normal?"

There had been times, of course, when my imbalance demanded so much of Arden, when my fears raged, when I clutched Pam and prayed that I'd never be able to hurt her as I sometimes feared that I might—that the answer could have been yes.

But neither Arden nor Dee—nor, I suspected, God—would have accepted that.

One of the most wrenching elements of leaving the city church had been also leaving Dee. Distance prohibited our meetings. Neither of us was dedicated to the art of letter writing. And our calls had become sparse.

But late that night, when the low rates had kicked in, I called her.

It was on its seventh ring and I was feeling guilty—surely she was in bed—when she answered. Excitement brightened her voice. "Wonderful you called! I'd been fighting a new design all afternoon and decided to wrestle it this evening—it might get weary and simply give up!—And I just now emerged triumphant! You'd be proud of me."

"I am." I could feel my voice altering with a smile.

"But first, thanks for the animal sketch. And by a teenager! She has a real future ahead of her. But back to me." She laughed ripplingly. "A new compote. You remember Mrs. Wright—*the* Mrs. Wright—who gives so many dinner parties?"

I didn't, but to keep the flow going I murmured what might have been assent.

It was enough.

"For some reason, the woman's obsessed with soup. Not just cream of mushroom—nothing so mundane—*creme* of mushroom, with scallops or scullions or whatever—*something* exotic!—and lobster-cheese-broccoli—well, you know how dim I am about recipes, or food, for that matter, but you get the idea."

"I get the idea." Adding croutons and crumbled bacon to spinach salad shaped Dee's vision of elegant cuisine.

"You're brilliant. Anyway, she decided to hostess a buffet with each compote reflecting the character of the particular soup. I mean, it could look truly five-and-tennish."

"Not in your tasteful hands!" I protested.

"Oh, you are a treasure! Why did you ever move?" Without breaking her patter, she said, "Of course there's Arden, but you could have visited the occasional weekend."

Laughter erupted.

She drew a long breath. "You are okay, then." When I didn't answer immediately, she said, "When I first heard your voice . . ."

"Well, I'm fine physically. And emotionally—so far, at least. No sign of another breakdown. But I will admit that I needed a booster shot of your unique brand of insanity. TLC. That kind of thing."

"Has Arden been beating you again?" and we both guffawed at that.

"Then," she asked weakly, "have you been beating *him?*"

And we laughed again.

"Seriously . . ." she invited.

"Seriously . . . it's been scary around here."

"Around here as in . . ."

"McClintock."

"Oh, yes! The Samantha Crane thing. Terrible. Our paper ran the articles by that young writer of yours . . ."

"Matt Culhaney."

"Exactly. Somewhat . . . graphic—in a literary way." She sighed. "Such a tragedy. And just after we'd discovered that poor lady—in a *tarp*. How callous!" I could sense her shudder.

"And now a third murder."

"A *third* . . ." Her voice drained off, then resumed on an intense note. "Come spend some time with me." She added, "Pam, too. And Arden, if he can get away."

"Abandon ship, you mean?" My tone had sharpened.

A beat of silence.

"Ouch."

I sighed. "I wasn't being fair."

Her voice caught. "It's only that . . ."

"You care about us."

"And—"

"You know what we've been through. What . . . my breakdown put everyone through. And really, I *am* okay, that way. If I were going to go over the edge again, I'd already've done it. There's been more than enough."

Another beat.

"Like . . . what?"

And I was sorry I'd mentioned it.

But hadn't that been the reason for the call?

"Mutilations," I said.

"Like . . . the foot?"

"Samantha's throat was slit."

"Dear heaven," she whispered. "I'd forgotten . . . hadn't made a connection. First a foot, used to work the organ pedals. Then a throat, slit to stop the song. What next?"

"Next, battered hands, with the drumsticks tied to them."

"Another musician? What's with this guy!" Then, without pause, "Paula, you've *got* to come!"

"I can scarcely carry a tune." Then why . . . that night among the oaks . . .?

"But can't you see—how large a leap is it from music to . . . other things?"

Like painting, she'd meant.

Had the murderer merged the arts, as well? Could Clint have been a *second* choice?

I sighed. "I couldn't leave Arden. Not yet, anyway. And we'll be very, very careful." And I would be . . . now.

She said stubbornly, "Very careful would mean removing yourselves from danger."

"If there is danger."

"Three mutilated corpses aren't enough?" She laughed self-consciously. "Or three corpses in . . . *good* condition, as far as that goes."

"I mean—danger specifically to us."

Extended silence. While memory—resisting suppression—spun.

"Then why *did* you call?"

I cringed. "To draw from the reservoir of all-rightness. I'm sorry. I shouldn't have leaned on you again."

"You should always lean on me. What are friends for?"

"To use as sounding boards."

"And then reject what they suggest?"

"Sometimes."

"As it should be," she said, more lightly. "Listen, evaluate, and make up your own mind. Just remember . . ."

"It's reassuring to know that there's a lifeboat there when I tire of treading water. Now describe those compotes to me. In agonizing detail."

"Well, actually, only the one is finished . . ."

While I diced cantaloupe, peaches, and bananas, I felt Arden's glance on me.

I turned.

He was smiling. "You look better this morning. More relaxed."

"I slept well."

"Thanks to Dee."

I sprinkled Equal over the fruit and handed him his bowl. "It's crazy. But yes."

He added milk.

"On cantaloupe?"

"It all mixes, sooner or later." He took a spoonful, made appropriate "yummings," and offered me a bite.

I declined. Whipped topping, maybe. But milk? On cantaloupe?

"What'd she have to say?"

I summarized pottery and weather, then added, "She invited us to visit."

Chewing suspended, he surveyed me. "Not a bad idea."

"But could you get away?"

"You and Pam."

"No."

He caught me to him. His hair, still wet, smelled of shampoo—something piney. Thoroughly masculine. Familiar warmth suffused me. I closed my eyes for his kiss. He tasted of cold milk and cantaloupe. Quite tasty, actually.

"Honey, you really should—"

I stiffened against his gentle touch. "You didn't desert me when I was . . . ill."

"That was different."

"Only that . . . *I* was the danger then—to you *and* to Pam! The sensible thing would have been to put me away. No one would have blamed you. Not me—" My voice broke. "But you didn't."

He hadn't, though through those long months when I'd watched his color fade, his shoulders stoop, his eyes darken, I'd begged him to. Not once had he drawn back—only drawn me closer. Held me. Soothed me. Assured me. And gradually my blackness had receded. My spirit had regained tentative wings.

And so had his.

"I love you," I murmured against his cheek. Milk fragrance mingled with Old Spice.

"God must love me, too," he whispered, "to have given me someone so precious. That's why I think—"

"No." I tightened my hands on his shoulders as—unbidden—my thoughts slid again to that evening in the park, when threat, no longer nebulous, had breathed and tensed and waited—for me. If I'd shared that with Arden—or even with Dee—there'd be no argument. I finished stubbornly, "If there's danger, we'll face it together."

"There's danger," he said flatly. "I can't agree that it left with the carnival."

The Saturday of the wedding couldn't have been more beautiful if Greg and Mary Lynn had personally placed their orders. There was no question of resorting to the sanctuary; the arbor behind Mary Lynn's apartment was sun-washed and luxuriantly green—freshened by a shower the evening before. Two days earlier, Mary Lynn's landlady, a fluttery round woman with a semi-Cockney accent, had tied rosebuds loosely to restrain their blooming; then, that morning, had waded dew-damp grass in runover moccasins to free them for full bloom. Apparently she'd commanded the robins and cardinals as well; they were in exuberant song.

Matt, already stiffly resplendent in his Prussian blue tux—the effect damaged only by the multicolored strap which suspended his heavy camera—had stopped by the parsonage to give us the details. "Neat lady," he'd said.

"The landlady—or Mary Lynn?" teased Arden, and Matt's cheeks colored.

"Both?"

It seemed that every time I saw Matt, it was his youth which most impressed me. How could one so young be so talented? Or how could one so talented be so young? In every other way than the maturity of his writing.

Arden was saying, "I enjoyed your story on the abandoned cemetery near East Danvers, Matt."

I'd seen it, too. "We've talked about walking there. Now, we will." In my mind I amended, Once we're past the fear.

Matt fumbled his camera out of Pam's reach while permitting her to stroke the colorful strap. "It was picked up . . . by some other newspapers."

"Wonderful!" I said.

"Deservedly." Arden tugged his shirt collar, and I went to straighten it and fuss with the lapels of his jacket. "You brought in some interesting historical points. Like the sandstone markers. I'd never realized—"

"Neither had I!" Matt warmed to his subject. "If teachers tossed some of the musty textbooks and took their classes to old cemeteries, abandoned grist and silk mills, ruins of canals—that kind of thing—there'd be fewer dropouts. And more people with an appreciation of the past."

Arden signaled for an okay on his tie.

"Handsomest man in the room," I said, and glanced toward Matt. "With one possible exception."

"Flatterer." Arden swooped Pam into his arms. "Most beautiful girl in the room," he said, "with *no* exceptions!"

She giggled and colored.

Matt glanced at me. Studying me for possible disappointment? I wondered.

"He'll get no argument from me!" I said.

"'Sides," Pam gurgled, "Mommies ain't girls."

Even Matt laughed.

"Everyone ready?" asked Arden, and led the way. Matt shut the door behind us. "Of course," Arden said, as though there'd been no interruption, "you realize you're making a strong argument for the demise of printed media!"

"Which could put me out of a job." Matt turned, waiting for me to catch up. "But there'll always be a need for newspapers. Don't you agree?"

"There'll always be a need for books, too." Arden descended the steps to broken sidewalk overhung by rampant ivy. "The problem comes when society fails to perceive a need and so allows important sources to disappear."

Abandoning me and my high heels to the uneven concrete, Matt secured his camera and scurried ahead, trying to make room beside Arden. "I've been considering a series of oral histories. Mary Lynn's landlady—about coming to this country as a war bride. Monique Toulouse, of course—for the circus and carnival backgrounds. That is, if she'll speak to me." He glanced back.

I became very busy with ivy strands which caught and twined in my hair.

"*Will* she, do you think, Paula?"

There was a tinge of testiness to his tone, and I realized—with some chagrin—that he still hadn't forgiven me for my comments on the phone that day.

So young.

"Paula?" he persisted.

I kept my voice light. "I have no idea," I said, "but it's worth a try, isn't it?"

"Would you . . . go with me?"

I looked up in surprise. "I . . . guess so," I said. Then, "Why not? I'd like to see her again."

11

Actually, we saw her that day, though not until the reception was well underway.

The ceremony had been charming. The flower girl—not much older than Pam—froze in mid-march, and though the ring bearer tugged and cajoled and onlookers encouraged, her bottom lip trembled, her eyes brimmed, and, when Matt knelt to take her photo, the entire basketful of rose petals erupted into the air, swirling and floating lazily before forming a small apricot drift where she'd been standing. Retrieving the basket, the insouciant ring bearer shrugged, juggled the pillow to place the empty basket on his own arm, and made the rest of his journey in unruffled solitude.

Returning to Pam and me, Matt patted his camera. "Should be a memorable shot or two," he gloated.

As her older brother escorted her down the avenue banked by blooming delphiniums and beaming well-wishers, Mary Lynn's foot turned on an uneven spot—but that only tilted the two more closely together, and he gave her a quick squeeze and bestowed a kiss on her forehead.

Another photo opportunity for the ever-alert Matt.

Someone tripped over an extension cord, silencing the organist's embellishments of "The Lord's Prayer," but the soloist continued alone—the richness of his tones intensified by the *a cappella* phrases which flowed unaided, unself-consciously, until a plug could be reconnected.

It might have been planned.

And though a bumblebee manifested an inordinate amount of interest in one bridesmaid's bouquet, evoking quiet terror in her expression; and though Greg spoke a bit too loudly as he voiced his vows, and Mary Lynn a bit too softly; and though a breeze riffled the pages of Arden's Bible and disarranged his hair so that a rusty lock hung boyishly on his forehead; and though Mary Lynn's father—wheelchair-bound with advanced multiple sclerosis—shivered so uncontrollably that his wife removed her lavender silk jacket and draped it gently about his head and shoulders; all of the inaccuracies or improvisations were endearing, and person after person in the reception line rated it the most flawless wedding in memory.

The breeze, having heightened by the time guests queued for refreshments, played havoc with stacks of styrofoam cups and apricot-colored napkins, gold-imprinted with Greg and Mary Lynn's names and the date. Even the surface of the punch in the large cut-glass bowl rippled.

"Time to post small-craft warnings," Dora Kuhn murmured as she half-filled a cup for Pam. Her blonde hair was disarrayed, and she wore small plugs of cotton in her ears. "Hope the tuxes are shrink proof."

But the white clouds scudding across the still-blue sky looked benevolent.

"Careful of that, honey," she said, as Pam struggled with her drink.

"No problem," I said. "Her dress *is* washable."

"Good thing, too," Dora observed wryly, and I sighed as cherry-colored punch drizzled down Pam's crisp pink ruffles.

"Monochromatic, anyway."

Dora frowned a question.

"An artist's rationalization," I apologized, "just in case."

"Rationalization is good, I guess," she grinned, and turned to the next in line.

While we perched on folding wooden chairs and juggled drinks and small decorative throwaway plates laden with wedding cake and flower-shaped mints, I noticed Monique. She'd made no effort to become a part of the group, but—partially obscured by glossy rhododendron foliage—clung to its verges. She held something larger than a napkin, but not by much.

"Lady." Pam pointed her icing-coated forefinger.

Thrusting her plate and sloshing drink toward me, she scrambled from her chair. I'd scarcely managed to protect my own dress before she reclaimed the plate and pattered down a path, veering to work her way through clusters of chatting people. I looked for a place level enough to hold the cups, decided on the seat of the chair, and was set to follow when I saw Mary Lynn detach herself from laughing friends. By the time I'd joined them, she was inviting Monique to come have punch.

"Thanks, dear, but I couldn't." Her voice was huskier than usual.

"I'd be so pleased."

"But look at you, so lacy and white . . . and at them." She nodded toward the well-dressed crowd, which seemed oblivious to our small group. She smiled uncertainly. "Probably not one of them lives under a bridge." And then, as though she might elicit discomfiting sympathy, she shrugged a misshapen shoulder and added, "Another time, I'll come visit, when you're settled."

Mary Lynn smiled. "I'd like that."

Of course, Mary Lynn would be in Germany.

"Here." Monique extended a small square of folded fabric. "I couldn't wrap it."

But Mary Lynn, carefully unfolding the piece, drew a breath of mingled delight and disbelief. "Oh . . . oh . . . oh," and then, in rising tones, "You *made* this, didn't you? But it's . . . more than lovely! It's . . . indescribable!"

And it was. Obviously a cushion covering, worked in row after neat row of ribbonlike pastel strips, it was centered by an embroidered cluster of satin-stitched roses, their sprays of sawtoothed leaves rambling toward each corner.

"Ohhhhh," purred Pam, reaching a grubby finger to touch, but I drew her hand gently back, and she didn't resist.

Mary Lynn's eyes filled with tears. "No matter how many wonderful gifts we receive—" Her voice broke, and she caught Monique into a fierce hug.

"Miss . . . I'm dirty."

"You're wonderful!" She drew back, still gripping Monique's shoulders. "Do you realize what a talent you've been hiding?"

A smile quirked the corners of Monique's lips. "Till now, it was holding performers' costumes together."

"And what a waste! You're an artist, Monique." She turned. "Isn't she, Paula?"

Wordlessly, I nodded. In the right shops, such work would bring a fortune. But I couldn't suggest that, not just then. While I knew Monique only in a surface way—grasping as much as she was willing to expose—I felt that such a comment would repel or frighten her.

Later. When we were closer. When she was ready to imagine a world where she could be acknowledged in a manner withheld since her accident, so many years before.

Mary Lynn said softly, "I won't use it as a cushion cover, you know."

Monique's glance wavered.

"I'll have it matted and framed and hung on a wall all its own."

When Mary Lynn had returned to show her guests the lovely workmanship, Monique also turned to leave. Tears streaked her cheeks—but I suspected that they couldn't be tears of sadness, nor even of exclusion. Such appreciation as Mary Lynn's required a rare comprehension of how deeply the artist resides in the product. To cherish the art is to offer love to the artisan.

Hugging Monique about the knees, Pam implored, "Lady stay."

Laboriously, Monique knelt to embrace her, their cheeks pressed together, their eyes shining.

And Matt's camera shutter snapped.

I'd never before witnessed such a transformation as occurred with that small sound. Monique's gray eyes chilled. The planes of her face hardened. Her body seemed inflexible as she rose. Certainly her arms were rigid, and her hands clenched at her sides.

Whimpering, Pam released her slowly, slowly moved to me.

Monique seemed not to notice. "Haven't you hurt me enough?" she asked Matt coldly. "You cost me my job, all the family I had left, all the life I'd ever known."

Her lip curled. Her eyes narrowed. I felt myself step involuntarily back, and Matt retreated also. "You leave me be," she said, almost gutturally, and one hand moved stiffly upward, one forefinger straightened to point. "You leave me be, or you'll be the next corpse found dead and damaged."

None of us seemed to know how to deal with what had just occurred. Pam's hand clutched mine. "Why lady mad?" she asked tremblingly, when Monique was already beyond sight.

And Matt said with a chuckle that seemed vulnerably self-conscious, "Mad is the appropriate term, I believe."

But no, Monique's reaction had come from deep pain, not from insanity.

"Guess that ends the chance of an interview," Matt added, his face still pale, his tone, though striving for lightness, still shaken.

Grow up, I thought, and wanted to say.

It was with relief that I saw Dean detach himself from his grandmother and hurry toward us.

He'd heard from Sylva.

"She says she misses me!" he said with creditable surprise. "It sounds like she really means it!"

I patted his shoulder. "You're a missable guy."

"Yeah," he said uncertainly, "but you'd miss me as a . . . kid who likes art. She misses me as a . . . friend." He took a letter, its folds already frayed, from his hip pocket, smiled at it, and replaced it without offering to let me see it.

Not that I would have read it anyway.

"Want more cake?" he asked. "I could get it for you. Mary Lynn said there's plenty." He confided, "I've had three pieces. But they're awful small, don'tcha think?"

"No more for me, thanks," I said, then noting his disappointment, "but you could get another that might be for me—and have it yourself."

His expression brightened. Then, "You don't think Mary Lynn'd mind?"

"I think she'd be delighted that you like it so much!"

"Pammie? Wanna come?"

She shook her head and shrank even closer to me.

Ordinarily, she'd have gone readily. I knew that she still puzzled over—perhaps mourned—the change in Monique.

"The lady won't be angry for long," I assured her. "Probably she isn't, even now." Besides, I thought a bit grimly, Matt had earned her anger.

Of course Mary Lynn would argue that his free use of the camera—as his incisiveness with language—was what made him the reporter he was and would be. "He's up for an award, had you heard?" she'd whispered in the reception line. Her voice was unshadowed, clearly delighted for him. "There'll be something major soon, I'd bet on it."

Glancing about, I saw him sitting with Minnie. I wondered if he'd told her of the encounter with Monique, and hoped not, but she seemed more intent on her teetering plate than on what he was saying—or even on his presence.

That would change with the awards.

If he'd decided not to share the incident with her, that at least showed good sense. Minnie was partisan enough on his behalf to stalk down to the bridge and single-handedly evict its resident.

I pictured Monique, huddled beneath that cheerless concrete arch, surrounded only by whatever clutter she'd managed to salvage from her past life and scavenge from the new. With only the interruptions of intermittent traffic overhead, an occasional scuttling of insects—or worse, rats—what thoughts of regret or recrimination had haunted her as she labored over the stitchery—her gift for Mary Lynn? Surely if any hope heartened her, it grew from the beautiful work she created.

And how could she feel safe there, how sleep past the knowledge of three murders so far and no killer found? What weapon might she keep close at hand? Or was life so burdensome, so dark and chill, that death held only a somewhat lesser terror?

Before winter, I thought. Before winter, something must be done about Monique. Already some evenings were cold enough to require sturdy covering. Was it possible that she built a fire to provide heat as well as a means for cooking food?

And I felt swift shame that I hadn't taken the time to visit her there. To ask—though delicately—how or if I might help.

Dean was back with one piece of cake for himself and one for Pam. Smiling, I wondered if he hoped she might be too full for hers as well—but she accepted it greedily. Perhaps the act of eating dulled her sense of dismay at Monique's disturbing anger.

After church at East Danvers, Amy caught me as Arden and I hurried toward the car for the final leg of our three-church appointment. "Would you mind a hitchhiker?" she asked shyly. "Our car's in the garage, and—Paula—I really need to talk with you."

"Hop in," Arden said. "Of course you'll be doomed to a rerun of the sermon."

"Fine." She settled herself beside Pam in the back seat and added teasingly, "Maybe I'll even listen this time." Her smile faded quickly, though, and I found myself sufficiently troubled that I paid scant attention during the McClintock service. Once, if Dora hadn't drawn me upward with her elbow, I'd have failed to stand for a hymn.

We took Amy home with us for lunch, a scant offering of microwaved leftover spaghetti, tossed green salad, and brown-and-serve breadsticks melting with butter and sprinkled with onion salt.

"Yum." She leaned back, looking more relaxed than I'd seen her all morning. Then her voice altered. "When the dishes are done . . . could we go for a walk in the woods?"

I stiffened. The woods—so far from town, so shadowed, its sounds foreign enough to mask footsteps . . .

Still, it was daylight. And there'd be two of us.

"Sure," I said. "I'd like that."

As we walked past pruned forsythia and the annex which housed Sunday school rooms, Amy seemed distracted, and though she hurried—keeping nearly a pace beyond me—I wondered if she might be reluctant to come at last to the point of discussion.

She led me to a spot I well recognized—a favorite place, she'd said, when she and Turk were courting. It was there she'd shown me the poem informing him of her decision to leave him. And it was there, I remembered, that not long ago they'd picnicked while he pressed his suit for reconciliation. Suddenly chilled, I looked about, but saw only the reassuring ordinariness of straight, sunstroked trees, undergrowth tremblingly spotted with leaf shadow, and small birds and animals, scurrying casually about their routines once we'd settled ourselves on a large, cool rock and they'd apparently satisfied themselves that we were two of them.

She asked, "You're not frightened, are you?" and then, "None of the murders has happened in daylight."

Unless, I thought, Mrs. Porter . . .

I resisted the urge to study the area even more diligently. After all, since the wildlife tolerated us, they might as easily ignore a lurking murderer—as long as he or she remained quiet. Unchallenging. Unthreatening.

Ridiculous.

For a time, we sat in quietness, and I enjoyed the stir of the breeze, the murmurings of woods life, and the semi-distant voices of water in its various moods.

Eventually, she cleared her throat.

A chipmunk, who'd been buffeting a maple leaf, tinted and fallen prematurely, scampered away.

Again, silence.

The chipmunk flirted his tail. Studied us, head to one side. Crept closer.

"I need to get this over with," Amy began, and the chipmunk was gone—perhaps forever—in a frantic scattering of pine needles.

"It's not what you might think," she said, "from the way I've been acting, I mean. It's not about Turk. Well," she corrected herself almost simultaneously, "it is in a way, since it's because of him . . . and the fact we're not living together, and money's so scarce—mine, not his," she interjected grimly. "It's because of that I've decided to tell him to take the house, and I'll move into town. Into McClintock. And I just wanted to get your feeling about it first."

My initial thought was that she would ask to live with us. My second was that my answer would be—of course. And that Arden's would echo it.

Instead, she said, "You remember where the fabric shop was?"

I nodded. It was standing empty when we'd come to McClintock but had since housed another abortive business venture. On either side of a recessed door, large front windows slanted outward at the top beneath dented aluminum awnings—striped green and beige. As I recalled, two small apartments backed the showroom. A split-cedar porch roof sloped from the store front toward the half-story, meant for storage, which topped the apartments. Half-lost behind, and in places beneath, a grove of untended soaring spruce trees—one of them skeletal, with dead orange needles—it had always struck me as a defeated, neglected place—save when heavy wet snowfall transformed the scene with Christmas-card magic.

"I know it looks sad," she said, and I experienced that sense, again, that our thoughts moved in sync.

And yet I'd had no inkling that she'd considered a major change.

"It's very isolated," I began. "Lonely." Of course, once the extra apartment was rented . . .

"No more isolated than where I am now."

True enough.

"It seems foolish even to think about it," she went on. "I mean, one reason I want to leave the house is that it needs repairs I can't do and can't afford to have done. And the shop looks even worse."

"We could help. And Dean."

She waved that aside. "Though I might have Dean do a mural," she said, as an afterthought. "Think he'd like to?"

I laughed. "He's been panting to get his fists in paint again!"

"But the other stuff—well, maybe somebody who's good with tools could firm up the shelves. And straighten the sidewalk. Maybe cut out the dead tree. But the building doesn't need a roof or anything major. Mostly little things, and a good thorough cleaning. New carpet, eventually, and . . ." She smiled self-deprecatingly. "I've given this a lot of thought."

"I can see that."

"The reason I didn't mention it before—well, I wasn't sure. I mean, my skills are mostly in poetry, and that's about as marketable as . . ." Apparently unable to think of an apt analogy, she shrugged. "I was going to say earthworms—but every fisherman buys those, while poems . . ."

"I remember some wonderful chocolate chip–mint cookies."

She leaned forward, her expression expectant. "Cookies and poetry, those I can do. So what does that suggest?"

I hated to let her down. Eventually, though, I had to shrug.

"Unfair, expecting you to get in two seconds what it's taken me weeks to plan. Add crepe paper streamers . . . pretty napkins . . . balloons . . ." An encouraging movement of her hand accompanied each suggestion.

"Parties?" I ventured.

"Exactly! How many working mothers have time or energy to arrange birthday parties? They could give me a theme—as long as it wasn't too exotic, as long as they didn't expect genuine orchid leis or live giraffes—and I'd do it for them! For a reasonable fee, of course."

I leaned back, hands flat on the roughness of cool rock. "Do you realize how exciting this is?"

"Yes!" she said, her eyes shining, her head nodding so energetically that her hair flopped. "Yes, yes, *yes!"*

I felt myself frowning. "Then why . . ."

"Why was I so worried? So tentative? So despairing?"

"Exactly."

She said soberly, "There's something very sad about giving up . . . home. And something extremely scary about committing myself to buying a building."

"You couldn't just rent it—perhaps with an option to buy?"

"The owner wants to sell. Now."

"But if Turk gets the house, surely . . ." I knew that vein of thought was fruitless. Turk would do anything in the world to sabotage such a definitive break with their past together. Such a cancellation of his plan for their future—together.

"Turk would rather see me dead."

Perhaps it was her calmness that caused a tremor to climb my spine. Or perhaps the chill sprang from remembered snatches of confrontation, torn into fragments by a coming storm—that night at the carnival. In anger, Turk had used the word dead. And it had throbbed with impatience . . . or intention.

"You're cold," she said, scrambling up—and then I noticed the intrepid chipmunk, having tried again after all, only to be terrorized again.

"A little," I said, though mine was inward cold, rather than anything born of late summer.

"We could talk on the way back." She skipped a step or two. "Oh, you can't know how excited I am that you're excited," and all the way through the woods, past the senior citizen housing complex, across a meadow toward town and home, she chattered on and on, while I listened distractedly, occasionally searching shadows for possible danger. Ears alert to unexpected sounds.

I paused, once, my hand on her arm. "Will you rent the one apartment?"

"It would be a way to help with payments," she said, but somberly.

I'd been thinking of another human presence.

She grinned.

"Yesterday, though, I thought of something better."

And instinctively I knew what that was. "Monique."

She studied me with a surprise that was merely mild. "It would mean losing the rent."

"For a while."

She waited.

"She could—if you had the space—display some of her work. And those same busy working mothers—"

She brightened. "Who never have time for mending—"

"Exactly!"

We resumed walking. "And besides, she's such a unique, interesting person! I can't think Matt Culhaney's right—can you? About her being dangerous?"

"Of course not!" I agreed, and then, unbidden, I remembered her cold anger toward Matt just the previous day. And her threat.

12

Gradually, that next week, I became aware of a solidifying wariness, a tightening security, throughout McClintock. It was as though the wedding had formed a respite, a small island of normality in a situation fraught with terror. Now—folding chairs returned, crumbs and birdseed devoured—the town seemed freed to fear once more. Perhaps even encouraged toward such darker moods.

Even before the wedding, there'd been small evidences of increasing caution. Drapes lifting before a locked door was opened to admit a neighbor. Salesmen and other strangers kept to porches. Children seldom seen in solitary play. Empty sidewalks after dinner. A reluctance to attend evening services or meetings which lasted past dusk. No evening baby-sitting, Connie's mother had ordained, even if we drove her both ways. And I understood.

Even the softball games had been scheduled for afternoons, and through the night hours Constable Joe's vehicle moved bulkily—pausing, engine throbbing, then creeping ahead. My ears had learned its habits.

Now, strange dog voices punctuated the night. Dobermans and German Shepherds strained from heavy chains or lunged against chain-link fences, newly erected.

"Sad," Matt said one afternoon as he stopped by, ostensibly for church news, but—I was convinced—for lemonade. "Too hot for brownies, I suppose?"

"Too hot to bake them."

"Never too hot to eat them."

"After the first frost," I promised.

And he suggested, "You'll put that in writing?"

Silence stretched companionably. Arden joined us and poured his own lemonade. The glass frosted comfortingly. "Doesn't anyone buy poodles anymore?" he asked.

"We were just discussing that."

"Sad."

"My word exactly," contributed Matt. "I've been thinking of doing a story along that line. No new murders, yet fear seems somehow intensified, rather than diminished." His voice drained off. Setting his glass sturdily on its coaster, he pulled a small pad from his pocket and began making notations.

Arden and I sat quietly, smiling at one another. I could hear Pam singing to her teddy bear in the next room.

The loudest sounds in the kitchen were the whir of the fan in the refrigerator and Matt's scratching pencil point.

He looked up once. "You're allowed to talk, you know." He shrugged. "I mean, it *is* your kitchen." And then he returned to his notes, and we might as well have been anywhere.

Arden caught my hand and grinned.

We didn't require speech, I decided.

Daisies still dot the meadow where childhood friends and I sought arrowheads long since depleted . . . or meteorites flung flaming from heaven to dim and darken there among the mosses and seeding milkweed. But few children gather daisies, now, roots and all, and carry them triumphantly for mothers to showcase—perhaps roots and all—in vases or

Mason jars. Few giggling teenage girls pluck and denude them, petal by significant petal, "He loves me . . . he loves me not . . . he loves me . . . he loves me not . . ." while pretending indifference; "it's superstition, after all."

No lovers—whose daisies, perhaps, foretold bliss—wander there; daylight discourages romantic dreaming, and after-dark dawdling is forbidden.

Except for an impromptu practice range, where occasional bursts of gunfire stutter and startle, the meadow stands silent. Deserted.

Deserted as well is the park, once dusk has threatened. The schoolyard—where recently teenagers bounced resonant balls until well past dark—still, now. Porches, surrendered to mosquitos. Even the custard stand shuttered prematurely.

Huddled behind drapes drawn and doors dead-bolted, we strain through the mania of paralyzing TV reruns for any foreign sound, any symptom of lurking or intrusion. Even the character of the pets we choose has altered. Wagging tails are discouraged. Hospitality—more than endangered—has become extinct.

"Nothing is so much to be feared as fear," wrote Henry David Thoreau, and Franklin Delano Roosevelt said, "The only thing we have to fear is fear itself."

Perhaps we in McClintock should take note, should find significance in the fact that our fear has somehow intensified during the *lack* of violence. Holding our breath until it happens again—if it happens again—is it possible that our waiting holds elements of expectancy? Of an ardent curiosity more enticed, more nurtured, by turbulence than by tranquillity?

Walking abroad at night I hear nothing more alarming than the sizzling of stars, the quiet purpling of thistles, the fisting of spent wild carrot. Soon children will resume their daily trek to classrooms. Goldenrod will signal a deepening autumn, opening to winter. Wrapped in our cocoons of hyperbolized dread, will we forego, as well, the wonders of icicles and snow?

"Well, certainly the character of the *Bugle* has changed," Arden said dryly, as he refolded the paper and laid it beyond range of Pam's pancake syrup. "Mary Lynn would never have suggested that we actually yearn for another murder."

"Maybe most people won't catch it," I said. "Hopefully, they'll get so caught up in 'purpling thistles' and 'sizzling stars' they'll never notice."

"That he thinks we're bloodthirsty?" He caught a fragment of pancake before it reached the floor. "Don't you feel a bit . . . resentful?"

"That he started to write it at our kitchen table?"

"Which makes us accessories before the—Pammie, if you don't want the pancake, let Daddy have it."

"Want it," she said, cradling the whole messy plate against her breast.

I sighed.

And as she turned a cherubic smile on me, I could see her curls tangling in syrup as well.

Oh, well. Better to consider Matt than the mess I'd have to deal with before Connie came and I could join Amy at the store. *Her* store, as of the day before. "He's so young . . ." I began, and wondered how much longer I'd be using that to excuse and explain him.

Or could it be construed as condemnation?

No, I hoped never to be one of those adults who found fault with youth.

Arden extricated the plate from Pam's fingers—not so difficult, since her hands were slimy with syrup and couldn't maintain purchase—then carried it to the sink. "I went to see Monique yesterday afternoon," he said.

"Monique! Under the bridge?" Where else? I thought, chastening myself for such a dumb question. And for not having gone with him. "Is she . . . all right?"

"Well . . . she's no longer grieving for Clint."

There was something about his tone. "That's . . . *good*. Isn't it?"

He turned on the hot water, at full force, and spoke above it.

"Now, though, she's decided who's to blame for Clint's death."

I asked quietly, "God?"

We'd seen it happen often before, of course—people in deep pain who'd demand, "Why? Why me? How could God allow this to happen?" and gradually develop a deep anger toward a deity who hadn't altered events to forestall tragedy and defeat evil. It was understandable. Such a little thing, it must seem, for an all-powerful God to zap a cancer or virus. To slow or hasten traffic—just a bit, just enough to cancel an accident. To stay the hand of a rapist, a mugger, a murderer . . . to mislead one or the other into another direction, another activity, so that paths failed to cross . . . or at the very least to grant a victim an additional measure of perception, precaution, or strength.

And yet He'd allowed His own Son to be crucified.

"Given time . . ." I proposed, but wondered. Monique had had the best part of a lifetime to question God. To blame Him.

I went to place my arm across his shoulder. "If anyone can help her, it's you."

"If anyone can help her," Arden amended, as he went to lift Pam down—so necessitating his own second change of clothing before he reported to his office—"it's God."

"I need to ask you something," Amy said, attention fully on the storefront windowsill she was scraping, "and I hate to."

"Are you okay?"

"Sometimes I think . . . never again." She did look up, then, and her eyes were red-rimmed, her cheeks tear-streaked.

Only Turk had the power—or the will—to hurt her so.

"For the first time . . ."

"You're afraid."

"Terrified," she said. "Truly terrified." She moved her paint scraper slowly, scaling great chunks of peeling white paint. "I guess there were moments before—many of them. But they were more sadness than dread. He says I stepped over the line when I decided on this place. Says it shows I'm determined to leave him forever." Her voice deepened. "He's convinced there's another man."

"When he's watched you so closely . . ." I found the broom and gathered a few of the worst cobwebs, draped like Spanish moss from the branches of the chandelier.

"He's sure that Clint and I—" She broke off. "Or that we would have, given time."

I said quietly, "He'd better keep that to himself. Sounds like a workable motive for murder."

She laid the scraper aside and reached for sandpaper. "Exactly."

Exactly? My broom stilled, then worked more slowly, until the soft grayness had formed an impromptu skein about the uneven broomstraws. I asked slowly, "You think . . ."

"I think it's possible."

"Earlier . . ."

"Earlier, I'd have staked my life that he was incapable. Heaven knows he can be cold. Even cruel. But to commit violence . . ."

Yet I'd seen him slam her against the corn-dog stand.

"What happened at the carnival—well, that wasn't the first time."

Stunned, I made no response.

Free of wisps, the chandelier showed other flaws—hundreds of spots where flyspecks had eaten the brass finish and allowed rust to develop. Scrapes and dents.

"I thought eventually I'd have it recoated. But for now, there's so much else to do."

I nodded. "What next?"

"The bookshelves?"

I ran a bucket of water, seething over detergent. Even through plastic gloves, it felt hot. Soothing. I wanted her to tell me how Turk had changed . . . or at least how her perception had altered. But I wouldn't pry. Dirt eddied about my sudsy sponge and dripped from a shelf-edge to form gray puddles on the stained tile.

"The difference is," Amy continued, "that always before he acted on impulse. Often, he'd even apologize, almost right away." She sighed. "Not always. But often. But last night—" Her voice broke. "Last night, he'd *planned* his intimidation . . . down to the smallest detail." She drew a long trembling breath. "Later, okay?" and with forced brightness, "Have you ever seen anything as filthy as this woodwork?"

Later, over delivered pizza and lukewarm soda, she told me. She'd been asleep when she'd heard sounds outside the house. It could have been anything, at first—wild animals rummaging, neighborhood dogs. A murderer . . . I was thinking.

Even when the lid of the garbage can clanged on the concrete, she was thinking raccoons. But then came the rhythmic scraping, as though someone dragged a branch or stick along the siding of the house. Around and around and around. Occasionally the scraping eased, and something tapped on a window. Then another. Another.

I shuddered, my breath catching.

But it was when she'd heard glass breaking that she'd fully panicked.

How could she *not* have—even *without* knowledge of three brutal murders?

"The laundry door," she was saying. "Even this morning, I couldn't find all the glass. It's a wonder he didn't slash a vein."

He. Turk.

A wonder, I thought, or a pity? And then felt warm with guilt.

"Of course the phone was dead."

Of course.

"Once I knew that, I just huddled in bed. I didn't know then it was Turk—though I guess I should have. It could have been anyone, though, and it seemed better—if he came to the bedroom—to seem to be asleep."

And of course he had come to the bedroom.

"Not right away. That was what was so horrifying! He did everything so slowly, and my nerve ends kept twitching, and inside I was shrieking, 'Get it over with! Get it over with!'"

First, after the shattering glass, there'd been doors and drawers opening and closing. Heavy footsteps through the downstairs—those even more frightening periods of quiet when he walked on carpet—or perhaps simply waited. Listening. Then he'd begun climbing the stairs. Changed his mind, going into the kitchen again. And later—much later—eternities later . . .

Of course. He'd wanted to delay, extend, refine her terror.

"He went to the closet first. Often, he seemed not to be moving at all. Just listening—and I was sure that he was. And, Paula, it was the hardest thing I've ever done to lie there still. Breathing quietly." She closed her eyes as though reliving those moments.

And—even with my eyes open—I felt her terror. How could he have subjected her to this, someone he claimed to love, when he'd have known that ordinary terror—if terror could ever be that—must be amplified by a trilogy of violent deaths?

Limp pizza drooped from her hand, congealing strands of cheese drooling to the dirty floor.

No matter.

Eventually, he had come to the bed and leaned over it. "Wake up, sleepyhead," he'd called quietly—softly, teasingly, as though rousing a favorite child. She'd recognized his voice, of course—for the first time had known firmly that it was Turk.

She said unsteadily, "And I'm not sure whether that made me feel less frightened . . . or more."

When she hadn't moved, he'd jostled the bed—gently, at first, then roughly. And turned on the bedside lamp.

"And it was terrible. Terrible. Terrible. The light shone up over his face—you know how it does, when you hold a flashlight under your chin, and you can look evil without even trying? And . . . he was *trying*. But the knife was worst." Lifting the pizza, she nibbled at it, her glance firm on mine.

I jolted. "The . . . *knife?*"

"One of the kitchen ones. He'd smeared it with catsup, or something, and he said, 'This could be your blood. And the next time, Amy, my love—the next time it will be.'"

Almost feverishly, seeming unaware of the processes of biting, chewing, swallowing, she finished the slice of pizza and reached for another. "And worse than the words, it was the way he said them. He could have been promising to take me out to dinner or buy me flowers." She sagged.

"You can't go back," I said firmly. "You've got to stay with us."

Her eyes brimmed, and she reached a sticky hand to touch my arm. "Just until I get a place cleared here—enough for a sleeping bag, get the gas turned on—in fact, I could do without that, since we already have water and electricity."

"As long as you need," I assured her. Hadn't she considered that he could terrorize her behind the screen of aging spruces quite as easily as at the home they'd shared?

She must not be alone again. Should not have been, this far. Why hadn't I insisted, earlier, that she stay with us?

But I knew that—then—she'd have refused.

Arden went with Amy to gather the things she'd need immediately, and we turned dinner into a party, with picnic foods and ice cream sundaes.

A delighted Pam insisted on being elbow-close to Amy and sharing bits of food. Later, as we sat together in the living room, we munched microwaved popcorn and watched some of the childproof comedy reruns. Pam resisted going to bed until at length she fell asleep in the crook of Amy's arm. Extricating her—and even asleep, Pam clung—Arden carried her upstairs.

"Thanks," Amy said. Her voice seemed clogged with tears.

I gave her a quick hug. "We enjoyed it, too."

"Enjoyed it, maybe. But for me—it was more. Deliverance—"

The telephone shrilled.

She shrank into herself. "It's Turk. I know it's Turk."

"I do have to answer it."

She sighed. "I know. But—I won't talk to him."

"You won't have to." I went briskly enough, for her sake, but wished desperately that Arden would pick up the bedroom extension.

Before lifting the receiver, I braced myself. I was being silly. It could be anyone.

But it was Turk.

He began without ceremony. "Let me talk to my woman."

"I'm sorry," I said. "You didn't say who is calling." I watched for Arden. Nowhere in sight.

Turk swore softly, then said—with what seemed almost like admiration—"As if you didn't know, little Mrs. Preacher. But you just tell that woman of mine that she ain't safe from me anywhere that has window glass. And you remember this—no one with her will walk away either."

I could think of nothing to say and lacked the will to hang up on him.

His laughter was low and chilling. "How old is that little girl of yours now, Paula? Close to three? Awful young to die . . . ain't she?"

13

Days passed, and Turk remained quiet. The waiting game—Turk waiting, while we sweated it out.

"Should we call Constable Joe?" I asked once. "Get a restraining order?"

But even before Arden answered, I knew that could be a dangerous idea. Turk would only be further angered, and what good was a paper anyway—signed by no-matter-whom—when someone was truly violence-bent? Perhaps in a city with well-staffed police forces and a climate which trained its personnel to sense and disarm such situations, but in McClintock, with a constable who already showed signs of unaccustomed stress?

Arden said, "I know that Amy's having her doubts about Turk—and no wonder—but I don't think he's made of the stuff it would take . . . to do what he threatened to do."

Still, it was a gamble, and—judging by Arden's increased care each night in locking up—he was fully aware of it.

"It could be a no-win situation," he said. "If we don't report it, it could be the wrong decision. But I have a deep feeling that if we do, it would be worse."

Again, he suggested that Pam and I spend a week with Dee. "Take Amy with you. Dee wouldn't mind."

"But I would." And my mind whirled with the inevitability of Turk's anger when he'd learn that Amy was gone from his sphere of terror. What might he do to

Arden? Closing my mind against it, I said, "As it is, I have to beat other women away from you with a stick."

He grinned—a wonderfully familiar boyish grin—and I recognized that stirring of joy and gratitude I'd felt when he asked me to marry him, when I first held Pam in my arms, so often during my breakdown, when he'd been there—unfailingly—to lend me courage, and thousands of times between. Wordlessly, I breathed a prayer of thanks that God had seen fit to bring such love into my life. "Besides," I said, quelling any reservations I'd entertained before, "it's important for Amy to get her place ready. The sooner she moves in, the sooner she can begin to build a business. And a life."

Paint drizzled from Dean's brush to the semiclean tile as he admired the newly coated wall. Its blue was so pale it might have passed for shadowed white. "What a background that's gonna make for a mural!"

Amy spoke around the serrated steak knife she'd been using as a screwdriver when her hands weren't juggling receptacle covers. "Any idea yet what it will be?"

He blushed. "Wild animals?"

Pam reached past her building blocks to gather her stuffed toys closer. We'd delineated an impromptu play area with crates and boxes to keep her out of reach of paint. "Teddy bears?"

"More like big cats?" Amy guessed. "Would there be . . . any people?"

She was obviously teasing, and Dean's heightened color showed that he knew it. He seemed to be weighing possible answers.

We waited, smiling.

Arden, braced on the third step of the ladder to reattach the chandelier, finally suggested, "Some people have a beauty that defies any paintbrush."

Dean laughed. "Right on." And then because he seemed unable to dissemble, he added, "Besides, I'm not good at drawing people. Maybe I never will be."

I reminded him, "A month ago, you were saying that about lions and tigers."

"Tigers!" repeated Pam, chortling. "Tigers 'n yions!"

Dean said with some surprise, "Yeah, I was, wasn't I?"

"I don't know, though." Amy's tone had grown cautious. "A warmer background color might be better. Light gold, maybe."

Paint flew in an arc as Dean laid his brush on the pan before insisting, "This'll be just *right* for deep jungle. All the greens and blue-greens. Humungous leaves. Rain dripping from vines. Even some of those bright blue butterflies—"

"Teasing," she said.

He hesitated.

"This wall is yours, not mine, and I don't care if you paint it full of warty toads and polka-dotted dinosaurs."

"I never would."

"So I feel safe in saying I wouldn't mind." She turned to look at each of us in turn. "Time for a break!"

It was only when we paused, when we settled on any available surface, that I noticed the sounds—sharp, echoing.

Frowning, Amy went to a window and peered out. "The dead spruce!" she said, her voice lilting. "Who . . ." She rushed outside, all of us following.

The woodcutter, back turned to us, worked forcefully, each cut of the ax exciting a shower of chips. Dead needles rained about his shoulders as limb after severed limb wrenched free, thudded to ground, and rolled to rest against a root of a healthy tree.

And then he turned.

Gasping, Amy lurched backward into Arden. *"Turk!"* The name jolted from her. *"Why . . ."*

"Just wanted you to remember," he called tightly, "I ain't forgot where to find you." His glance flicked to Arden, then me. "Day *or* night," he finished grimly, and returned to his work. He must not have realized that despite our pleading, she'd begun to spend her nights there.

Later that afternoon, Matt stopped by. Wearing shabby coveralls and a threadbare shirt, he offered himself for any task available.

Amy, still pale and a bit shaken, suggested, "Help Dean with the sink?"

"Glad to." He paused by the blank wall. "What's it going to be, Dean?"

"Jungle." Dean set down the squirt bottle with which he'd been attacking grime. "Here," he said, "in the foreground, moving diagonal, right toward the floor—a tiger. Prowlin'. There's gonna be a boa constrictor wrapped around a high limb, right about there . . . and maybe a jaguar . . . there—snarling. I'm not quite sure what birds, but a cockatoo, almost certain, the color of the wall, with just some lighter white for highlight and a kind of bluish-gray for shadow. And flowers—orchids and . . ." He shrugged. "I've gotta do some research first, but I thought I could get started early next week, when the paint's clear set."

"Tell you what," Matt said, conspiratorially, "when it's finished, I'll take a photo of you standing by it. One copy for the *Bugle,* one for you . . . and an extra, just in case you'd like to send one to . . . you know . . . anyone." He winked at me.

The remainder of the afternoon, working at double speed, Dean grinned and hummed all the while, until—following a long respite of quietness outside—the ax blows resumed, proving that Turk had returned.

Matt looked up brightly. "Some good neighbor, taking out the old spruce skeleton?" he asked. "Everybody's getting in the act!"

Amy and I exchanged glances suggesting that the "act" Turk was performing had nothing to do with kindness.

But Arden said mildly, "Guess I'll go offer to help stack."

That night, a cold front came through, and early morning found a patina of frost on grass, flowers, and shrubs. The marigolds shook off the attack; the petunias didn't, nor could many of the other gentler blooms. Once the sun had melted the frost away, gardens looked darkened and limp, more dismal than graveyards, with just a few stalwart plants still standing.

Frowning, Pam reached to touch each withered blossom.

"So early," I sighed to Arden, "and school not even beginning until next week. So much to do."

But what troubled me most was the thought of Monique, shuddering beneath the bridge.

Later that morning, Connie watching Pam, and Arden committed to a crowded schedule of appointments, I went to Amy's alone.

It was a pleasant walk—sunlight slanting through foliage already beginning to wither toward fall. What effect might the change of seasons exert over McClintock's mood of terror? With a sinking sensation, I admitted that it might only intensify as winter approached.

But that morning . . . that morning my spirit was energized by the tingling of frost in the air. My lungs felt clean and clear. God's in His heaven . . . my thoughts sang.

As soon as Amy had admitted me to the store—now remarkably clean and welcoming, and neat even though her sleeping bag still lay unrolled in its corner—she said, "Let's ask Monique today."

"Yes," I breathed. I wondered how—convinced that Turk hadn't veered from his intentions—she could have slept the night before.

"Turk needs to learn he can't control me," she'd said earlier, and added thoughtfully, "I need to learn that, too."

At least if Monique accepted, Turk would have to terrorize two, as opposed to one—and Monique might well prove impregnable to any tactic he might devise. She'd dealt with tougher situations. And tougher men.

"Are you as . . . nervous as I am?" Amy asked.

"Petrified. Should we wait for Arden?"

"No." She spread her hands. "I keep thinking how *I'd* feel . . . I mean, even the two of us could look like a delegation!"

"When?" I asked.

"Now?"

If we delayed, our tension could only grow.

"I'll take some cookies with me." She plopped a few into a plastic food saver. "Soften her up." She sighed. "I baked early this morning, when I couldn't sleep. I kept . . . hearing things."

I threw her a sharp look.

"Only night sounds," she said, "but—you know. In a new place . . ."

I nodded.

The sooner Amy had company, the better I'd feel, with Turk capable of appearing at any moment. And the murderer, of course, I realized with a start. How could we—even for the slightest moment—forget the murderer? Even though she'd already refused our urging that she stay with us, at least until her apartment was occupied, I yearned to insist.

I didn't have that right.

And in the frost-nipped sunlight, my fears seemed deceptively groundless.

The breeze, like the grass, was still damp and cool. I was glad for the hood on my light jacket—and once again thought of Monique, unprotected by walls. Unwarmed by any heat except what she might coax from dried twigs and whatever other tinder lay at hand in or near the dry wash beneath the bridge.

We saw her as we mounted a slope where—in shadowed areas—frost still crackled beneath our soaked sneakers.

Sitting in sunshine, she huddled in a voluminous blanket. She was turned away, apparently watching with taut intensity.

Watching . . . what?

As we drew closer, Amy drew a harsh breath and caught my arm.

Twin fawns, their rusty coats still splotched with creamy spots, frolicked in a sloping meadow already predicting autumn's hues. Short spired weeds—dock? ragweed? I'd never been sure—thrust burnt-umber tones against beige and ochre grasses. Against fading milkweed, clinging only to shreds of the silken treasure so recently swelling its pods, the teazel also clawed and empty. Against lanky stalks of wild carrot, their once-lacy blooms clotted and dry. Saucy goldenrod—in flocks, in herds, in nodding swarms—defied dullness, denied death. And poison ivy, scarlet against gray, wreathed a weathered fence post and entwined its upper strand of barbed wire. Behind and beyond, the arc of the bridge abutment tunneled darkly to further sunshine. Further color.

I wondered if Amy might not be thinking—as I was—that it was perhaps not so terrible a place to live as we'd expected. Only local traffic utilized the country road leading to and from the stone bridge.

Slowly, quietly, we moved forward. Monique sat motionless, except where the blanket stirred in the breeze. The fawns moved with the quiet grace of ballet dancers—save that instead of some small thump of slippers landing, an occasional hoof clicked on pebbles.

"Beautiful," breathed Amy.

Surely, a poem already took shape in her mind . . . as a painting formed in mine.

And then—swiftly and still gracefully—they spun and, white tails flagging, eventually disappeared within mauve-tinged brush.

"They saw us." Amy's voice was heavy.

"Or heard us."

I wondered if Monique had also been alerted to our approach. If so, she gave no sign, only gathered her blanket more closely about her, rose somewhat stiffly, and descended in a slow, careful shuffle toward the undergirdings of the bridge.

Her bridge.

When we reached it—and her—she was pouring coffee into styrofoam cups from a battered enamel pot kept steaming on a grid above smoldering charcoal.

"Sugar and cream?" she asked, without turning. Her voice sounded hoarse. Unused.

Amy started. "Just cream."

"Both for me, please," I said.

She took her own black. "Sit down."

Surprisingly, there were thick cushions—a bit chilly, but neither as cold nor as damp as the concrete beneath my thin soles. I wondered if, at night, the cushions combined to form her couch.

Monique sank to an opposite seat and raised her cup to her lips. Steam, swirling, obscured those eyes I found startlingly beautiful. "Why have you come?" she asked, without further ceremony.

Amy extended the cookies in their plastic container.

"Only for that?" Monique asked dryly, and set them to one side.

Amy's sigh sounded ominously like a groan. She glanced at me—imploringly, I felt—and took a gulp of coffee.

Still, it was not my invitation to deliver. I decided only to give her time to gather her thoughts.

"There was frost last night."

"I was warm enough here." Monique shifted the blanket from her shoulders, and I saw that she wore a man's flannel shirt, checkered red and black, and—beneath that—a bulky ribbed turtleneck. Laid neatly on a wooden crate which held a wind-up alarm clock, several lighters, an embroidery scissors, her hairbrush, and an open book were an orange knitted cap and a pair of heavy gloves. "I'll be comfortable here, long after snow."

"But wouldn't you rather not?" Amy's question burst from her. Her face colored quickly, neck to hairline, and she lowered her glance. "I'm sorry, but . . ." She looked up, but her hands were awkward on her cup, and the coffee sloshed.

Carefully, Monique took it and set it on a level spot of concrete.

"We worry about you," Amy finished awkwardly.

Monique's face broke in a gentle smile. "And I appreciate that, dear child. But—truly, I'm fine. And . . ." Her hand swept the area with unexpected grace—as it once must have gestured when she acknowledged applause. "You can see . . . my options are limited."

"Not as limited as you think!" Amy half-stood, then sank back and leaned toward Monique. "I'd like for you to come live with me."

Monique's eyes shadowed, and I could see the beginnings of refusal.

"Not charity," I said.

"Not charity!" Amy reinforced, one fingertip rising to her chin.

"You want me . . . to pay rent?" Monique's lips quirked.

"Not in money."

"In . . ." prompted Monique.

"In being another person in a too-large, too-empty building."

It wasn't going to be enough. Monique had no way of assessing the breadth of Amy's need.

Amy cleared her throat and continued, "In allowing me to . . . to agent . . . the sale of your handiwork. And—if you wouldn't mind—to help with cooking and straightening up."

In the end, Monique accepted.

Her reluctance melted, I was certain, in the warmth of Amy's obvious sincerity. "I'm really being selfish," Amy said once. "The place is so lonely, otherwise. Last night I couldn't sleep."

Monique's eyebrows raised, and I thought of her own total lack of protection.

Perhaps Amy had, as well, for she hurried on, "And if I'd happen to be on a job, you could take calls." Her face and voice brightened. "You could even help, for bigger parties!"

"I could clown."

"You could . . . *clown?*" Amy's second cup of coffee seemed in jeopardy.

Saving it, as she had the first, Monique smiled gently. "I have done . . . long ago." She hitched her stiff shoulders, as though to test their limberness.

Still, clowning wouldn't require the suppleness of trapeze art.

"Wonderful! I hadn't even thought of clowns . . ." Amy's voice trailed off, and the glazing of her eyes, the widening of her smile, suggested that related possibilities jelled. "I can't wait!" she said at last. "There's already one party scheduled—this weekend. Could we be ready by then, do you think?"

"Carnival folk are never unready." Monique returned Amy's coffee, stood purposefully, and began to gather her meager belongings.

Arden was scrubbing potatoes when I finally got home, after helping Amy and Monique settle in. "Baked potatoes," he said, "grilled pork chops, and broccoli and cheese."

"Sounds wonderful!" I sank to a stool.

"Not so fast!" he warned. "You do the pork chops."

I groaned.

He grinned. "Most women would think they'd struck the mother lode just for potatoes."

"As I do," I said mildly. "Garlic bread?"

"Then I'd think *I'd* struck . . ."

". . . the mother lode," we finished together.

While we worked, I recounted our day's triumph.

"So Turk faces a new ball game."

In silence, I placed the chops on the rack of the stovetop grill; he chunked broccoli into the steamer.

"You're not worried about Monique?"

I frowned. "That . . ." and suddenly I knew. "You mean . . . what Matt suggested?"

"She does come from a tougher world."

Tougher. The term I'd attributed to her experience earlier that day. "She's not violent, Arden." Unbidden, I recalled her threat to Matt. Her expression . . .

"Anyone can be violent, given provocation."

Not you, I thought. Not Amy.

And yet, at one time, I'd feared myself—in the throes of depression—capable of some unspeakable act.

"Where's Pam?" I asked, needing to change the subject. And yet—had I? For it had been Pam I'd feared I'd hurt.

Dear God.

"Watching Barney tapes," Arden answered, and smiled. "We ran Connie home right after the soaps."

He handed me the garlic powder. "If *you're* sure Amy's safe with Monique," he said, "then I'm sure."

"I'm sure."

He kissed me.

Pam was in bed, Arden watching the late evening news and I half-listening while I sketched—for the dozenth time—twin fawns frisking against the background of a bridge, when a knock rattled the back door of the parsonage.

Arden hadn't seemed to hear. "Get it, honey?" I wanted to suggest—but my throat felt dry. Heartbeats hammered my rib cage. My voice felt unresponsive.

Besides, did I truly intend to sacrifice Arden—

Ridiculous. Though disliking myself for it, I surrendered to the almost paranoid mood of nighttime McClintock, switched on the porch light, and lifted the curtain before releasing the deadbolt.

My precautions weren't lost on Matt.

"And yet," he said, with a twisted smile that failed to light his face, "you're wise."

That he wasn't quite himself was obvious from the start. He seemed distracted, his movements disorganized, his conversation disjointed. But it wasn't until Arden, he, and I waited while the kettle warmed that he arranged his lanky frame at the kitchen table and said, "I think I was supposed to be murder victim number four."

Arden jolted.

I felt my breath congeal. Suddenly requiring the warmth the kettle promised, I turned the burner to high.

"When?" asked Arden.

"Where?" I added. "How did it happen?" And how wonderful, how miraculous, that he'd escaped.

"Last night. Coming from East Danvers." He ran his fingers through his hair. Fussed with the collar of his jacket. Finally clasped his hands on the tabletop as though to still them. "Where the road curves on itself with woods on either side."

Arden nodded.

Not far from the bridge, I thought. Monique's bridge. And she, so close to such danger. Thank God she was safe, now, with Amy.

Or at least as safe as Amy, if Turk accelerated his harassment.

"I hadn't meant to tell anyone—not wanting to raise fear to an even higher pitch." Matt glanced toward the door, which I'd locked. Double bolted. "But all day, I've been ducking shadows. Having cardiac arrest if a fly buzzed."

The kettle approached a whistle, and I lifted it, finding comfort in its weight. Its warmth. Chocolate swirled and seethed beneath streams of boiling water. "You didn't call . . . anyone?"

"Not even Constable Joe?" Arden asked.

"No one." Matt shrugged. "I didn't have any proof—unless you call a dented fender proof of anything but awkward driving." He grinned, but not convincingly. "I took the ditch to avoid her."

Her?

"Or him," he added quickly. "I couldn't tell. There was just something . . . womanlike . . . when she shrieked after me." He shuddered. "More like an animal, actually. High pitched. Piercing. Rapacious—and defrauded. I knew that if anything happened—if a tire blew . . . anything—she'd be on me, rending. Tearing." Another shudder shook him, and when I set his mug before him, he clutched it. Lifted it greedily. Drained it. Extended it for a refill. "Or he," he added, very much an afterthought.

When the drink had relaxed him, when he fitted his stool more naturally, Arden suggested, "From the beginning."

Matt sighed.

I tensed to listen.

"I'd been interviewing in East Danvers—a man who raises prize-winning pumpkins. Feeds them milk, it seems."

Arden nodded.

"And we got to talking. Turns out he has more than pumpkins in his arsenal. There's a swordfish over his mantel." He measured with his hands. "Well," he laughed shortly. "Perhaps a bit smaller."

Arden smiled. "That did seem more whale-size."

"And his wife bakes apple pies." He licked his lips. "Though no better than your brownies, Paula." He spoke, it seemed, almost with gentle accusation.

"We're not twenty-four hours past frost!" I said. "Give me a break!"

"A promise is a promise." This was the old Matt, I thought—this young giant with the appetites of a child.

"Anyway," he said, sighing, his eyes dulling, "it was well past dark, and I was driving a bit too fast—and remembering apple pie. It was all so unexpected! Suddenly, just as I turned the curve, she—*it*—loomed in the roadway. Ax raised—" Again, his shoulders quivered, and he clutched the empty mug.

I moved to extricate it, to refill it, but he shook his head. His grip, if anything, tightened.

An ax, I was thinking. An ax . . . and in my memory I could hear the thudding of Turk's ax in dead spruce. Could see the spraying chips.

I forced my mind to turn to Matt.

"I've never been so scared. It was just instinct made me veer from the road. I imagined the brush of cloth against the side of the car, felt the thud of fender against . . . something. And waited for that ax to come through the side window, then the rear one, but as for calling the constable—or the state police . . . or anyone—all I have to report are the ax and the checked shirt."

"Shirt?" Arden asked crisply. "You saw what he was wearing?"

Matt nodded, looking down, turning the mug in his long fingers. "A flannel shirt," he said. "Checked. Red and black."

14

That next week, the *Danvers Bugle* carried Matt's feature on the gigantic pumpkins . . . and the swordfish. He'd also written a meditative piece on school's reopening. On the ripening of autumn's colors. Beautiful writing—but I doubted that most city papers would be seduced by beauty alone. Blood seemed the magnet for wider than local interest.

In the center section, a short report on the first party Amy had orchestrated was topped by a photo of Monique—as Que Clown—posing with the birthday girl. And a half-page ad invited everyone to Amy's grand opening, slated for the weekend.

But I found nothing anywhere concerning the threat against Matt. Nothing, in fact, to allude to the danger so close to everyone's mind.

Arden guessed, "He saw how his last article incited more fear. Still . . ."

Still, I finished the thought in my mind, perhaps people deserved to know that violence continued to lurk. And—remembering that Mary Lynn and I had wondered if his articles might not encourage the murderer by granting him publicity—I felt hypocritical. Was there no pleasing me?

Once again the image Matt had created for us rose in my mind. That figure—perhaps a woman—raising an ax, shrilling the rage of a predator deprived of its prey, wearing a red-and-black checked flannel shirt.

Close on that thought came remembrance of the midmorning visit beneath the bridge. Monique and hot coffee. Monique and a gentle acceptance of Amy's friendship.

Monique in a red-and-black checked shirt.

Ridiculous, I told myself.

I'd seen her angry only twice. True . . . both of those times angry at Matt.

But at the bridge, she'd left behind only a few rags reducing to ash on the cooking coals, and she'd brought no ax with her—just a small hatchet she'd used to break her kindling.

Ax. Hatchet. Could the two seem interchangeable when filtered through panic?

Perhaps.

Especially when the viewer was so young.

Outwardly, things seemed to be returning to normal. Each morning, clusters of children giggled and danced their way to the elementary school, while older students, comparatively silent and sleepy eyed, waited in clumps for the arrival of their buses.

After school, Dean galloped toward the shop, dropped his books, shrugged into a giant paintshirt, and continued work on the mural, while I worked at sheets of masonite braced across sawhorses.

"Sew No Longer" read the sign for Monique's window, where her small store of embroidery would be showcased, and for Amy's display—"Parties, Ltd."

"For goodness sake don't make it *un*limited," Amy had begged, "or they'll want real giraffes for sure!"

"Whattaya think, Paula?" Dean would ask occasionally, into the near-silence of slapping paint brushes and Amy's scratching pencil point.

"Wonderful," I'd assure him. "More lifelike every minute. I can nearly hear the water dripping from those vines! And hasn't that boa constrictor moved since yesterday?"

He'd laugh—but his pleasure in his work was palpable.

And with good reason. One tiger, in particular, uncompromisingly gripped the gaze of all who paused there. Fortunately, he seemed more placid than menacing.

"He just ate," Dean assured small children who tiptoed in to watch but cowered behind a parent or older sibling.

I suspected that preteen girls were more interested in Dean than in the painting. Poor things, I thought. His heart's been taken.

As if his thoughts ran in tandem, he asked, "Sylva'd sure be pleased, wouldn't she?"

Amy's grand opening was an unqualified success, garnering five orders for Monique's handiwork—primarily mending—and reservations for three additional birthday parties.

One customer—someone I'd never met—a tall woman with dark hair pulled severely back to exaggerate prominent cheekbones and a large straight mouth, spoke in contralto tones. "I hear that you furnish a clown."

Amy nodded toward Monique.

"Not . . . the *carny?*" The words were delivered with muted distaste.

Though she never broke the pattern of her stitches, Monique's sudden stiffening showed that she had heard.

"She loves children," Amy defended. "And Miranda's guests were delighted."

"Not at *my* party," the woman said firmly. Then, "Surely there's someone else."

"Another clown?"

"Precisely."

"Not that I know of. No one with the skills." Amy's demeanor had definitely chilled.

"Skills?" the woman snorted. "What's so difficult in wearing a red wig and acting idiotic?"

Amy's pen poised over her paper. "No clown, then?"

The woman straightened. Propped her hands on her hips. "Perhaps you really don't want to book this party. Of *course* there must be a clown. Miranda had a clown. *Brandi* must have a clown. Just not . . ." Her eyes shifted, and her voice lowered—though insufficiently. "Just not that one."

Amy sighed. Closed her book. "I'll get back to you in a day or so."

"See that you do!"

When she was gone, Brandi in tow, Amy turned to me. "She heard," she whispered.

I nodded.

"What do I do?"

And of course anything she said might only make things worse.

"Ignore it?" she asked.

But then another influx of people laughed and jostled their way past bobbing balloons and swirling streamers toward the refreshment table. And, like so many other groups that day, they paused to admire Dean's mural—no more than one-half complete. He stood near it, his face gleaming, and explained what remained to be done.

I stood by watching—smiling until my jaws ached—and thought, as I had at Mary Lynn's wedding, what a welcome break such gaiety provided. It could almost seem that murder had never touched us.

I felt a sudden chill.

Perhaps such relaxation shaped our greatest danger.

Apple crisp cooled on metal racks that following Tuesday when both Matt and Dean dropped by.

Drawn by the fumes, I thought—and smiled.

They wore twin expressions of contentment as they settled themselves at the table.

"How's the mural going?" asked Matt. "Ready for those photos yet?"

"Not quite. But," Dean's voice throbbed with excitement, "I got another . . . what ya call it?"

"Commission?" guessed Matt. "Another mural to do?"

Dean nodded, and said more forcibly, "Paula, we got another commission!"

"We?" asked Matt.

"Paula and me."

"I'm his assistant," I interjected. "Only when he needs me to hold the ladder or something."

"Awww," growled Dean. "It is a big one, though."

"Where?" Matt seemed distracted.

Anticipating the apple crisp, no doubt.

"Almost ready," I said, and went to the freezer for ice cream.

Even Dean's concentration seemed to waver, but he managed, "That old abandoned church, outsida town."

I paused, freezer door ajar. So isolated.

Matt said quietly, "There's a lot of activity, Paula. Bulldozers. Construction. Near where the new mall's going up, right?" He directed the query to Dean. "The one they plan to make into apartments?"

"And offices." Dean accepted his bowl and clutched his spoon. "Oh, boy! Do I haveta wait?"

"Only if you're polite," Matt grinned, and grabbed his own heaped plate. "Ready, set, go!"

"We're not gonna wait for Paula?" Dean's spoon was suspended, Matt's fork already in action.

"Only if we're polite," Matt mumbled around a huge bite.

We all burst into laughter. Matt looked decidedly youthful, his mouth bulging, a drizzle of ice cream on his lower lip. I resisted the urge to touch a napkin to it as I would have for Pam.

Perhaps even for Arden.

"Where's Pammie?" Dean asked, his dessert already half-consumed.

"She and Arden went to the post office."

"More for *us!*" squealed Matt, and Dean convulsed in embarrassed giggles. "And Paula," Matt said, half-seriously, "you really need to watch your weight—don't you?"

"Vandal," I said—and thought of Dee. That was one of her favorite words.

I'd have to call her again, one day soon—to let her know that things seemed to be moderating.

And then I remembered Turk—attacking a dead spruce. And Matt's recent brush with disaster, and wondered how long it would be again, how deeply we'd be lulled into an illusion of all-rightness, before something else occurred to shake us.

Though please, dear God, I prayed inwardly. No more murders.

It was deep night, moonless, and Arden had not yet returned from a men's weekend retreat miles away. He'd hesitated before leaving, asking if I was *sure* we'd be all right. If I'd double-check the doors at night. If maybe he shouldn't call Dr. Connelly and ask . . .

Submerging my own fears, I'd managed to defuse his. Fortunately, he'd had a ride, and our station wagon waited in the driveway, in the event I'd need it.

As it seemed I would.

Pam lay listless and murmuring, her forehead dry. Burning to my touch. When I'd tried everything the doctor suggested and her fever persisted, when he said, "Well, then, bring her to the emergency room," one of my first thoughts was of probing that pernicious darkness—and with my arms immobilized by Pammie's weight.

When Amy called, asking, "What can I do to help?" I felt almost pathetic gratitude. But of course she couldn't help. Only Arden could, and he beyond reach.

"Then . . . Matt?"

I hadn't thought of Matt.

His answering machine—which he revised weekly—opened with an Ernie Pyle quotation and closed with three dings.

Why bother with a message when I needed to leave almost at once?

Nevertheless, I did.

I checked the stove and lights. Wrote a brief note for Arden. And then, whispering comfort ostensibly for Pam, I gathered purse and keys and light quilt and pseudocourage.

It was difficult to weigh which was greater, my fear or my self-ridicule.

Why should a murderer who'd struck in a shadowed carnival ground and near a deserted cornfield—and threatened along a lonely country road—suddenly choose to lurk beyond a parsonage porch, within the hearing of witnesses?

Of course, Mrs. Porter had lived in a residential area. And there lay another discrepancy. What had I to do with music? What had *Matt* to do with music?

Ridiculous.

God, please let my fears be ridiculous.

Carefully, Pammie draped against me, I locked the kitchen door behind us.

The blackness was deep. Pulsing. Venomous. Crowded with unidentified stirrings and breathings. Terror a palpable presence. Heart-thumps thrummed in my ears. My breath puffed raggedly. You're getting heavy, Pammie. The glow from the porch light reached anemically toward the wagon, barely glinted on its windows. And the flashlight, too awkward to handle with Pam, hung heavy and useless in my purse.

The car doors were, of course, locked.

I fumbled the keys.

Next door, a dog barked sharply. Startled—by me?

Or by someone foreign, someone sinister?

A chorus of barking developed, built to crescendo. Not the high, nervous yapping of pets, but the purposeful baying and howling of guard dogs. No tenors here. No obbligatos. Baritones and basses.

Dear God.

The key turned. I struggled to open the door, to arrange Pam's yielding weight into her car seat.

She seemed boneless.

So difficult. If the murderer stood there, he could at least offer to help.

Dumb thought. Cancel that, God.

"Pammie, honey."

So hot. Murmuring.

The barking.

There. Finally. Secure. Pam's door locked. Now . . . around the car.

A shadow—deeper than darkness.

Surely, imagination. I stopped. Peered into velvet. Into black mush. Into nothingness that swirled with my concentration. Besides, if I couldn't see him . . .

Or her.

But I had to pass through light, however scant, to the driver's door.

My breath was nearly a sob, my fingers rigid. Clumsy.

Dear Lord.

The keyhole elusive.

Please. Please.

The turning. The click. At last.

Praise You.

The door resisted. Then yielded, creaking. I banged my knee on metal, stumbled in, tugged the door shut and locked it in a single motion.

And dear Lord, yes, there was someone there, some bulk, an arm extended, a shout—more noise than words—a thudding against the side of the wagon, a banging at window glass.

I didn't look. Couldn't look.

Without lights, by feel, I backed, swerving, then roared recklessly forward, sensed the stroke of shrubbery on the car, the texture of grass, rather than gravel, under tires, prayed that if the assailant couldn't get out of my way, he would at least be disabled—incapable of another attack. Of pursuit.

And how could I pray for the injury of another human being?

No time for guilt just then. Escape was paramount. Safety—especially Pam's.

The station wagon bounced over broken sidewalk, veered onto the street; only then did I switch on the lights.

There was, of course, nothing in the rearview mirror. If anyone stood there, shrieking imprecations, the drone of the engine, the noise of tires on pavement, shut out the sounds. And the streetlights were too dim to reveal shapes.

We were free.

But—what of returning to that dark danger? And what of Arden?

Arden, returning unsuspecting to . . . whatever waited there.

If it waited.

Dare I pray that it move on to seek other prey?

Certainly not!

For what, then, could I, should I, pray?

Of most immediate concern was Pam, feverish in her car seat and a ten-mile drive between us and the hospital.

"Let her be fine," I prayed aloud. "Let Arden be safe. Let this horror—whatever it is—be found and stopped."

Pam was resting sweetly, her fever broken at last—hospital personnel bustling about in comforting precision, and Joe Derrick long since alerted to what I had not fully seen—when Matt arrived with Arden in tow. "Got your message," Matt was saying, as Arden interrupted, "I was just unlocking the door—"

Rushing to them, I hugged them indiscriminately.

"Well, now," said Matt, nearly stammering, and I stepped back, embarrassed to have embarrassed him.

I paused, weighing how much I should disclose.

In the end, while nurses settled Pam into her bed, just for the night, I told them everything.

Arden's jaw tightened, and his hands opened and closed nervously.

Matt was more difficult to read. At last he said, "So even in McClintock itself—" He broke off. "Do I write about it, or not? Is it worse to increase the dread, or allow people to relax their guard—perhaps at their own peril?"

Arden suggested, "Since Constable Joe's investigating, you may not have a choice to make."

Matt nodded, then tentatively, "Paula, you're sure . . . I mean could you . . ."

"Could I have imagined it?" My throat tightened. "Did *you* imagine the attack on you?"

"Fair enough." He reached out, but I withdrew my hand.

"What I hate most," he said, his young face fractured with lines of concern, "is what this thing is doing to all of us. The death of trust."

Amy was alone in the shop when I dropped by late one afternoon on my way from grocery shopping.

"How's Pammie?" she asked.

"Fine, thanks." Since we'd brought her home a week earlier, she'd been improving steadily. "Just a bug, they think. Something going around."

"Dean's grandmother isn't feeling well either, so he went straight home from the bus. And Monique decided to take a walk. To the bridge, I think." She shook her head. "I guess anywhere can seem like home."

"It was the most stable of any she'd had—probably for years," I said. "Until here, with you."

"I'm really enjoying her!" The sponge with which she'd been cleaning the counter plopped into its sudsy bucket. "She promised to get back well before dark."

I felt a twinge of uncertainty. I hadn't broken confidence with Matt, hadn't told even Amy about the scene on the road from East Danvers. Had, in fact, tried to discount—even in my own mind—the "evidence" of the checked flannel shirt, and the possibility that our assailant—Pam's and mine—might have been similarly dressed.

After all, most farmers owned at least one such shirt.

And most hunters.

Most men into outdoor winter sports.

Turk.

And Turk owned an ax as well.

So would most hunters.

All farmers.

Besides, in Matt's state of mind, in the darkness, he might well have been mistaken. It might have been a jacket, not a shirt. Or some other related color. Perhaps not even checked.

After all, he wasn't certain whether his intended assailant had been a man or a woman.

As I was uncertain about the person who had terrorized me.

There was within me something basic and sturdy which denied any possibility that Monique could be so violent . . . someone who loved color and beauty so deeply.

And yet Van Gogh had cut off his own ear.

Amy was continuing, "She's . . . not like a second mother, but like a favorite aunt. She's been asking about Turk."

I'd been both surprised and pleased that he hadn't come to the grand opening.

"He was nearby, though," she said, "did you know that?"

I jolted. She was reading my thoughts again.

"Across the street, half-hidden by the trees." She paused. "Monique told me. But when I went to look, he was gone." She shuddered.

"Couldn't that mean that he's resigned to your new life?"

"For most men, it might." Her eyes held a haunted look. Then she shook herself. "Forget Turk! I've been practicing—and sometimes it even works. Hardly a nightmare a night now." She reached to wring out the sponge. "Remember the woman who wants a clown, but not . . ."

I nodded.

"Problem solved!" she said. "Monique suggested I get someone else. Oh," she hastened to add, "she'll still do the other parties. She loves them! She loves the children."

Remembering her sweetness with Pam, my conviction firming that she couldn't have been the threatening figure that night Matt drove from East Danvers, I determined never to entertain such doubting again.

Monique's sharing the store was the best thing that could have happened for Amy.

"And if Turk bothers me again," Amy said, almost smugly, "I'm fairly convinced that Monique will kill him."

Into my shock at the inconsistency of her offhand comment and my carefully crafted disclaimer, she intruded,

"You'll never guess, though, who's going to clown for Saturday's party!"

"I'm just glad you didn't ask me."

"I thought of it."

I grimaced. "I love clowns—when I'm on the outside, looking in."

"Matt's a clown—inside and out!"

"Matt?"

"It's hard to imagine, isn't it?" she asked brightly. "That string bean? His legs stick a yard below the ruffles—but that's fine! The striped socks show that much more. And he and Monique worked out his makeup."

"He and *Monique?*"

She propped one hand on her hip and grinned. "Do you realize how much like an echo you're becoming?"

I couldn't help it. "An echo?" I parroted, and we both convulsed in giggles.

"It's time I go," I said, at last. Monique still hadn't returned. I paused at the threshold. "Lock up after me?" I tried to keep my voice light. "And call me—okay? When Monique gets back safely."

"There's something magical in makeup," Matt's next article began.

> Perhaps any woman could have told me that—but I always wore masks for trick-or-treating, never tried out for school plays, and felt more repelled by than drawn to the combat paint of football. Therefore, the closest I'd ever come was to swipe suntan oil on my face and arms, or Vaseline during chickenpox, or calamine lotion on those few unhappy occasions when I'd consorted with poison ivy.
>
> Clown makeup is something quite different. It alters the inner person as substantively, as wholly, as it transforms

the outer. First the base, the chalky white, whereby I became a death's head with alarmingly ecru teeth. Flinching, vowing never to smile again, I thought of Dr. Pinter, my dentist since childhood, and envisioned his reaction. "I told you, young man, floss each day—and don't forget the hydrogen peroxide and soda."

Gradually, the various blue triangles, the circles and ovals of red, the black outlines—for emphasis, for laugh wrinkles, for starry eyes—dissolved my resolve, and I grinned widely at this mutation in my mirror, this melding of mirth and monstrosity—of warmth and weirdness.

A wire-springy red wig, a stovepipe hat, broken in midsection, a large economy-sized polka-dotted bow tie and a red nose the size and shape of a tennis ball completed the transfiguration of my upper body—a process which progressed gravitationally to modify limbs, stance, even shoe size.

These conversions were observable and obvious. I chronicled them as they occurred. More significant by far were those immeasurable alterations of mind. Of spirit. Of attitude. Plato, describing death—though in a positive, even anticipatory way—referred to "a change and migration of the soul." "A change came o'er the spirit of my dream," someone—perhaps Plato again?—once said, or wrote, and better than anything within my vocabulary or my philosophy, these expressions characterize the metamorphosis of that part of me which had always been unalterably Matt Culhaney.

No longer. Not then. The being, the creation, the—whatever—who adjusted oversized yellow gloves and accompanied Amy Turkle to a child's birthday party bore no relationship to Matt Culhaney, reporter. True, it moved with his muscles and tendons, spoke through his vocal chords—even saw through his eyes and filtered sound through his ears. But this spirit was freer and more freeing than his could ever be. These emotions were more sensitive, more sensitizing. There survived no compulsion to impress. No inhibition warned of status, of ego, of professionalism. There existed only a deep impulse for reaching out. For loving—unconditionally. For amusing, for comforting, for pleasing.

It was with deep regret, once the party ended, that I removed the gloves, the gigantic shoes, the hat, the striped socks and ballooning pants, the tie, the nose—and, reluctantly, the makeup—to view in that unforgiving mirror once again the person I had been satisfied enough to be . . .

. . . before the magic.

The next afternoon, while Connie baby-sat and Arden made sick calls, I hurried to Amy's to help inflate balloons for a midweek event. Matt, there too, was uncharacteristically quiet.

So was Amy.

"I loved the article," I ventured.

He grumbled his thanks.

I raised an eyebrow, but Amy avoided eye contact.

Only Monique—off in a corner, humming tunelessly as she mended by hand—seemed herself.

Something had happened.

Or was about to happen?

It was a relief when Dean arrived. "Hey, guys!" He shucked off his jacket and reached for a paintbrush. "What's up?"

No answer.

He turned a quizzical glance toward me, and I shrugged.

"Oops," he said.

Oops, indeed. I thrashed through my mind for possibilities. The article? Surely Amy hadn't disliked it! Perhaps the editor had? But how could anyone?

I cleared my throat, wanting to ask something, anything.

The smell of burning cookies predated the smoke alarm by seconds.

"Great!" Amy scrambled from her chair, and a balloon whooshed in manic gyrations of escape.

I yearned to follow it.

Instead, I followed Amy to the kitchen. Each cookie was a well-defined lump of ashes, but at least the alarm had quieted.

Amy sighed, and one tear dropped, carving a crater in the nearest charcoal mound.

"What's wrong?" I asked.

She peered at me numbly, her eyes blurred.

Fear knotted my throat. "Turk?"

She shook her head.

Not Turk. Surely nothing else could be as bad. "Then what?" I removed the cookie sheet from her still hands and tapped its contents into the garbage can.

She spoke at last. "I'm not sure. It's just—"

Monique spoke from the doorway. "I could make another batch."

Amy slumped against the counter. "No use. No use."

For a moment, Monique remained, her expression denoting awkwardness, I thought, and—concern? Even *fear?*

No, surely to read fear was stretching.

When she'd returned to the showroom, I said, "Amy, please let me help—"

"No use."

And Amy's words, her tone, were so reminiscent of those months I'd spent in emotional blackness on blackness on blackness that I shuddered.

She roused. "Don't worry." Her smile was a ghastly parody of all-rightness. "It's probably nothing."

And as though to prove it to herself as much as to me, she straightened and led the way to the others. "Bad news, troops," she said with a lightness that might have seemed unfeigned had I not heard her hopelessness, nor seen her tears. "Or good news, depending on your viewpoint. The cookies are casualties. Dean, run to the grocery and get reinforcements, okay? Your choice." She handed him a few bills. "Matt, how are you at lemonade? Monique—do you know where the leftover party napkins are? And Paula—don't just *stand* there! Inflate balloons!"

Dee called just before bedtime.

I stifled a yawn. "How are the tureens going?"

"Don't ask." She sighed. "But you already did, didn't you?"

"Then cancel the question."

"No. It was fair. And things aren't as bad as my vicious mood might suggest. Actually, three of them are show worthy. Too bad they're going to hold slimy soup, and nobody will look past the smell. They'll think the ladles are simply for . . ."

"Ladling?" I suggested.

"Exactly," she drawled.

"Disquieting," I agreed. "Works of art should be for admiring, not for using."

"Despite what museum curators say." She laughed. "I'm burned out, is all. The crazy lady calls three times a day—usually when I can least afford to be distracted—to check on progress. When this job is finished I'm getting an unlisted number."

"Until then . . . have you considered taking the phone off the hook?"

"But what if my agent calls. Or . . ."

"Or?"

"Or my best friend. And how is she doing these days?"

Briefly, I thought of the strangeness at Amy's—and dismissed it. After all, by the time we'd parted, everyone had seemed restored.

No need, either, to mention the two tentative attacks—on Matt. On me. These would necessarily renew her campaign to draw us to the city for safety.

"Fine," I said.

We chatted for the better part of an hour—about important things: Arden and Pam, Amy's shop, Dean's mural, the town's quietness. And—as ever—we gave equal time to trivia. Long before we said good-bye, Arden had waved, thrown me a kiss, and gone to bed. Even from downstairs, I could hear his even, heavy breathing.

I'd no sooner hung up than the phone rang again. I caught it quickly, before Arden could waken.

"Hello," I began, then listened closely to the nearly incomprehensible words spilling, buzzing, blurring, shrilling erratically into my ear.

"Tried to call when she first heard . . . You've got to come! Got to! Horrible—and they'll blame me."

"Who is this?"

The voice was flat. Grating. "Dead, I think. Yes—almost certain, so much blood. Scared him off, though—or maybe not."

"Monique?" I guessed. I'd never heard her voice on the phone before. Had never heard, on any phone, any voice so frantic. So disjointed. When her only answer was a babbling incoherence, I said, "We'll be right there," and hung up quickly.

Dear God, I prayed, as I hurried to rouse Arden, to bundle Pam into a blanket, "please protect Amy." As close as we were, so parallel our deeper thoughts, surely I'd have sensed trouble if anything serious threatened her. Wouldn't I, God?

Unbidden, thoughts of the afternoon rose, and I suppressed them. Please God. Promise me that Amy's safe.

But if an answer came—either in assurance or in sadness—I was too rushed and too frightened to sense it.

15

Amy's spruces—brooding, dense, faintly tossing—spoke in mournful murmurs. The dead trunk, denuded of limbs, soared baldly among them, contributing nothing to their chorus save a blunt thrumming when struck by some tendril of breeze.

Behind and below the massed, moving darkness huddled her building, its door ajar. Faint light—candles?—flickering within threw ghostlike, unintelligible shadows across the broad, slanting show windows.

Arden, plucking Pam from her car seat, urged, "Don't go alone."

He'd parked the car on the other side of the street. I waited, shivering. Then, on impulse, locked all the doors.

Why would anyone be burning candles?

Of course no one was.

Something, stirring in the breeze, created that insubstantial quality. Amy's streamers and balloons. Monique's needlework, on hangers and easels.

Pam limp against his shoulder, Arden moved with me toward that gaping door.

I shuddered. "Monique?" I called. Then again, more staunchly. *"Monique!"*

And in my mind replayed fragments of the troubling scene that afternoon. What had distressed Amy, caused her to express such uncharacteristic hopelessness? And what had Monique to do with it?

In the distance, sirens throbbed.

Sirens were wrong for McClintock. Still, strengthening as they neared, they established their reality in this unreal setting. Their relevancy to this surreal landscape.

Where was Amy?

"Amy?"

"Honey, don't."

I spoke around tears. "She can't be. I misunderstood."

Just as I entered—tentatively, fearing what I must prepare for, must expect, could never accept—Monique burst from the back, her misshapen arms flailing, her face a ghastly gray, and the constable's car, its sirens undiminished, wheeled onto the sidewalk and reared to a stop. Its garish lights flared. Pulsed. Invaded dull caverns of neglected spruce boughs. Repeatedly exposed then abandoned the letters of Amy's sign. Of Monique's. Caught a bird in flight.

What kind of bird would be flying now, at this time of night? In a climate of such tragedy?

"Where—" I began.

Monique croaked, "Leave the little girl here."

"Honey—" Arden reached to hand Pam to me.

But I shrugged him away and followed.

Even before I saw her, my mind roared dissent. Raged in denial.

Amy lay, still and disordered, in blood. After one quick glance, I turned away.

So much blood—vivid, virulent.

Surely one slight body could never have held so much.

It violated her white cotton nightgown, tarnished her fresh-painted woodwork, speckled her thick-pile throw rug, traced a sluggish stream down the glass face of her wedding portrait.

Closing my eyes, I held my cupped hand over my mouth. To cap a scream? To discourage vomiting?

Monique was beside me.

What might it mean that she was bloody, too?

She caught me solidly as I swayed, as I sought the comfort of blackness.

I would not faint, I ordered myself.

Amy needed me.

Clutching awareness and stepping in concert with Monique's erratic movements, I gave room to Constable Joe—who entered with obvious reluctance—and watched almost abstractedly through a protective film, a scrim used on a stage, as he and Deputy Jones knelt. As they examined, as they discussed, as they made notes. As they snapped the essential photos from all angles, as they measured, as they drew a chalkline—where the blood would allow chalk to adhere. Poor Constable Joe, I thought, forced by repetition to learn these grim tasks. But his face was drained of color, his lips clamped tightly. And I continued my numb observation even as he covered Amy's body, masking the blood—for moments only, until it carved a muted repetition of its obscenity through the sheet.

I hadn't been aware of Matt.

Suddenly, he was looming over me, gripping my elbows, transferring my weight from Monique's support to his own.

She made a sound—almost of loss.

I looked past his bulk to reassure her, but she was already gone.

"Are you all right?" he asked. His voice wavered.

I nodded. "Are you?"

He'd apparently knelt near Amy. Surely, I thought, with a shudder, not to take a photo. Somehow, he'd swiped blood across one cheek.

He swallowed noisily. "This is the toughest yet."

I felt the tears surge. Lord, I said within myself, trying not to reprove. Hadn't I asked Him to protect her?

Reason told me that she'd been dead prior to my prayer.

And fairness noted the similarity of my reaction to Monique's after Clint lay dead—chastising God for not having interrupted the flow of universal laws to neutralize human inventions.

"She was killed with an ax," Matt said, rubbing my arms.

I winced, sensing the ferocity of such a blow, the destruction so quickly delivered.

Turk had attacked the dead spruce with an ax.

And Matt had been threatened with an ax. By someone who might have been a woman. Someone wearing a red-and-black checked flannel shirt.

Like Monique's.

And Monique had been bloody.

But she'd brought only a hatchet with her.

Suddenly, I recalled Amy that afternoon—how long ago?—saying that Monique had taken a walk. Perhaps to the bridge.

What if she'd hidden an ax there? Had gone to retrieve it?

No. Monique had every reason to love Amy.

But what had reason to do with murder? With any murder, but especially those which had plagued McClintock?

Even numbed by personal grief, my mind, my heart, refused to accept such a possibility. Monique's grief was as genuine as my own. As wrenching.

"No mutilation," Matt was saying.

Wasn't murder—especially when the weapon was an ax—mutilation enough?

He shook me lightly.

And then it sank in. "No muti . . ."

No mutilation relating to the talent of the victim.

"None," Matt affirmed.

"But . . ." What did that mean?

"It may be only that there wasn't time. That he—or she—was frightened off before . . ."

"Or . . ."

"Or," he said, swallowing again, "this could be different."

Dear God, yes—so different! This was Amy, my friend. This was Amy, who wrote poetry, who delighted children.

". . . a different murderer," he finished. "Not one of the serial killings at all."

I shuddered. One unknown murderer had been unthinkable. But . . . two?

"They're going to question Turk, of course," he said.

Poor Turk.

"You need to go home," he said firmly.

"Arden's . . ." I nodded vaguely toward the showroom.

"I saw him. Let me help you."

My knees required his steadiness as we left the grisly scene. When I turned to look back one last time, he blocked my view. "Enough," he said gently. "You can't help her now."

I thrust a wordless prayer toward God, and as Arden, Pam, and I walked unsteadily to the station wagon, then rode slowly homeward, I knew—as I needed to know—that the appalling figure in that blood-spattered apartment had been only a shell, that since the first fatal fall of the ax, Amy—the real Amy—had been with Him.

The next week passed in a blur.

When the body—not Amy, I reminded myself constantly; Amy was elsewhere—when the body had been released by the coroner, when Amy's family—distant in blood ties and attitude, as well as in geography—had gathered and gone, when Turk had been arrested on suspicion and led—unprotesting—away, when a brief, uncharacteristic flurry of outside interest had stirred, had diminished and departed, when Matt's touching memoriam had been published, absorbed, and folded into scrapbooks, when all that had been endured, the real work began. The mechanics of coping. The tightening of defenses. Throughout the area, new, grim protective barriers bristled. For those who'd loved Amy, the girding was emotional and spiritual, nonetheless stalwart for its invisibility.

Repeatedly, I found myself on the verge of censuring God, then swerving guiltily toward pleas for forgiveness. Repeatedly I caught myself adopting the body language of depression—the pacing, the bouts of undisciplined weeping, the clutching of one hand in the other, that dense, swirling darkness in the mind. Of the spirit.

Arden tried to help, and I wanted to accept his comfort. But whenever I came close to calm, to acceptance, the horror closed in, and disbelief warred with rage.

"It's so . . ."

"Unacceptable?" Arden suggested. "Too pallid a word."

"Too weak a concept. Arden . . ."

He enclosed me in his arms. Whispered against my forehead. "It's all right, honey."

"Never. Never again all right."

"Not her death! All right to cry, I meant."

"How can I bear . . ."

"We'll help you. Pammie. God, me."

"I'll never be able to forget."

He didn't remind me that he'd tried to hold me back, but only patted, murmured, assured.

"Who could do such a senseless, brutal thing? So insane."

He agreed gently. "Feel sorry for him, too, honey."

But I could never feel compassion for Amy's murderer—whoever he was.

Or she.

With that admission, the spirals of pain compressed and tightened.

You've got to defeat this, I told myself. Depression is a place you've visited once. Nothing is worth the return trip.

Yet the patterns continued. Pacing. Prayer. Pacing. Tears. Pacing. Denial, a refusal to accept the absence of her laughter. Pacing. Rage. Anger that crepe paper streamers still framed her show window with their obscene gaiety. That balloons—though somewhat shrunken—still bobbed in the slightest breeze.

One day, after funeral flowers had decayed over the mound of her grave, I half-ran, stumbling through tears, to the shop, where I battered at the side entrance. "Monique! Monique!" My knuckles throbbed. "Monique."

The door opened slowly.

I'd frightened her. "Sorry," I said.

"What's wrong?" Her tone was one of resignation.

I laughed harshly.

Hadn't she noticed? The *world* was wrong! Pushing past her into the showroom, I tugged at streamers, yanked at strings, ripped tape from fresh paint—leaving rectangular wounds—snapped the slender dowels which anchored balloons and overturned the urns that had moored them. Pulling the sign, the sign I'd painted, from its fastenings, I slammed it to the floor. It vibrated across tile, ending at a table leg, where it shuddered and died.

Once past initial shock, Monique helped me dismantle the landscape of Amy's dreams.

"I wanted to before," she whispered, "but hadn't the heart to attempt it alone."

When, satisfied, we sank wearily onto stools at the counter, only Dean's unfinished mural remained unchanged—and its brooding quality of suspended violence seemed fitting.

"This may be the wrong time," I began unsteadily, "but I've wanted to ask . . . I've needed to know . . ."

"What happened that night," she finished.

I nodded.

She shifted. Closed her eyes as though gathering images. "I blame myself," she said, "not hearing at first. Thinking it her TV. She'd been quiet at dinner."

As she had been that afternoon, I remembered.

"I felt she wanted aloneness, to think. I supposed it was over *him*." Her lips firmed.

Turk, I knew.

"By the time I heard her scream—heard that awful thudding . . ." She cringed. "And I was awkward, hurrying."

She trembled, and I reached to comfort her. Whether she rejected my touch or just happened to move at that moment, I couldn't know.

"I think I knew she was dead."

"You saw . . . no one else?"

"The door still closing, I think, though can't be sure. All I can be certain of is . . . "

Blood, I finished in my thoughts.

And Monique had herself been bloody.

"I knelt down," her knees bent as though in memory she repeated the action, "and tried to lift her. To hold her. Young as she was, she was more like my dear mother than any other I've ever known."

Tears filled Monique's striking eyes.

I wanted to, but didn't, take her hands in mine.

And I thought how much like platitudes "appropriate" words of comfort sounded. I'd mouthed them myself a thousand times—most recently to Amy's relatives, who had seemed bored by the whole proceeding. Always before, I'd considered such phrases sufficiently soothing. Now, they tasted like baking soda on the mind.

"We go on," I said at last. "Not because we want to. Because we have no other choice."

In the past, I might have added, "Amy would have wanted us to."

That, too, lacked truth.

Amy would not have chosen for us to proceed without her. She'd planned to make the journey with us—infusing our experience with her eager joy. Enriching us with her poetry—and, in turn, absorbing all we might contribute.

If cancer had occasioned this death, or multiple sclerosis, or AIDS—or any from the arsenal of debilitating, encroaching diseases which at least permitted time for summation and preparation—then surely Amy, of all people, might have encouraged and enabled those to be left behind. Would have eased their transition into an Amy-less world.

But this harsh wresting of life from a still-vibrant body was different. There would be those who'd suffered loss from other, slower dyings who'd argue the senselessness of any youthful termination, who might cite the benefits of surprise, of not suffering, of leaving life still at the pitch of it.

That I could ever embrace such consolation for Amy's murder was unthinkable.

Monique wiped at her eyes.

And I tugged myself from personal grieving to consider her. After all the adjustments she'd been forced to make in her lifetime, what must she fear—a return to her home beneath the bridge? For while I'd lost a cherished friend, Monique had lost that and much, much more.

"She was buying the property . . ." I began, knowing that some real estate agreements included life insurance.

And while no will had surfaced as yet, while Turk—unless he were found guilty—would be the logical heir, Amy might have provided for Monique.

Would have—had she sensed a need so immediate.

Still, when she'd feared Turk . . .

What a blessing if some paper, some letter, some jotted notation should secure Monique's residence in the apartment—even her rights to the store!

And the afterthought came swiftly. Beyond the blessing—a respectable motive for murder.

"Whether you like it or not," Dee said, "I'm coming."

"But your work . . ."

"I've fired the final tureen—perhaps the last in my career!" she added with what might have been relieved disgust. "Mrs. Wright's accepted delivery, and I've accepted payment—which can't begin to cover pain and suffering. Or," she added grimly, "the cost of the vase I slammed against the fireplace one night."

"Oh, Dee," I said, half admiringly, "you didn't." I'd never been seized by a fit of artistic temperament—and so was convinced that as a painter I'd never exceed mediocrity.

"I did, indeed," she said, somewhat smugly. "It seemed preferable to murdering the lady—" She broke off, and I heard her gasp. "Oh, Paula, what a monster I am! Forgive me."

"For what?" But my voice sounded strained, even to my own ears. "For not being obsessed with death—as all of us here are?"

"So thoughtless."

"Quit beating yourself!"

"I could bite my tongue out."

"Dee," I said firmly. "Just tell me when to expect you."

"I'll try to choke back any other gaffes."

"They may be just what we need to get us past this," I said. "A dose of normality."

"Normality . . . What are they doing to find the murderer?" she asked.

"The county's involved. State police."

"Comforting."

"They're looking for ways to pin everything on Turk."

"You don't sound convinced."

"I'm not." I paused. "This isn't a safe place to be, Dee. Not for artistic types, at least. Are you sure—"

"I'm sure."

And she certainly sounded convinced.

"You need me," she said. "You said so. What else can matter?"

The first afternoon of Dee's visit, she stayed with Pam while I went with Arden to visit Turk, still held in the county jail.

Arden tried but could never have prepared me totally for the changes I'd find. Turk seemed a broken man, his posture slumped, the lines of his once-handsome face strained. Drawn. Drained of all arrogance.

"I didn't do it, Paula," were his first words. "I loved her. You know that."

And although I'd also seen his violence against her, I believed him.

"It was my ax, they say. My fingerprints were on it. Well of course they were; how could they not be?"

I recalled the power of his blows against that dead tree, how they had seemed to shape a warning.

"Has anyone finished it?"

I started.

"The tree."

"It's just as you left it," Arden said. "When you get out—"

Turk snorted.

Arden reached to cover his clenched hands, and Turk didn't flinch away.

There alone was evidence of great change.

"You will," Arden promised. "They'll find the real murderer—"

"They think they have," Turk said bitterly.

"But they can't hold you for long—not without more evidence."

Matt, who'd been doing a great deal of research on the matter, had reported that they'd either have to bind Turk over, or release him. And soon.

"And then I'll help with that tree," Arden promised.

Turk visibly relaxed. Then asked, "And . . . Amy's building?"

"Monique's keeping it up."

"That carny . . ." His lip twisted briefly.

"We . . . straightened the showroom," I said. "And Monique's cleaned the apartment."

"Amy was so excited about that business of hers."

"It was growing," I said. "She was doing good work."

"She always did good work." His voice broke. "I should've encouraged her." His glance touched Arden, then me. "The way you two do," he said, and sighed.

"What did you think?" asked Matt. He was folded into a low chair in our living room while a game show murmured and Pam shared her popcorn equally among herself, her teddy, and Dee.

"Off the record?" asked Arden.

Matt grinned. "People never seem to trust newsmen."

Dee drawled, "And with good reason—especially those up for prestigious awards."

Matt colored.

"What's this?" Arden and I asked together.

"A possible citation," he mumbled, giving undue attention to his popcorn. "Statewide."

"Well! Congratulations!" Arden offered his hand, and Matt accepted it half-heartedly.

Arden raised an eyebrow.

Dee grew very busy with Pam's teddy.

I empathized with Matt. Recognition was fine, when it hadn't been bought by the blood of neighbors and friends.

He looked up then, and his eyes were shadowed.

"It's all right, Matt," I said gently.

He said wryly, "Tell that to Aunt Minnie. She's still holding out for the Pulitzer."

Television laughter filled the shocked silence. So his pain was for that ancient grief, rather than for the raw tragedy surrounding us.

Then he cleared his throat. "But about Turk. How was he today?"

Arden rallied with admirable ease. "Broken. Regretful. A bit bitter."

"But not guilty." Matt paused. "Right? At least not guilty of . . . what he's being accused of."

"How does anyone tell?" Dee asked, more in curiosity, it seemed, than in any tense search for answers. "It isn't as though murderers are labeled."

"The mark of Cain," Matt supplied.

"Exactly. Look how often some baby-faced, clean-cut person admits to the most horrible acts, while the grisled, pockmarked, stooped—"

"Are full of good deeds toward their fellowmen," I finished—in the way Dee and I had often, in the past, paralleled one another's thinking.

And more recently, Amy and I.

"Okay?" Dee asked softly.

"Ok—" I began, and finished with a nod. Why hadn't I known that Amy was in danger? Why hadn't I sensed it? Why had I dismissed the tension of that final afternoon as just an unfortunate alignment of moods?

Matt reached for his pad and pen.

"Oh, oh," I said, shaking off regret. "Watch out. Newsman in the throes of inspiration."

"Not exactly," he said, deprecatingly. "What I'm doing here is making a list of . . . of victims. And then finding somebody—anybody—who might have had reason to want each of them dead."

"If," Dee supplied grimly, "reason is a word that can apply anywhere here."

"Oh," Matt said comfortably, "there's always a reason. Once things are untangled, you'll see. Now, take Turk. His motive against Amy is obvious. Not that he didn't love her—but a crime of passion and all that. Now—supposing there's one murderer, rather than two—"

"Two?" gasped Dee.

"Because she wasn't—" and I couldn't shape the crucial word.

"Mutilated," Matt supplied. It hadn't seemed easy for him either. "Supposing there's one murderer," he repeated, "why could Turk possibly have killed the others? Let's brainstorm. First . . . Clint Wyse."

"Turk hates drug dealers?" I suggested. "Even reformed ones? Those who've served their time?"

"The vigilante twist. Not bad." Matt wrote it down.

"Or maybe wanting to set up a pattern?" That was Dee.

"And there was that night at the carnival, when Clint—"

Arden said evenly, "I'm taking Pam up to bed."

A bit uneasily, it seemed, Matt looked after him. "It must appear," he said raggedly, "that we're playing God here." For long moments we were silent; then Matt settled more comfortably in his uncomfortable position. "Samantha? What would Turk have had against her?"

And I remembered the look of rage he'd leveled at Samantha as she sang, as she swept the audience into her joy. Suddenly, I too found the procedure unpalatable. These were real people we were juggling about—as on a game board—and Arden had been wise to withdraw.

We broke up soon afterwards, Dee helping me carry bowls and glasses to the kitchen, Matt saying that he intended to repeat the process with other possible suspects. Monique. Mr. Wyse.

"Mr. *Wyse?*"

"Oh, yes," Matt said, "for the first three. Hadn't I told you? Seems there was more to his familial turmoil than expelling a son. Ten years earlier, his first wife died in an automobile accident—but there's good cause to question the accident part. Seems someone may have tampered with the brakes."

16

After a night of tossing—both physical and mental—my first morning thought was of Mr. Wyse. Poor man. I'd felt compassion for him in the death of his son, so long estranged, so newly rediscovered. But to have lost his wife as well—and so tragically. To have been suspected in her death—as Matt had suggested.

How much more painful a life-changing loss when suspicion tempers even the sympathy of neighbors.

And I remembered Clint's pain, his anger that he hadn't been informed of his stepmother's death. Had he even known of the shadow dogging his father? Would he have cared? Tragedy on tragedy—the man must feel that relationships could bring only further anguish.

Quietly, still in bed, I prayed for his peace of mind.

For Turk's.

For my own.

And drifted into an uneasy sleep.

When I finally got up, Dee was making toast.

"Fine hostess I am," I said, and, yawning, accepted the orange juice she set before me.

"I didn't come to be hostessed to," she said. "I came to hostess." She settled onto a stool. "Isn't that biblical?"

"I believe the word is minister."

She shrugged. "Maybe in newer translations."

We sat in companionable silence.

"You're tired," she accused.

"Understatement," I argued.

"Pam not up yet?"

I glanced at the clock. "Another ten minutes or so, and her inner alarm goes off."

"She's so sweet."

More silence.

And then, "I've been thinking about Mr. Wyse—" We'd said it together.

Our laughter merged as well.

"We haven't lost it," she said. "Scary, isn't it?" But she was smiling. "It's good to be here."

I reached to clasp her free hand. "It's good to have you." I blinked rapidly.

"No tears, though," she insisted, and went to the refrigerator. "I came to help you past those."

"If anything ever can." But even as I said the words, I knew they weren't true. Just moments before, we'd laughed—companionably. Lightly. Though it seemed, somehow, disloyalty to Amy, the edge of mourning had already begun to dull—as it must, I knew. No one could sustain that overwhelming grief, that exquisite peak of pain, for long. As with mountaintop experiences, there must be a descent toward plains of normality.

"The trick is to avoid the valleys," Dee said.

I jolted.

Again, she'd paralleled my thoughts!

Spooning raspberry jelly onto her toast, she asked, "What do we do today?"

"Whatever you like."

She raised a brow and took slow bites of toast with jelly—or, rather, jelly with a little toast.

Clearly, she was waiting for me.

"I'd like to plant a chrysanthemum, I think. On Amy's grave."

"Then we plant a chrysanthemum!"

She finished her toast, ran water over her fingers, and dried them on paper towel. "And then?"

I drew a deep breath. "Couldn't we just . . . visit?"

Later, when Pam had been fed, bathed, and dressed, I looked for Dee.

Surely just in the kitchen, I thought.

Not there.

The sanctuary?

Not there, either.

My heart constricted.

Even the meadow edging town wasn't safe.

Nowhere was safe.

Arden was in his study. I thrust Pam toward him. "Dee's gone," I croaked.

The smile with which he'd greeted me died.

"In her room?"

I hadn't checked. I would.

He half-stood.

I said urgently. "If I'm not back soon . . ."

He did stand, then, to catch me in a quick embrace. "I'll wait five minutes. No more."

Her bedroom was empty, as I'd known it would be. The bathroom door, ajar—mirrors still steamed from the warmth of Pam's bath, the air a bit stifling.

Clattering down the stairway, I paused near the cellar door. Of course not—but I looked anyway and called her name, feeling foolish as well as frantic.

Through the kitchen again. Down the back steps.

Where next?

I saw Dee waving from the far edge of our lot.

She was smiling.

How dare she smile when she'd frightened me so? I propped my hands on my hips.

Hurrying to me, she caught me in a hug. "You're not my mother, you know."

"I was *worried*."

"Probably had me murdered—" She broke off. "I'm doing it again," she said ruefully. "Sorry."

"You *would* have been sorry if . . ." Sighing, I allowed her to lead me toward shade, where the brick walls of the annex overshadowed pruned forsythia fronds, stripped even of their lowest leaves, and a third of the lawn, littered with dried maple and oak leaves.

"I know you think I'm paranoid," I said. "But—it isn't safe here. Not now." I said quietly, "You'd be safer in the city."

"One of Matt's articles mentioned that," she said. "'Far from the expected killing fields.' I told you, didn't I, that he's been in our daily?"

"He's stringing for quite a few of the bigger papers."

"Sad it had to happen this way."

"He's a fine writer."

"Marvelous!" She paused. "But so are thousands of other writers struggling to be read."

Arden appeared at the kitchen door, Pam close beside him. "Ah, safe I see!"

"Rescued," she called, almost gaily.

When he'd gone inside again, she said, "You know where I've been?"

"Not really." I felt my eyes widen. "Not—to Monique's?" I hadn't thought to call there.

She said gently, "To the cemetery. I . . . wanted to say hello to Amy. And now—could you tell me about Clint?"

I didn't trouble to lecture her on how foolish she'd been to walk alone. With Dee, lecture was fruitless.

Besides, I was struggling with a renewed emotion that had, along with Clint's image, receded into the semicomfort of memory, a poignant pattern of wounds dealt with and shelved. With thoughts of Amy still so raw to the touch, I wasn't certain how I could accommodate a resurgence of other, less personal griefs.

Still, as I spoke of him, I found myself smiling.

I felt Dee's hand on mine. "Acceptance will come with Amy, too," she promised.

Perhaps. But that, I knew, would take much, much longer.

As it happened, we asked Monique to go with us to the cemetery. We chose a lavender chrysanthemum, and Monique, tears streaming, placed it.

"She's no murderer," Dee said as we returned in time to fix lunch.

I agreed. "No one will ever convince me."

"And Turk?"

"Im—" I'd been going to say impossible.

"Improbable," I finished.

Dee opened the kitchen door and gestured for me to enter first. "And that leaves?"

I sighed. "No one we've thought of yet."

"In other words . . . anyone."

"Afraid so," I said, and reached for the colander.

"Not everyone though," she insisted. "Only a few people could be that evil."

"Or insane?"

Dee had always insisted that the insanity plea was overworked. It was a discussion we'd often had as she worked. Once, she'd insisted, "There are people who are just innately evil, Paula. Think about it. 'The bad seed.'" A pause. "You can't envision that, can you? I swear, you'd find good in . . . in Judas Iscariot."

"Actually," I admitted, "I've always had great sympathy for Judas."

She clapped her hand to her forehead—apparently forgetting the wet clay on her hands. Mopping her face with the tail of her smock, her voice faintly muffled, she mumbled, "Tell me why I'm not surprised."

"His betrayal was foreordained. Somebody had to do it—according to prophecy. What motivation had he?"

"Good old-fashioned greed?"

"There's a theory he was trying to force the kingdom."

"Insubordination. Right? If not insurrection."

"Remember—'The Devil entered into him.'"

This time, apparently remembering the clay, she stopped her hand in midair. "You're doing it! The insanity plea! For *Judas!*"

I shrugged. "There's more. How many of us aren't as guilty—every day? And how much better was Peter? Huh? Maybe Peter's was the *greater* sin—since he was close to Christ in a way Judas was never invited to be. Maybe the only thing that kept Judas from an equal forgiveness was his unbearable guilt."

"I give *up!*" She'd made a clay-smudged gesture of surrender. "I give up! Is there anyone—in all of history—so depraved that you'd accept the bad seed theory?"

"Probably not," I'd said, rather enjoying her discomfiture.

Even the hardier plants succumbed to the next killing frost. Dedicated gardeners quickly cleared their patches of blackened vines and snarled stems, once tall and supportive, then sagging. Defeated.

As we are defeated? I wondered.

Surely journalists worth their paychecks would draw the analogy between nature's decay and the dark events which had blighted—perhaps forever—the way McClintock thought and lived.

Matt had certainly made the connection. His articles—appearing almost daily now in the *Center City Times* and periodically in more distant newspapers—were clipped and displayed wherever a bulletin board surface offered itself: in the laundromat, the grocery store, the post office. I'd seen Minnie shift other items into a huddled grouping to give his clippings prominence.

More than ever, Matt himself was omnipresent—sometimes talking to individuals, more often to small, attentive groups, his gestures, his expressions intense.

"He's basking in celebrity," Dee observed. "He's become his craft."

Mary Lynn would have named that one of the qualities which set any genius apart.

But I disagreed.

It wasn't that Matt seemed to enjoy it; his air of quiet sincerity disputed that. But . . .

"He's in his natural element," Dee said.

And that was it. He *belonged* in that bustle, that single-minded pursuit of facts, however sordid. That glare of publicity. Apart from it, he'd be incomplete. And just as tissue and muscle required periodic infusions of nutrients, a newsperson's creative vitality must be replenished—repeatedly. Mary Lynn had raised a valid concern. How could Matt, having tasted the heady wines of notoriety and acclaim, be content with a diet of school board meetings and town council sessions?

How could *Minnie* accept that inevitable descent to normality?

Dee was saying, "I'd hate the constant submersion in tragedy."

Me too, I thought. Depression courted me even when, surrounded by love, I observed the darker events. And when they intruded, as Amy's murder had done—was still doing—I felt battered. At risk.

Dee stood and stretched. "Journalists are a different breed."

"Like potters," I teased, and raced her to the kitchen.

17

Eventually, Dee left.

"We potters," she said fondly, "don't rake in the big bucks the way ministers do."

Arden joined our laughter. "Fortunately, money isn't the most important factor."

"Sometimes not important at all." Quickly, she inserted an amendment. "Except at mealtime."

"Speaking of which," I said—not without malice—"will you be attending Mrs. Wright's soup extravaganza?"

She grimaced. "Case in point," she said. "May I never be tempted toward another such project simply for monetary gain."

Though she'd gained in other ways as well. Quietly proud, she'd shown us photos of her favorites among the tureens. And Matt had been impressed that two would be featured in a spring pottery journal.

Matt . . . He'd seemed quite enchanted with Dee. Actually, I'd expected him over to say good-bye.

Then, just as Arden closed the station wagon gate against Dee's luggage, Matt came loping up the street, his jacket zipped high against the deepening chill.

"I'd go with you to the station," he said, "but I have a deadline."

Dee offered a gloved hand. "It was nice," she said, then giggled as he kissed the back of her wrist.

"Chivalry isn't dead," I observed dryly.

"Only gagging," laughed Dee.

Matt grimaced. "What's that taste?"

"Probably moth repellent. Paula?"

I'd loaned her the gloves.

Matt swiped a hand across his mouth. "I hope to see you again. Soon, maybe, when . . . *if* I happen to be in the city."

The way he had spoken, almost secretively with a quick glance in my direction, caused me to wonder.

"Interviews?" Dee guessed, giving my thoughts form.

He shrugged. "A journalist never knows."

"Good luck, then." She settled into her seat beside Pam.

Arden nudged me around the front of the wagon. "She'll miss her bus," he said.

Matt stooped and blew another kiss. "For now, then," he said, and stood huddled against a sudden breeze while we drove away.

A headline in the next *Bugle* announced that McClintock would hold no Halloween celebration this year.

"It seemed unfitting," one interviewed elementary school teacher said, "to glorify imagined murder and mayhem when we've not yet recovered from the real thing."

"What do *you* think, Arden?" Matt asked. His pen was poised over that ever-present pad.

"How does 'Amen' sound?"

"Appropriate," he grinned, and scribbled quickly. "Paula?"

When I didn't answer immediately, he said, "Or maybe you're a member of the anti-Halloween-ever league."

I said, a little stiffly, "Given a healthier climate, I'd dress Pammie in a pumpkin or Snoopy costume and be out trick-or-treating with the rest of them."

"You feel cheated then?" he persisted.

I'd give him nothing controversial for his article. "Matt," I said gently, "I'm still grieving for Amy."

He sighed, pocketed his pad and pen, and looked eagerly toward the freezer.

And despite myself, I had to laugh. "Butter pecan or macadamia nut?"

"Both?" he asked, hopefully.

We saw Turk only seldom that month. Usually, he put in an appearance at church. One Monday afternoon, he appeared to ask Arden if it was a good time to finish the job on the dead spruce. While they worked, Pam and I visited with Monique, who indicated that Turk had been staying in Amy's apartment behind the storefront. I wondered why he'd abandoned the house. Perhaps it held too many memories—although it was difficult to imagine any more chilling than those surrounding the site of her murder.

"He's different," Monique said. "Sadder. But mellower, too. But then," she added with a sigh, "most of us have changed."

We had, indeed. But perhaps none of us quite so profoundly as Turk—still not entirely cleared of suspicion and obviously not over Amy's loss. When Dr. Connelly called to get our thoughts on serving still another year at McClintock, Arden paused and asked for time to consider. I could imagine Dr. Connelly's reaction—an unease, a period of questioning, of possible argumentation. Arden said little during the remainder of the call except to restate his need for time.

Our need for time.

"For your sake and Pammie's," he said as he hung up. "I hate this living in fear. And, worse even than the fear, the not knowing."

Waiting for the other shoe to fall, I thought. Wondering if the series of murders had run its course, if the unknown murderer had, perhaps, moved to some other area, or if he'd died in an accident somewhere, or if—sated with blood or vengeance, riddled with guilt—he'd altered his life course.

Too much to hope for, God? I asked in my thoughts. You could do it. If You invaded his heart . . . or hers.

The waiting continued. Past Halloween—unnoted in McClintock, save for a few jack-o'-lanterns and stray spatterings of corn. Into early November. Past the first light snow, which dappled still-green grass, crested the tight puckers of long-dead wild carrot, and clotted in the curls of brittle oak leaves.

When Pam insisted that we make a snowman, I explained, "Not enough snow, yet, honey." I dressed her for a walk instead.

We set off down the sidewalk toward Amy's transformed spruces and Monique. Two months earlier, I'd have searched the shadows for lurkers. Listened for footfalls. We'd relaxed prior to Amy's death as well. I shivered, and proceeded more alertly.

When we returned home—our faces pinked with cold—to jerk off our boots and wriggle wet toes, Arden told me that Dee had called.

"No need to call back," he said. "She's probably elbow-deep in clay by now. But . . ." He paused, frowning. "She asked about Matt. When he was coming to the city."

Pam thrust her tiny foot into my hand—a signal to continue rubbing. "I'd forgotten. He did seem to think that . . . something was imminent. He'd have told us, wouldn't he?"

"Or Great-Aunt Minnie would have."

I laughed and rubbed vigorously enough to please even Pam. No mistake there!

But more important matters pressed.

Although Dean had decided not to finish Amy's mural—at least not until spring, and then only if Monique and Turk insisted—we'd been given the go-ahead for the one in the abandoned church, soon to become an apartment-office complex. The developer wanted it ready for occupancy well before the new mall opened behind it, possibly in March.

"So whattaya say, Paula?" Dean asked eagerly. "How's your schedule?"

"I can work around yours," I said. "But—" Again, caution jolted me. True, construction seemed to be in full swing at the proposed mall, but the church itself stood apart. Not truly isolated . . . but how much space did it take—with saws whining and heavy equipment roaring—for a killer as efficient as ours to accomplish his bloody work?

Or hers.

After all, Clint had been murdered while carnival gaiety waned within easy shouting distance.

"Saturdays," Dean was saying. "Week nights'll be hard, with dark coming so quick. Just an hour or two after school." This to Arden, delivered in a man-to-man style. "And I promise I won't keep her out past dark."

Arden said as soberly, "I appreciate that."

Our glances met, and I knew that his thoughts paralleled mine—that with the climate of fear only suspended, not alleviated, we wouldn't have stayed out past dark on any account.

The developer, who'd seen Dean's work in Amy's shop, had asked for an English country garden with songbirds and butterflies among the flowering herbs.

One of the scheduled offices was for a health food chain.

"No wild animals, they said," Dean informed me. "Guess that means not even toads or earthworms. I can live with that. Can you?"

I assured him that I could live a lifetime lacking both.

"Makes me wonder, though, what he thinks birds and butterflies are—if they ain't wild animals."

We began on a Saturday just past mid-November. The half-finished buildings of the nearby mall reared into depressing gray skies like bombed-out shells. Several trucks perched on unleveled ground near the largest complex. Hammer blows and the agonized shrieks of power saws punctuated what must otherwise have been an almost eerie stillness.

Arden's expression eased. "Not alone out here." Then, helping us with our supplies, he promised lunch and a late afternoon pickup.

Pam purred, "Daddy and me goin' to a movie."

"Later," Arden reminded. "After lunch."

I stooped to give her a giant hug.

Holding me, Arden whispered, "Maybe I should stay."

But a telephone shrilled, a gruff voice answered, and I assured him, "There's someone here. Right in the building."

He hesitated, then surrendered to Pam's tugging.

Soon after they'd gone, as we assembled our paints, the developer wandered in, asking to check our sketches.

"The background's perfect," I said. It was a blue just below brightness, merely milder than medium. Swatches of carpet cluttered a windowsill. "We'll pick up the carpet tones, too."

"Mmmmmm," he muttered.

Dean swallowed hard and twitched. Paint spattered past the plastic beneath the cans, and the developer looked up in annoyance. Quickly, Dean swiped the spot with a damp sponge.

No harm done, I thought sullenly, as the glare continued. Give him a break.

Did he think for one minute that we'd be able to cover that vast wall without a few spatters and spills?

"It's latex," I said tightly. "Soap and water cleanup." Besides, the installation of carpet would make such concerns academic.

"Mmmmmm," he mumbled, but glared at the sketches instead.

By midday, when Arden and Pam brought us lunch from McDonald's, we'd roughed in the mural and decided on a style blending modern and traditional. "Not photographic," I explained. "More design than that."

"Sounds wonderful," Arden said.

What did he know? I thought comfortably. He had trouble distinguishing Picasso from Winslow Homer . . . except for the seascapes.

Still, his affirmation meant everything. "Thanks," I said, and kissed him.

Dean and Pam giggled.

"He tastes like sweet and sour sauce," I said. "Yum!" And the giggles intensified.

Once they'd gone, taking the lunch litter with them, we resumed work.

We'd painted steadily, without speaking, for some time when I glanced toward the window and realized that I hadn't seen or heard the developer since lunchtime. No loss in his grumpiness—but he *had* been another human presence.

Dean said, "It's gettin' awful dark for . . ." he glanced at the wall clock and finished weakly, "for so early."

And though it was later than I'd have expected, it was indeed early for the murkiness graying the huge windows.

"Must be gonna snow?" Dean asked, already scraping leftover color into one of the baby food jars we'd brought for the purpose.

I did the same, but took a moment to admire the clump of foxglove I'd just completed. "Digitalis," I said.

"Heart medicine."

I glanced up quickly, and Dean shrugged.

"Gram takes it sometimes." He leaned closer to the painting. "It's nice, though, that something so pretty can save lives, too."

Something pinged on window glass.

And with an inward shudder, I recognized that only that rattling broke the silence.

No hammer blows. No saws.

We'd been painting with such concentration . . . had we missed the sounds of departing trucks?

My eyes closed briefly in frantic prayer. Not alone here, Lord. Please, not alone, with darkness gathering.

"It *is* snowing!" Dean said, momentary alarm mitigated by a childlike pleasure. Slyly, he added, "Bet Pammie's driving Rev crazy, wantin' to build a snowman."

But Arden had taken Pam to a movie. I felt a clutch in my heart when I thought of the dark theater, of their pleasure in the film, in the popcorn, in one another—their blissful ignorance of our dangerous isolation, if darkness continued to deepen.

As it did.

If the construction workers were gone.

As they almost certainly were.

In mere months, mall life would teem about the area, offering the comfort, the presumed safety, of crowds. Not always an accurate presumption, I knew, from acquaintance with city life. Muggings, rapes—even murders—could occur unnoticed within scream's reach of hundreds of self-absorbed passersby.

But at least there was the potential that someone would hear . . . would care . . . would help. Now, the hulking, empty structures only increased my apprehension. Our vulnerability.

"Leave the rest," I said abruptly.

In Dean's eyes, alarm deepened.

"I'll wash the brushes. Then we'll walk." I swallowed noisily.

Even the distance through dusk and curtained snow along a narrow road edged by brooding evergreens would be preferable to helpless waiting.

"Rev—" Dean began comfortably. Then his eyes widened. "The movie!"

I caught up our brushes, and he swabbed at the paint pans with paper towels.

The hallway was littered with the debris of newly installed drywall. Grit moved beneath my sneaker soles as I side-stepped a heavy ladder, collapsed and leaning awkwardly against a baseboard not yet nailed in place. I pushed the washroom door inward. Flicked the wall switch on with my elbow. The door swished closed behind me. Still, as I ran water into the lavatory, I could hear the clatter of cans moving. Newspapers crumpling.

And then—chillingly—another sound intruded.

Footsteps.

Somewhere.

On the upper floor? Maybe.

Maybe not. In an empty building, sounds warp. Echo.

But footsteps—any foreign footsteps, anywhere . . .

Dear God—help.

And I felt a deep anger that mere knowledge of another human presence could initiate such fear.

It's all right, I told myself—yet listened avidly over the slim splashing of water. Just the developer returning. "Who's there?" I called, striving for pleasantness.

And heard nothing.

Of course, if he were on the upper floor . . .

It's up to you, God.

And there I was, doing it again, expecting Him to zap an enemy.

If it was an enemy.

Someone held the washroom door ajar.

I stiffened.

"Did . . . did I hear you . . . c-callin'?"

Dean.

Whew.

I had to reassure him.

Why? I asked myself. So he'd be nice and placid for the kill? I left the brushes in the lavatory, left the water running, wiped my slimy hands down my smock, and spoke to him as I might have spoken to Pam when there was something I needed to impress upon her.

"There's someone else in the building," I said, striving to keep my voice level.

Still, he gasped.

I patted his arm, leaving paint marks on his sleeve. Better paint than blood.

Still, I tugged the rag from my smock pocket to smudge the paint, then replaced it. "It's probably just one of the workers."

He seemed to be struggling to believe.

At last he nodded—or was that only a tremor?

"I want you to hide."

"But . . ." He caught my hand.

Oh, dear God—was he hoping to protect *me?*

"I can run faster without . . . without us trying to stay together. You can see that, can't you?"

For a moment, he seemed to consider. Then he nodded, slowly. "Hide where?" he asked.

Oh, where, where, where? Lord, show me where.

"The closet. Right near the entrance, remember?" Once, it held choir robes—now, painting and cleaning equipment. "You can even watch from there, if you're very, very careful. And when you're sure you're safe—"

"I'll run like fire and get help!"

How much precious time had we expended?

"Hurry," I said.

And turned off the water to listen.

Nothing, once Dean was fully silent.

Perhaps I'd imagined the whole thing.

Perhaps as Dean closed and stored paint cans, the convolutions of an empty building had caused me to cite another source for his footsteps.

Let us pray.

And yet, as I resumed the cleaning—striving for calmness—I felt the hairs on my neck stiffening in that indescribable, primal knowledge that I was observed. Not as when at home I turned to find Arden watching, that warm smile touching his lips.

Would I ever experience that loving smile again?

But as just over a year ago, when another danger threatened, and before that, in the hospital as I'd endured the indignities of emotional therapy, and in childhood, when a classmate—jealous of my grades and my family, complete in all its parts—had spent our recesses expressing silent hatred.

There was no mirror on the wall yet.

Could that be a blessing?

Better not to know the assailant until those final seconds, when the blade descended?

Oh, merciful Father, would it be the ax?

And would there be time enough for careful mutilation?

What would the murderer find appropriate for a painter? Hands? Eyes?

Shuddering, I tapped the brush handles. Watched—distractedly—as the bristles shaped.

And then he spoke—almost casually, yet with an undercurrent of coldness. "What are you doin' here, alone, near dark?"

Turk's voice.

And—thank God!—he'd said alone. He mustn't realize that Dean was with me. Praise You, Lord, I found my thoughts chanting.

I placed the brushes on a slender shelf.

"Answer me!" He caught my wrist, forcing me to turn. His face pushed close to mine. "You want to happen to you what happened to . . . Amy?" His voice broke.

Why? I wondered. From guilt that he'd killed the woman who'd once loved him? The woman he'd once loved?

Well, he'd never even *liked* me.

This should be easy for him.

If I allowed it to be easy. Something I was determined not to do.

He was relaxing his hold. His glance had left me. It rested—not where it seemed to, I was sure, on the wall beside, beyond me—but on the past. On his pain. "If she'd stayed with me," he was saying, "if she'd been content to be my woman—"

"You wouldn't have had to kill her?" I asked softly, and knew immediately that I'd gone too far. The rage—growing in his face, burning in his eyes—exceeded anything I could have imagined. But his hands . . .

His hands were at his sides, clenched and working.

And if God planned to give me opportunity for escape, this had to be it.

Lunging at him, banging my head against his diaphragm, I knocked him off-balance, to slam against the wall. While he huddled there, I tugged on the door, slamming it behind me, dragging the heavy ladder across it. No. No. The door opened in. *In!*

I could hear Turk moving heavily.

Lord, help me. Clear my thoughts.

The door opened in. In. In. Any barrier would be ineffectual.

What else . . . what else . . . *what else!*

A rope, paint-streaked and stiff, wrapped the top rung of the ladder.

No time. Surely, no time.

Yet it came free easily. With clumsy fingers—still slimy with thinned paint—I looped the door handle—once, twice. My mind, whirring, struggled to recall knots from my Girl Scout days.

I heard Turk grumbling.

Ignore him. Ignore him. Now, to anchor to the ladder, to tug it close, and the harder Turk pulled, the more tightly the ladder would hug the wall.

For a little while only, I knew.

But a little while might be enough.

Looking over my shoulder at the then-throbbing door, listening to its banging and Turk's nearly unintelligible syllables of frustration and threat, I sought the light switch.

The switch. The switch. The switch—*where?*

In those seconds, the lights flickered once . . . twice . . . and extinguished.

Moving swiftly through near-darkness, I whispered a prayer of thanks.

Forget the light switch.

God was still on the job.

18

Paula?"

Dean's voice.

Shhhhh, I thought. Not safe yet. The rope might give any moment. Or the door handle.

Or the door itself.

Would Dean be safer with me—or here alone? Where surely Turk must discover him in his search for me.

My heart curdled.

"Quick," I said, and tried to resurrect any memory of the terrain around the former church. To identify spots of safety. The new, empty buildings? No, too obvious. Far too obvious. Untended shrubbery—scant cover for me, but enough, perhaps, for Dean. A broad, broad—too broad—expanse of what had once been, and would be again, lawn. Trees—where were the trees? Bare now, though, wherever they stood—even stubborn oak leaves shriveled by the frost. And the evergreens, those evergreens which had threatened my thoughts as I'd pictured our walk home—now potential sanctuary—far, far too distant. My thoughts screamed to God for help. For calm in which to think. Perhaps the mall complex, after all, would be safest.

Dean was with me. "Where, Paula?" he asked in what seemed perfect confidence.

Misplaced, I knew.

Please, God.

"Outside," I whispered. "Then we'll see." Where had we put our jackets—

The washroom door thumped. Splintered.

Quickly!

We thrust open the entrance door. Turk's truck! Parking lights partially obscured by snow. Driver's door ajar.

"Quickly!" I nudged Dean. If he'd left the keys . . .

But it became all too obvious that we'd not escape in it—keys or no. It slumped unevenly, one tire flat.

Just as I'd adjusted to that and turned, a figure loomed before us.

For an instant, we recoiled.

But Turk was imprisoned in—or just now breaking free of—the washroom.

And Turk was only slightly taller than I. Stocky.

Despite the near-darkness, I recognized this slender height.

This was Matt.

Here was safety.

Within, another shriek of rending wood.

Any moment now.

"I've called the constable," Matt said, his hand gentle but insistent beneath my elbow.

"You knew?"

"I've been watching Turk."

"Thank God!"

I felt, rather than heard, Turk's frenzied search through the darkened hallway.

"Hurry!" My voice sounded strangled.

"Over here."

Matt's pickup, on the far edge of what had been the church's parking area. Matt's clutching was more hindrance than help as we slid and sloshed through slush.

"Dean, my man, you'll have to go in the bed, I'm afraid."

"No problem." Dean scrambled in with the ease of youth. He'd freeze, I thought. But better that than—

Inside the building, lights flared.

The electricity had come on. Why hadn't I anticipated—

"You're safe," Matt said, reassuringly. "Get in. The door's unlocked."

Such relief, settling into that seat—though vinyl-covered and cold.

Now, it was up to Matt. Hurry, hurry, hurry.

The engine turned over just as I heard a bursting of sound—a mingling of shouts and clanging metal—

"He's thrown something at my truck!" Matt said, more in surprise than in anger. He gave a short burst of laughter, then patted my arm. "Don't worry. We're already out of range. Unless he has a gun?" His voice had taken on a slight edge.

"I don't think so."

"Well . . . guess we'll know soon." He switched on the headlights, flicked them to high, but falling snow formed a partial barricade, like swaying curtains of crystal beads.

The truck moved, swiftly and joltingly, along pavement in need of repair.

Still I could hear, or thought I could hear, Turk's screams behind us.

Matt peered into the rearview mirror. "The tenacity of madness," he said mildly.

I turned to look through the back, seeing nothing but Dean, huddled there. "He's . . . following us?"

"Angled across the parking lot. Lucky I disabled his truck."

Of course. The flat tire. I felt both relief and admiration. Matt had suspected Turk, then. Had been watching out for us.

He laughed shortly. "Could we ever have used him on my college track team!"

I shuddered. "Is he . . . carrying anything?"

An ax, I was thinking.

"Nothing."

But perhaps it was the ax he had flung.

We threaded a narrow track, footing a rocky slope. Gravel pinged beneath the truck. Low branches scraped.

"Poor Turk."

I hadn't meant to say it. But, surprisingly, it had sprung from the heart.

Matt snorted. "Misplaced pity, wouldn't you say?"

I didn't try to justify my sympathy. Turk, from the beginning, hadn't known how to measure his wealth. How to nurture love in a culture that still, far too often, trained its boys that to be dominant was to be fulfilled.

"You're different, Matt," I said.

"I'd certainly hope so."

We were traveling smoothly, then, on highway. I heard wet snow spraying from the tires.

"You value yourself. Someone did something right."

He said a bit stiffly, "I'd like to think that . . . *I* did."

I said tentatively, "I meant in raising you. In teaching you values."

"Oh, yes. My parents taught me how to be alone. To be my own companion."

I said softly, "But is that bad? Most artists—most people in any of the arts—grow from lonely childhoods. Don't they?"

"Did you, Paula?"

"Yes!" My vehemence surprised me. And, it seemed, him.

He asked softly, "And did you choose to be alone? Or was solitude thrust upon you?"

Sorry I'd initiated the subject, I answered as honestly as I could. "A little of each, I guess."

"And then there was Aunt Minnie."

Glancing at his profile, I winced at the tightness, the tautness. The anger.

"She . . . idolizes you."

"She makes an idol of me. There's a difference." His lips twisted in what might have passed for a smile. "She wants me to be my best."

"I . . . want Pam to be her best." My voice wobbled as he turned a fierce look on me.

"Then I'm doing Pam a favor."

By saving us from Turk, he was doing *all* of us much more than a favor.

But why that strangely hostile tone of voice?

Of course he was tense—worried about Dean and me, about what Turk might do when he finally found us.

But he couldn't find us now.

Matt would be stopping—any moment now—and calling Constable Joe again to tell him we were safe. Telling him where to find Turk.

Poor Turk.

But I wouldn't say it aloud again, not when it distressed Matt. We owed him too much.

He'd have known Turk before, since they'd both been raised in McClintock, and though Turk was older, who knew what earlier tensions might have—

Matt swerved to avoid something in the road, and I braced myself against the dashboard and the door.

"Sorry," he said—the old Matt again—and smiled.

Smiled . . . his glance on me longer than it should have been at such high speed.

Why was he driving so fast?

"I'm all right," I said. "It didn't even shake me up." Glancing through the back window, "Dean's all right, too."

"Oh, yes," he said in a tone of surprise. "Dean."

At least he was watching the road again.

Where were we anyway? Far out of town, by the look of it, though snow alters landmarks.

A sudden thought jarred me. "Arden and Pam—they'll be coming to pick us up at the church. What if Turk—"

"Turk won't bother them."

How could he be so certain? Certainly, Turk hated me more than Arden, since from the beginning he'd blamed me for supporting Amy's independence. But what better way to hurt me than through those I most loved? And I recalled his violence as he'd shoved Arden against the pole that night at the carnival.

I laid my hand on Matt's arm, and it stiffened beneath my fingers.

"Yes, Paula?"

"Could we go back?"

"No, Paula."

That simply. That tersely. I waited for an explanation, but none came.

And then, as cold knowledge crept up my spine, as I felt my blood congeal, my breathing quicken, then still, then catch, I knew that Arden had nothing to fear from Turk, that neither had Dean and I. That our danger was here, close enough to touch, beside me on the seat of this speeding pickup.

I determined to clutch the insight to myself, to monitor my breathing, to give no slight sign.

But he asked in a light, friendly voice, "You finally figured it out, didn't you, Paula? But you can't imagine why?" He patted my knee. "Don't worry. I'll explain everything, in time . . . just as I did for the others."

19

I had often told friends—in what might have seemed flippancy, but wasn't—that in those moments when a plane has left the runway and is slanting at perilous angles, when my inner sense argues, "Impossible that anything this huge, this heavy, could fly!"—that in those moments, my prayer life accelerates.

And yet never had it achieved such velocity as at that moment of enlightenment, of comprehending for the first time the nature of my danger, of realizing that Matt knew. That he would anticipate some desperate action on my part. That he was more than my match physically, and that he'd realize that, too.

More than my match emotionally as well.

After all, *he'd* known from the beginning that he was the murderer.

Why?

Why would a talented young man—a nice young man, in every way but this—what could have motivated him toward murder? What could desensitize someone as sensitive as his writing proved him to be?

Proved?

Or suggested? And I remembered those times when he'd seemed if not callous, at least a bit self-serving—traits I'd attributed to his youth.

"What are you thinking, Paula?" he asked, almost casually.

At length I said, "You realize that no one else knows my brownie recipe."

He laughed boyishly. "Well, that's a startling twist! I'd thought you might try to reason with me."

"A waste of time," I snapped.

"Exactly." He negotiated a curve at a slightly slower speed. The headlights caught clumped shrubbery. Searched and released shadows. "Or plead with me," he added. Almost hopefully?

"Forget it!"

"Too proud to beg for yourself. I'd have expected that. But . . ." he jerked his head toward the darkened rear window.

Dean!

"Dean has nothing in this!" I said. Actually . . . I wasn't sure what I had in it either.

He said reasonably. "I could scarcely release him, could I?"

"You might as well release us both."

"Ah . . . that sounds like a prelude to pleading."

"Turk knows you have us."

A short outburst. Of amusement? Of scorn? "And who's going to believe *Turk?*"

A good question. Turk was still a suspect. I wondered that he wasn't under surveillance. Perhaps he had been, and even now—

Matt repeated the question, with a more insistent inflection.

"Arden will," I said—but my tone lacked conviction.

"Think so?"

"And Monique," I added. "Monique and Turk have . . . reached an understanding."

"Ah, Monique. Yet another unimpeachable witness!"

He eased past a stop sign so plastered with snow that only faint red showed, and made an abrupt right.

I heard Dean bump roughly against the side of the truck bed, but peering through gathering darkness, I could see only a huddle reshaping.

"Oops. An unplanned bruise, I'm afraid. No matter. It won't even be noticed."

Carefully, I kept my voice level. "You're insane."

"So we've reverted to reasoning, have we?"

The snow was slowing, combining in pulpy flakes. Great snow for snowmen.

I swallowed what tasted like grief. Who'd build snowmen with Pam when I was gone? Arden wouldn't feel up to it.

"It's a game with you, isn't it?" My voice was vibrating, but not with emotion. The truck thudded, veered, throbbed along a single track, rutted and frozen, where snow delineated mounds which looked innocuous, but battered the oil pan. Challenged the springs and axles.

And directly behind my feet, something jarred loose. Rolled. I tried to test its measurements. Its stability. Its potential as a weapon.

His voice had hardened. Dulled. "I was always good at games. Never quite good enough to satisfy Aunt Minnie, of course, but . . ."

Instinctively, I sensed that here lay the pulse . . . of something. Dividing my attention between him and the object—even through my sole it felt long and hard—I said, "She's unswervingly proud of you."

Silence.

"She speaks of you with such . . ." I shrugged. What was the best word?

What was the object on the floor?

"Ownership?" he suggested. "No, more than that. As though I were her creation—not yet perfected." He slowed, and the truck bounced and scraped less volubly. The headlights had become less like strobes than spotlights, briefly dramatizing each spray of drooping, snow-laden shrub. Each length of white-traced bark. A flash of brown. Perhaps a deer. In softer circumstances, the patterns of light and dark, dissected by falling snow, would have delighted me.

But I'd caught the object between my feet. Long, almost certainly. Cylindrical—perhaps.

Matt touched my arm, and I tried not to flinch.

Had he caught my fumbling movements? Even guessed their motivation?

"You can't imagine, Paula—no one could—" His voice broke. "I tried to please her in every possible way—and always fell short. Just as I had with my parents."

Surely those were tears in his voice.

"First it was the piano lessons. Every week, all the way to Simmons, I'd plead with her to allow me to quit. Before I'd learned my scales, she was planning my debut at Carnegie Hall. Oh, how I despised those scales! And Mrs. Porter and her *tap*-tap-tap-tap, *one*-two-three-four, *tap*-tap-tap-tap, *tap*-tap—until I wanted to scream! And I would, once the lesson was over, once Aunt Minnie had brought me home, once I'd get a street or two beyond hearing. I'd park my bike and scream and scream." He shuddered. "And when I told Aunt Minnie, she'd coo, 'I hated it, too, at first, dear—and then I learned to love it.' Only I noticed that she never went near the piano herself, just took me back, each interminable Saturday, for that *tap*-tap-tap-tap."

I forced myself to pat his hand. "So sad, when children—"

He slid his hand away. "Don't patronize me, Paula." There was no anger there. "It's been tried before."

"I'm not. I can truly understand—"

"Of course you can," he hooted.

"My brother—"

"So we're manufacturing relatives now!"

Surely I'd told him.

But of course I hadn't. Those childhood wounds, still sensitive to the touch, had been revealed only to Dee and to Arden. And, of course, to Dr. David, during my therapy sessions.

Almost sullenly, I insisted, "You're not so unique, you know. Everyone carries battle scars."

"Not like mine!" Then more softly, in a moan, "Not like mine."

"And so self-pity's why you decided to . . . to *create* news? To *force* prize-winning coverage?"

I heard his shuddering breath but steeled myself against sympathy. "You couldn't trust in your talent alone, could you? The rest of us did. We knew that awards would come, even for purpling thistles and gentle interviews. But you needed more, didn't you? And if success was going to be so sluggardly—"

"Please," he whimpered. "Can't you understand? Aunt Minnie—"

"But it hasn't worked, has it? Being a stringer wasn't what you had in mind, was it? Rather, to be on *staff* of a major publication—to be sent on assignment? To be read by *millions!* How many offers have you had, exactly, from city papers?" I hated what I was doing—like tearing the wings from a living butterfly. "Let me guess. Exactly—*none?* All that blood for nothing, Matt. All those people grieving—"

"Stop!" No whimpering, then.

"All a waste—"

"Shut up!"

He lunged for me, and the steering wheel spun crazily.

The truck swerved. Jolted. And he gave full attention to it. Too late. It pitched wildly, shuddered, lurched. I was certain a tire had blown just before the passenger side lodged firmly in a ditch.

I reached for the door handle.

He caught my left wrist. "Not . . . quite . . . yet!"

But my door was open—not far enough for escape, but far enough for shouting—before it snagged on dirt and stone and snow-curded turf. "Dean! *Run.* Get away. Matt's the mur—"

Matt's hand clamped roughly over my mouth, jerking my head against his chest. I tasted blood.

His . . . or mine?

But Dean had heard—perhaps had already suspected—and was already out of the truck bed and scrambling frenziedly up a bank, beyond which stretched a wooded area lost in slashing snow and darkness.

Run, I thought. Run! Run! Dear Lord, give speed to his feet, strength to his legs.

Matt barked one short, very ugly word—then shoved me against the door. *"Out!"*

But even he must see that the truck was jammed against the solid bank.

Another curse. A fist, banging the steering wheel in a nervous tattoo.

And I knew—without studying his expression in the dim glow of the dome light—that this uncharacteristic anger could prove more immediately deadly than any cool deliberation.

Tugging, thrusting his shoulders against metal and vinyl in great wrenching explosions of breath, he finally managed to force his door creakingly ajar.

He was distracted.

His back was to me.

I reached beneath the seat.

Something metallic and slender. Yes, as I'd hoped—cylindrical. A grooved wooden or plastic handle. A screwdriver? Extricating it carefully, I winced lest it clink.

Too late?

He was out, had switched off the headlights, had released a flashlight from its securing straps, was reaching for me with his free hand, commanding my cooperation.

In the process of sliding backward across the seat, I managed to slip the tool within my full smock, to semi-anchor its thick handle within the band of my slacks.

I flinched at the cold length of metal, but warmed to its potential if—only if—I could keep it hidden.

But the point protruded, pressing conspicuously near the copious pocket where the dangling paint rag could scarcely hope to cover should any light fall fully on me.

"You're hurting me," I said.

He sighed, but waited, fingertips tapping on the door frame. He stopped, banged the wheel again. "Just like old Mrs. Porter. *Tap*-tap-tap-tap, *tap*-tap—" Suddenly, he laughed. "That was why I cut off her foot, you know."

I froze in horror.

"I'd gone to see her—for an interview—not because I wanted to, because it had been assigned. And she was giving a lesson. And tapping. That foot kept *tapping—*" He broke off, and his voice resumed coolly, "But you think you'll keep me here while the brat escapes. *Move!*"

Bracing my feet at the passenger door, ostentatiously pressing myself slowly backward on the slanting vinyl seat, wet with snow, I fussed with the point of the tool until it had slipped beneath my bra. Securely enough?

Not if he continued to drag at me.

"I could get out better myself, I think."

"Sure," he said, "and a slow show you'd make of it." His hands closed firmly at my waist, and I thought, Please God, no farther forward.

Or he'd surely find the tool.

"He can't escape. You know that. No matter how you procrastinate. After all, where could he go?"

I had no idea.

But God would. Please, Lord, give Dean safety.

"You're a fool," Matt said, gave a few brutal yanks, and hauled me free of the seat.

"I could kill you here," he said with less expression than when he'd often asked, "More coffee, please?" He continued, "And I should. You know too much about me now—the pain of my soul."

I could feel his effort to regain control. Poor Matt, I thought, so desperately afraid to be vulnerable.

"I *may* kill you here—*then* find Dean."

Shrugging, I forced myself to sound clinical. Disengaged. "That would be easier, I suppose. Not as dramatic here, though—for your story. Too much like—" I choked on her name.

"Samantha's? Not really. Cornfields, woods . . . and I've never hung anyone before." Although his flashlight beam raked the nearby woods, where shredded, dead vines looped and tangled, I could sense his close surveillance, his awareness of me—and I determined to grant him no satisfaction.

"Possibly," I said. "'Paula Templeton, minister's wife, was found snow-shrouded and storm-stiffened, hanging from the limb of a wind-hewn oak. A noose formed of wild grapevine is presumed to have been the cause of death. Suicide is a possibility.'"

"Not bad," he said, laughing, and lighted me around the hood of the truck. "Great imagery, really. But rest assured—there'll be no question of suicide. Now . . ." We were crossing the rough track. "Let's find Dean, shall we? A double feature should make for an even richer headline."

His persistent facade of civility was perhaps most unsettling, for I found myself relaxing. Liking him as I always had.

His gentleness was nearly hypnotic.

And insane? Or merely calculated to disarm?

And was there a difference? Matt. Dear Matt. How we loved you.

Even as the terror stalking McClintock had grown familiar through necessity, so through laughter, through shared times, he had become familiar. Cherished. Trusted.

I remembered Antonia Porter's severed foot . . . and shivered.

"Cold, Paula?" he asked. "Let me give you my jacket—"

"No!" Remembering the screwdriver, I'd spoken too harshly. "Really. But—thanks."

"As you wish." I could hear the shrug in his words.

Surely, surely, insane.

His concern for my safe footing merged on chivalry. Wasn't that in itself insane—to preserve so carefully what he later planned to mutilate?

"When I think of madness," Dee had said during our indeterminate discussions on the insanity plea, "I think of Hitler, raving, hammering on the podium."

"Watch your step," Matt urged, his hand beneath my elbow.

Inches farther, and he might have encountered some portion of the tool.

I jerked away. "I can manage, thank you." And promptly stumbled.

He laughed. "Temper, temper."

Oops, I thought. If I fell full-length, I might well impale myself. A shame, I thought wryly, to cheat him of choreographing my death.

Again, he chuckled. "The fool's circling around on his own tracks. There, see?" He aimed the flashlight beam. "He was walking backwards!"

No raving there. Perfectly in control.

A madman? Or someone whose goals were simply out of sync with the rest of society?

"I think we'll find our little friend very soon," he said. "In fact—" and he swished the light upward.

And there, huddled on a limb midway up a hemlock, was Dean.

Oh, Dean, I thought in dismay. Oh, God, please . . .

And then, suddenly, in a shower of snow and sound, Dean was catapulting—not jumping free, but swinging on a thick, frayed vine.

"Tarza—" began Matt in a tone of admiration before the wind was knocked from him, and he swept backward against a tree where he paused, slumped, and slid to the snowy ground.

The flashlight had spiraled away wildly, then crashed and blackened, so I couldn't see Dean's expression. But satisfaction oozed in his words.

"Guess we showed *him*, Paula."

"You certainly did!" and I caught him in a quick hug made quicker because Matt was moaning. I could hear, rather than see, his sluggish movement.

Now what?

"Get a rock," I said. "The biggest you can hold. Or—wait—better yet a limb, if you can find a fallen one."

Dean moved away.

"No," I said, and heard desperation in my voice. "Vines. As many vines as you can pull free."

He didn't hesitate. Didn't question. I could hear his tugging, his panting.

Matt was standing. Oh, dear Lord—see that? He's *standing!*

"One and a half against one," he was mumbling. "And what were you . . . going . . . to do—bash me over . . ."

"Put your hands around the tree—behind you," I said in as harsh a voice as I could summon.

"Dear Paula, why would I?"

"Because if you don't," I said, pressing the sharp end of the screwdriver against his throat, "I'll perform a tracheotomy, here and now."

I could hear Dean's indrawn breath close at my shoulder.

"Hands behind the tree." I couldn't be certain whether Matt was following my instructions. But he hadn't tried to wrest the tool from my hands. Surely that was a good sign. Wasn't it, God? He must not question—as I was questioning—my will to follow through. "Carefully, Dean. Circle way around him. Take a vine. Tie his wrists together as tightly as you can."

"Square knots?" he asked.

"And then some."

A moment later, he said in some surprise, "He did it, Paula! He did what you said!"

Matt laughed softly. "I'm terrified, of course." His voice sounded steadier.

Not good, I thought.

Dean hesitated.

"Don't let him throw you," I urged. "Tie his wrists."

There were small sounds of activity. Of straining. Surprisingly, the darkness—so total after the flashlight's demise—seemed to be lessening. My eyes, adjusting to the blackness. I could distinguish Matt's bulk, deceptively obedient. Dean's movements.

"There," he puffed.

"Good! Now—his ankles. And watch he doesn't kick you."

Matt said lazily, "My feet are yours."

He had something planned, I knew.

But what?

"Now, wrap the rest of the vine around and around. Here," I set the screwdriver against a tree. "I'll get more."

With Matt immobile, I helped with the wrapping.

"Really, Paula! I feel like a mummy!"

Dean stood, hands propped on his hips, and panted, "Now what?"

A good question.

"Go for help?"

"And leave me alone with this vicious woman?" Matt asked. And laughed. "Have mercy!"

"Ignore him," I said. "And yes. Do you have any idea where we are?"

"We passed some houses before we turned off."

"Are you afraid?"

"'Course not!"

"'Course not!" mimicked Matt.

I yearned to kick him.

"Go for it," I said.

Dean asked uncertainly. "You'll be okay?"

"No problem," I said, sounding more confident than I felt.

"No problem," laughed Matt.

I stationed myself at a nearby tree, hunkering, for a time, until stiffness set in, then standing—always with the screwdriver clutched in my hand.

I'd never been colder.

Strange, in the excitement of fear, I'd not noticed, but now . . . I was, after all, not wearing a jacket or boots. No gloves. No cap or scarf.

"Freezing to death lacks drama," Matt drawled. "Now admit it. Wouldn't you rather hang?"

"Shut up." I shivered.

If help didn't come soon . . .

I yawned.

"That always happens. First, you go to sleep."

I ignored him.

Then nothing.

For a long, immeasurable time . . . nothing.

Snow sifted down slowly then—no new fall, just that released by the movements of limbs. Making small plops on the ground. Only that and the creaking of branches, an occasional soft footfall of wildlife, and my own breathing broke the stillness.

Matt shifted, releasing a fresh small avalanche.

"Keep still," I cautioned.

"I am." He moved again. "I thought you'd dropped off."

I braced. As tight as those bonds were, surely . . .

"Just easing my weight," he said.

But it seemed more than that.

"Don't be paranoid, Paula. You have me trussed up like a Christmas ham!" Again, movement. "After all, *you're* the one with the weapon." And he laughed.

I prayed frantically; he couldn't have a knife, could he?

Of course, he'd planned to kill me—and Dean—with something! Hanging had been an afterthought, designed to heighten horror.

Hadn't it?

If not, he'd still have needed something to cut the vines.

Dean had tugged them down.

But Matt would be prepared.

"You should have frisked me," he said. "Of course, you were afraid to get too close." He grunted with some sudden effort. I heard a vine snap, then another.

Dear, dear, dear Lord.

I backed against my tree. Braced myself there.

"Poor Paula," he said, softly, "you're going to die violently here after all, aren't you? No time for freezing, I'm afraid."

But nothing happened. He grew very still. "I thought you might want to know about Amy first. Why I killed her. The others are self-evident—Mrs. Porter for that *tap*-tap-tap-tap."

He stretched, and I braced myself.

"I swear, Paula, you're as nervous as Mrs. Porter's cats!" He paused. "Samantha—well, of course it occurred to me that the music theme was provocative. But there was more. She possessed that poise—you saw it!—something I'd struggled for all my life. With all that gyrating, she didn't even sweat. And I presumed the sexuality was intentional, but later—"

"You tried to seduce her!" I accused.

"Later, I saw that she was hopelessly innocent. Aunt Minnie was wrong, for once. Not a slut at all. Clean as driven snow. But arrogant."

Another vine snapped.

"Oops," he said, "I do believe the mummy's unraveling!"

"Just . . . keep . . . still!" I commanded.

"Clint—well, of course, I hadn't planned Clint. He was a fill-in."

A substitute for me, I knew, that early evening among the oaks.

"Amy was hardest. And not a musician. Hadn't you wondered about that?" He waited. "Not talking, I see. Actually, I'd developed a personal interest in Amy—though she couldn't see anyone but Turk. But you haven't asked me what you must be *dying* to know." He laughed. "Dying . . . that's good."

And I knew he referred to the two attempts on me. "You hated me," I said. "I'd thwarted you . . . how you planned to exploit Monique."

"That caricature! And you defied *me* on her behalf? If I'd killed you then—at the height of the carnival—it wouldn't have been for effect. It would have been for enjoyment, purely."

Despite what I now knew of him, I cringed. We'd been so close. Or so I'd thought. "You hated me . . . that much?"

"Oh, yes, dear Paula. But . . . past tense? I . . . think . . . not." His voice had altered with strain. What was he doing? Hurry, Dean.

"The second time," he said in more normal tones, "anyone would have sufficed. It was time, you know. People forget. You just happened to be . . . available." He laughed. "So thoughtful to call and leave a message! I barely had time to get there!"

And later he'd met Arden. What if *Arden* had seemed an acceptable victim?

Of course, Matt couldn't have known whom I'd have alerted once I'd reached the hospital. Or even on the way.

Another pause. Dear God, he must be nearly free, and no sound of help coming.

Perhaps if I kept him talking—not about me. About Amy.

"You propositioned Amy, too?" I asked coldly.

"I . . . thought of it. That day I clowned for her, I saw a different Amy. Vivacious. Imaginative. *Fun!*"

He stood quietly, apparently waiting. "You aren't going to ask why I killed her?"

Hating to humor him, yet coveting the time, I asked woodenly, "Why did you kill her?"

"She'd begun to get on to me. To what I was doing. Hadn't she said anything?"

She hadn't, of course. But there'd been that afternoon of distraction, of hopelessness.

"She might have been waiting to be sure. Or—I could have been wrong, in which case, too bad for little Amy, I guess!"

"You have no regret."

"Only that I didn't have time enough to—you know. To do what I'll do to you—very soon!"

And he launched himself toward me.

In the slight light, I could see the upraised blade gleaming. Arcing.

Where had he hidden it? How retrieved it?

I swerved to one side, and it stapled my sleeve to the tree.

"No hurry," he said, and pinned me with his shoulder while he extricated it. "Dear Paula. You're *freezing.* You should have accepted my jack—"

I thrust him away with my knee. The screwdriver was too long for close combat, I knew. Kicking, I pressed him farther back.

"Spunkier than I'd thought." And he lunged again.

Meaning to put the tree between us, I'd sprung to one side. The root tripped me and sent me sprawling.

"Clumsy, clumsy," Matt said.

Somehow I'd managed to retain my hold on the tool, to protect myself from it in falling. I twisted on my back and waited. The ground was hard and uneven beneath me, the snow unbelievably cold.

Carefully, I braced the handle of the screwdriver against my breastbone. Supported it with both hands. Breathed a prayer that I could deflect the knife thrust, that there would be time to chart its path.

He threw himself toward me, the knife raised for what would, I was sure, be its final descent.

Cringing, I felt weight on the screwdriver, the resistance of fabric, then of . . . flesh? Flesh? Despite rising nausea, despite a buzzing in my mind, I held steady, allowing the tool to drive home—dear God, what other choice had Matt left me?

He grunted obscenely under the easier slide, then, of metal—between ribs? Wet, sticky warmth flowed over my hands, soaked into my shirt, crawled on my breast. Blood? Oh, God forgive me—*blood?*

What else had I expected? I wondered. And sobbed.

Something plopped to the ground nearby. The knife? Pray God, the knife. Even dying, he'd surely try to finish the job.

Dying?

I sobbed. Asked, "Why? Why? Why?" Why had he forced me to kill him?

His weight, limp and sprawling, lay fully on me. His breath came in harsh moaning bursts.

Please God, don't let him die.

And it was then, as I freed my left arm and lifted it to embrace him, perhaps to comfort him, that I heard voices.

Dean's, shrill with terror and hope.

Turk's.

And Arden's.

20

Matt hadn't died.

How could I have lived with myself if I'd killed him? How could I erase even his wounding from memory?

Leaning against Arden in the merged light of several vehicles—Joe's red and blue slashing rhythmically and uselessly against the peaceful scene—I'd watched as paramedics lifted Matt's stretcher toward the open ambulance doors. Quiet and ashen, faintly confused, he'd motioned me to move closer.

The EMTs paused as I bent over him.

"You should have finished me," in a whisper. "A real friend . . . would have." He turned his head as though in rejection of a traitor.

As the ambulance pulled away, I struggled with grief and guilt. What was left for him? If not a cell on death row, at least perpetual imprisonment—worse than death.

Poor Matt.

Poor, poor Matt. How could such a talented, personable young man have housed the monster capable of such horror? I traced back through my memory—finding signals I might have caught, had I been alert. Periodic moodiness. Comments which lacked compassion. Self-centeredness I'd marked against his youth.

Minnie Kelp had nurtured his obsession with success—had, in fact, designed it. For what purpose? To bask in another's triumphs? Yet—in fairness—many adults attempted to live through their young, to recapture lost opportunities, yet few of their children and grandchildren chose to channel their frustrations, their angers, through violent acts.

Was Matt insane? Had he, perhaps, always been? I'd read that genius lies a scant hair's breadth from insanity; was his hold on stability so precarious that he simply slipped over the edge occasionally? Or was he so skilled at subterfuge that he juggled dual personnae—skimming at will from one to the other as it suited his purpose?

And what had shaped that compelling purpose? A hunger for attention. Adulation. Awards. Or, simply, finally, for Aunt Minnie's total, unconditional approbation? Had he planned the steps toward achieving that goal—or been caught in a spiral he saw no way of escaping? It had seemed, as he spoke of Mrs. Porter's murder, that it had been unpremeditated. That suddenly the rages of the past had consumed him. Perhaps remorse had shaped his gentle memoriam to her. And after that—

Arden was saying, "Thank God Dean reached us in time." His hand was heavy at my waist.

Turk laughed harshly. "Didn't seem little Mrs. Reverend needed our help." He added self-deprecatingly, "Sure put *me* out of commission!"

My cheeks warmed. Strange, when the rest of me was nearly rigid with cold despite the worn red blanket Constable Joe had draped over my shoulder. "I'm sorry, Turk. I thought—"

"I *know* what you thought, and who could blame you?" It seemed his turn to hesitate. "After Amy . . . after Amy . . ." He moaned.

I covered his hand with mine. He reversed our touch, stroking my fingers to warmth.

"Especially in jail," he continued brokenly. "Time to think. To know how wrong . . . about Amy. About everything. About everyone."

After a heavy pause, I asked, "Then you came to suspect Matt?"

"No. I just—" He cleared his throat and lapsed, again, into silence.

Arden finished quietly, "Just decided to keep an eye on you. And for that he has my undying gratitude."

"Little enough to do for Amy," Turk said unevenly, "protectin' her friend."

"Twenty of you aren't worth one of my sweet Matt," Minnie Kelp said that next Sunday. She would have snarled, I was sure, but for that trembling lip.

"We loved him, too," I said, putting her momentarily off guard.

Then—"Some love, stabbing him with a screwdriver!"

"Be reasonable, Minnie." Sara Bancroft's not unsympathetic voice intruded. "What was she to do? Allow him to kill *her?*"

Minnie's head went up. "*I* would have," she insisted. "Gladly."

"Pish-tosh!" And Mrs. Bancroft led her away, but gently.

But Minnie would not be hushed. "Like the Bible says, 'What greater love than this . . .' You'd think a *minister's* wife would have known that!"

None of this eased our decision about remaining at the McClintock charge, and Dr. Connelly was pressing.

Arden said, "Maybe we should just ask for a move and be done with it."

"Is that what you truly want?" I shifted a sleeping Pam for greater comfort—hers and mine.

"What do *you* want?"

"I'm not sure."

"That's just it." He was up, pacing. "So many things are unfinished here."

The mural.

Dean and I had spoken of continuing—and once had gone as far as the door of the building, then turned back.

"Dean would miss us," I said. "Someone new might have trouble understanding him."

And Turk seemed to be reaching past his grief.

"Turk tried to save us," I said. "I was just too dense to see it." Pam stirred. "He said he hadn't suspected Matt. How do you suppose he figured it out—that Matt was the one?"

Arden shrugged. "Maybe he didn't truly know—until he saw the truck pulling away. All along, he'd thought it was Monique. But he'd seen us drop you off, and saw it grow dark."

I shuddered. If Matt had found us alone, Dean and me, in the old church—defenseless and unsuspecting, welcoming him . . .

Arden added softly, "He's offered to plow the parking lot this winter."

"Really?" How could we leave Turk, with signs of his mellowing?

"He's renting Amy's half of the showroom—to anyone who'll promise to keep it the same."

"Planning parties?"

"Or selling crafts of some kind."

"Nice."

"Monique will be all right—whether we leave or not."

Monique was a strong lady.

I stood carefully, Pam's weight sagging.

"Let me." Arden shifted her into his arms, and I rubbed mine to relieve their numbness.

He started toward the stairway. "And then there's Minnie Kelp."

So we were back where we'd begun, I thought, sinking to the couch to wait.

To go . . . or to stay.

There was so much to hold us. Even the accumulated terror and grief of these past months had shaped a bond difficult to break.

How could I bear not visiting Amy's grave?

The churches were growing. Friendships firming. Ministry opening. People already asking about next summer's craft show.

But our presence, more than ever, would be an irritant to Minnie.

Lord, what are we to do?

And the phone rang.

I caught it quickly before it could disturb Pam.

The soft voice was Sara Bancroft's. Trembling. Close to tears. "Minnie needs the Reverend," she said. "She's in a real state and askin' for him—and for you."

And as I called to Arden, I suspected that God had given us our answer.

Evelyn Minshull has retired from a long career as a public school teacher. Since 1962 her published books have appeared on the lists of more than a half-dozen publishers, including Parents Magazine Press, Westminster Press, David C. Cook Publishing Company, HarperSanFrancisco, and Thomas Nelson Publishers.

Her most recent works are *Eve: A Novel* (Harper, 1990), *And Then the Rain Came* (Thomas Nelson, 1992), and *Familiar Darkness* (Baker Book House, 1994).

Minshull currently serves on the board of directors of the St. David's Christian Writers' Conference. She is also a licensed lay speaker in the United Methodist Church. She and her husband, Fred, are longtime residents of Mercer, Pennsylvania. Minshull is a frequent speaker and workshop leader at local churches and at writers' conferences throughout the eastern states.